Praise for *The Notebooks of Malte...*

"The short heart-pounding sentences, the ...aginative illustration of unseen events, the conveyance of first thoughts and unfiltered experiences—all of these elements elevate the prose into something close to poetry. . . . [Edward] Snow transfers the complexities of [Rainer Maria] Rilke's story and language out of the German and into moving and readable English." —Warren Frye, *New Criterion*

"This book has been central for many young poets, in many languages, for generations. Now, Edward Snow has created a fresh, inviting version in English."
—Robert Pinsky

"Reading Rilke in English, one faces three doors: read Edward Snow, read a lesser translator, or learn German. Just as Snow has produced masterpieces in the past, his rendering of *The Notebooks of Malte Laurids Brigge* is a revelation. Though I had read the volume before with curiosity, I found Snow's version a page turner. I devoured it like a velociraptor."
—Mary Karr

"This brilliant new translation walks right off the page into the streets of Paris and into the recessed corridors of memory and impassioned imagination. . . . Sentence by sentence, Snow releases the hallucinatory revelations of a mind creating its own indelible tracks between 'curiosity and dread,' between shocking estrangement and almost unbearable sympathy. I first read the *Notebooks* in earlier translations fifty years ago; they have never felt so radiant, so nuanced, so immediately yet enduringly prophetic."
—Peter Sacks

THE NOTEBOOKS OF
MALTE LAURIDS BRIGGE

RAINER MARIA RILKE

~

The Notebooks of Malte Laurids Brigge

TRANSLATED WITH AN INTRODUCTION AND NOTES BY EDWARD SNOW

W. W. NORTON & COMPANY
Celebrating a Century of Independent Publishing

For information about permission to reproduce selections from this book, write to
Permissions, W. W. Norton & Company, Inc., 500 Fifth Avenue, New York, NY 10110

For information about special discounts for bulk purchases, please contact
W. W. Norton Special Sales at specialsales@wwnorton.com or 800-233-4830

Manufacturing by Lakeside Book Company
Production manager: Anna Oler

Library of Congress Control Number: 2022949561

ISBN 978-1-324-06608-8 pbk.

W. W. Norton & Company, Inc., 500 Fifth Avenue, New York, N.Y. 10110
www.wwnorton.com

W. W. Norton & Company Ltd., 15 Carlisle Street, London W1D 3BS

1 2 3 4 5 6 7 8 9 0

CONTENTS

ABOUT THE AUTHOR

RAINER MARIA RILKE was one of the twentieth century's greatest poets. He was born in Prague on December 4, 1875. In 1897 he fell in love with Lou Andreas-Salomé (who was fifteen years his senior), and the two trips they took to Russia in 1899 and again in 1900 would provide inspiration for his first significant volume of poetry, *The Book of Hours* (not completed and published until 1905). When they separated in 1901 he took up residence in a writers' colony in Worpswede, where he met and married Clara Westhoff, a sculptor. A year later they moved to Paris, where they remained married but led separate lives. During the following years Rilke traveled widely throughout Europe and beyond, but Paris remained his home base through 1912, and his poetry flourished there: *The Book of Images* (1902, 1906), *The Book of Hours* (1905), and the two books of *New Poems* (1907, 1908). In 1910 he published his only novel, *The Notebooks of Malte Laurids Brigge*, which he had been working on fitfully since 1903. His last years were spent in Switzerland, where he completed his two masterworks, the *Duino Elegies* and the *Sonnets to Orpheus*, in February 1922. He died of leukemia at Valmont on December 29, 1926, and is buried near a little church overlooking the Rhône Valley.

ABOUT THE TRANSLATOR

EDWARD SNOW is a professor of English at Rice University. He is the recipient of an American Academy of Arts and Letters Award in Literature for his Rilke translations and has twice received the Academy of American Poets' Harold Morton Landon Translation Award. He has also written groundbreaking studies of Vermeer, Bruegel, and Shakespeare.

TRANSLATOR'S
INTRODUCTION

St. Vitus

Rainer Maria Rilke completed *The Notebooks of Malte Laurids Brigge* (*Die Aufzeichnungen des Malte Laurids Brigge*) in the winter of 1910, a full six years after he had begun work on the book. It would be the only novel-length piece of prose fiction he ever wrote. The book ends oddly but beautifully with an unnamed "I" retelling the story of the Prodigal Son. Toward the end of this retelling (which slips into the third person immediately), a long extended simile describes a period of "great changes" in the protagonist's life:

He was like someone who hears a magnificent language and feverishly resolves to write in it. Still ahead was the dismay of learning how difficult this language was; at first he refused to believe that a long life could be spent constructing those first short practice-sentences that meant nothing at all. He threw himself into this schooling like a runner into a race; but the density of what had to be mastered slowed his pace. It was impossible to imagine anything more humbling than this apprenticeship. He had found the philosopher's stone, and now he was being compelled to transmute ceaselessly the quick gold of his inspiration into the dull lead of patience. He who had adapted himself to infinite space now burrowed like a worm through long winding passages without exit or direction. Now, as he learned to love so laboriously and with such pain, he was forced to understand how all the previous love he thought he had achieved was peremptory and trivial; how nothing could have come of it, since he had not begun to work upon it and translate it into something real.

I can't help but hear in this passage an oblique but very deliberate comment on the language of *Malte Laurids* itself and how hard Rilke had to work (against himself, as it were) to achieve it. Both during and after its composition he characterized it as "my most difficult work." He spoke in retrospect to his French translator of "the dense weave of this prose, which was completely new to me."* Of the several contradictory things he said about the book on the verge of its completion, his remark in a letter to Sidonie von Borutin stands out: "It is my hardest and most cherished work [. . .] a true alchemy of suffering [. . .]: but ultimately the gold is nothing but gold, the purest gold, gold through and through."†

Certainly in *The Notebooks* one encounters "a magnificent language" that has been worked into a fictional prose that over long stretches takes one's breath away. The aliveness of narrative voice and

---

* Reported in Maurice Betz, *Rilke in Paris* (Zurich, 1958); quoted here from Hartman Engelhardt, *Materialien zu Rainer Maria Rilke "Die Aufzeichnungen des Malte Laurids Brigge"* (Frankfurt: Suhrkamp, 1974), 164.

† Letter of November 1909; quoted by Robert Vilain in his translation of *The Notebooks* (Oxford, 2016), iii.

the states of mind that emanate from it, the musical interplay of long winding sentences and terse fragments, the hypersensorial descriptions and visualizations, the amazements of metaphor, the adroit, reader-friendly storytelling—and all this fully under control in the work at hand: one would be hard pressed to think of another book that sounds and reads like this.

Often *Malte Laurids Brigge* is termed "a poet's novel" because of the ways its language-magic comes to the fore. But there is a sense (thinking again of the labor the Prodigal Son passage describes) in which it is the very opposite of that. Rilke the poet never *worked* for such an extended period on any text he wrote, before or after *Malte*. His major books of poetry owe their existence almost exclusively to "the quick gold of inspiration." The 1899 part of *The Book of Hours* (sixty-seven poems) was completed in three weeks; the second and third parts (1901 and 1903) in a week each. The *New Poems* he remembered as marking "my best time in Paris . . . when I anticipated nothing and no one and the whole world streamed toward me increasingly as pure task and I responded clearly and confidently with pure achievement."*
He received the *Duino Elegies* in 1912 as a quasi-mystical "dictation," and when that dictation broke off after a few days, he could only wait, for almost ten years, till it resumed.

But *The Notebooks* would engage his *worst* time in Paris, and he was very conscious of being without help, either as a writer or as someone who might be losing his mind. The germ of the book can be found, I

---

* Letter to Lou Andreas-Salomé of December 28, 1911. All quotations from the correspondence between Rilke and Andreas-Salomé are taken from *Rainer Marie Rilke and Lou Andreas-Salomé: The Correspondence*, trans. Edward Snow and Michael Winkler (W. W. Norton, 2006).

think, in an exchange of letters during July 1903 between Rilke and Lou Andreas-Salomé, his former lover and (at least in his mind) his lifelong confidante and would-be therapist. Newly returned in 1903 to his home in Westerwede, he wrote her a July 18 letter of many desperately eloquent pages describing the fears that invaded him in Paris. He alludes briefly to encounters that will eventually appear in *The Notebooks* (e.g., a dying man arriving in a carriage at the Hôtel-Dieu, a sitting woman with her face buried in her palms, two outcast old ladies, one with a drawer of pins for sale, the other with a pencil that extrudes uncannily from her closed hand), and finally settles into a long account of walking down the Boulevard Saint-Michel one bright morning and inadvertently falling in behind a man who, it turns out, is struggling to fend off an incipient attack of St. Vitus's dance. Rilke's account of his own growing fear and fascination as he is drawn along behind the man is a detailed narrative, pages long, and so polished that it seems ready for immediate entry into a *Notebooks of Malte Laurids Brigge* that has yet to be conceived. (A revised version *will* become a key episode in the finished book.) At the end of the narrative, when the St. Vitus victim finally gives in and begins convulsing helplessly amid a crowd of onlookers, Rilke transitions back to Andreas-Salomé: "I was as if consumed, utterly used up; as if another person's fear had fed on me and exhausted me—that's how I felt." Then he continues:

> Had I been able to *make* these fears I underwent, had I been able to shape *things* out of them, real, steadfast things that are bliss and freedom to create and that, once created, stand there calmly and exude reassurance, then nothing would have befallen me. But these fears that were my daily portion stirred a hundred other

fears, and they arose in me and against me and banded together and I could not get beyond them. In striving to form them I became creative *for* them; instead of making them into things of my will I gave them a life of their own, and they turned that life against me and used it to pursue me far into the night. Had it been better with me, been quieter and friendlier, had my room stood by me . . . I might have succeeded even so: succeeded in making *things* out of fear.

Lou responded promptly on July 22—not with solicitude for his fears (which is probably what he wanted) but with enthusiasm for what she saw as a breakthrough in his writing:

As I read your last letter there were moments when what you described made such an impact on me, came alive through the smallest physical detail and yet grew beyond it into the tremendously human, that I forgot about *you* completely. And I felt that odd process of "ensouling" [*Beseelen*] that can emanate even from impressions of misery when they come not straight from life but channeled through the life of that person creating them, transmuting them. For you are wrong when you say that you merely suffered through those things as a helpless accessory without repeating them in some higher process. They are all *there*: no longer only in you, now also in me, and external to both of us as a living thing with a voice all their own,—no different from any poem that ever came to you.

His letter, she continues, left her with a twofold impression: first, of the neurasthenic, easily distractible young poet of their earliest days together, but also of an artist undivided from himself (her phrasing), whose unified consciousness "bend[s] down, like an adult to a child, toward the impressions arising from the earlier, more helpless world of experience, in order to lead them all upward into the light, clothed in its most difficult memories as in genius for everything that has ever suffered." This latter impression, she says, now dominates, and she sees him as *one whose work has arrived*; "the poet in you creates poetry out of man's fears":

> [Earlier] you would have seen misery in a falsified way. To take an example: the man in Paris, the one struggling against St. Vitus's dance—you would have taken on something of him, poetically and psychologically speaking, by being in his company, and you would have observed things in the manner of a St. Vitus's dancer: *now you describe him.* But only in your doing so does the martyrdom of his condition open up in you, seize you with the clarity of insight,—and what then truly distinguishes you from him is the very *power* with which you experience it along with him, a power that is without any of the mitigating self-deceptions of the primary sufferer.

Rilke wrote back on July 25, basking in Lou's praise but protesting that she is overestimating him, that he is not up to it, that "it was only a letter and as yet nothing has come of it," and that in his present state describing things is part of his problem:

> There is still nothing but confusion in me; what I experience is like pain and what I truly perceive hurts. I don't seize the image: it presses into my hand with its pointed tips and sharp edges, presses deep into my hand and almost against my will: and whatever else I

would grasp slides off me, is like water and flows elsewhere once it
has mirrored me absent-mindedly.

Nevertheless, the idea for a book has formed, and by earliest 1904
work on what will be *Malte* is underway. In May 1904 he writes
Andreas-Salomé (trying to diagnose a new complaint) about the work
he accomplished in February on "my new book," which may have
caused him "a certain overexertion":

> I made an effort back then, in connection with my new book, to
> write down and give form to many things from my difficult Paris
> impressions, and occasionally I would feel, while I was doing this, a
> stab of pain in my soul similar to what one feels in one's back when
> one lifts something too heavy.

Later in the same letter he makes a "to do" list, and the second item
is "my new book, whose firm, close-knit prose is a schooling for me."
If Lou has released him into this project, she has overestimated the
degree to which the Apollonian stance with which she credits him has
been achieved. She has unwittingly sent him back to school. There are
always more things to learn about *description*. (Perhaps "a stab of pain
in my soul" balances out her too-easy talk of "ensouling.") There are
limits to her understanding. It will take a *new* book to make good on
those powers of empathy and descriptive insight that Andreas-Salomé
prematurely celebrates in him.

We are fortunate to have Rilke's 1903 letter to Andreas-Salomé, with
its complete early version of the St. Vitus episode (i.e., the version she

responds to), and hence a true first draft of one of the most memorable of the many narratives in the published book.* One can follow Rilke's "work" of intricate revision, and watch the text rethink itself with each new choice. More importantly, we can experience how the feelings in the letter's version shed their confusion and deepen in the book, perhaps even reverse course. *So much changes.* Even the first-person narrators ("Rilke" in the letter, "Malte" in the fiction) take us in different directions. Consider the concluding passages:

> I was as if consumed, utterly used up; as if another person's fear had fed on me and exhausted me—that's how I felt. [*letter*]

> I was drained [*leer*]. Like a blank sheet of paper I drifted along past the houses and up the boulevard again. [*book*]

Both versions describe a defeat, but the extreme derangement in the former is replaced by a clipped despondency in the latter—and *that* feels almost healthy. In the letter the observing "I" is dominant, and yet without agency, as the other's fear becomes an insatiable appetite that threatens to devour the defenseless self. As the account unfolds, Rilke the observer becomes more and more singular and fixated ("No one paid any attention to him except me—and I couldn't take my

---

* Rilke would have had the earlier account at hand. He had asked Andreas-Salomé, his wife Clara, their mutual friend Ellen Key, and others to lend him copies of the letters he had written them from Paris, so that he would have access to them while writing his book. See Ralph Freedman, *Life of a Poet: Rainer Maria Rilke* (Farrar, Straus and Giroux, 1996), 210.

eyes off him for a second"). His description of the afflicted man and his convulsive missteps conveys not the empathy with which Andreas-Salomé's letter credits him but the taking-in of a fear imagined to be increasing in the other: "I felt this whole man filling up with anxiety, felt his pent-up anxiety expanding, felt it mounting, and I saw his will, his fear, and the desperate expression of his convulsive hands . . ."

The book's version, by contrast—as if to counter such phobic introjection—creates an odd but authentic version of genuine empathy. Fear almost ceases to be at issue. If Malte is "drained" in the book, it is because he has used up all his will in his striving (always fantasmic, to be sure, but still poignantly sincere) to *help* the other. He even decides to stumble when the other stumbles, not because he is caught in some sick mimicry but because he wants to lend credence to the other's desperate charade (logic dictates that the nonexisting object will be more convincingly *there* to curious onlookers if two successive walkers appear to trip over it). While Malte is racking his brain trying to think of "ways to help," the man is making his cane into a spinal support; when Malte notices this, he admires it as an "ingenious solution," and observes that "now all went well. Blessedly well." When all this wishful thinking inevitably crumbles, Malte reaches out with one of those great "inner" gestures whose language Rilke had not yet become master of in the middle of 1903:

> And I, who was following along behind him with my heart pounding, I gathered together all my bits of strength like coins, and, with my eyes still fixed on his hands, I begged him to please take it if he needed it. I think he did take it; there was so little, but how could I help that?

More moving still is the change the book makes in the St. Vitus dancer's climactic moment, as he gives himself over to the force he has been resisting. Here is the passage in the letter:

By now I was close behind him, without a will of my own, drawn along by his fear that was no longer distinguishable from my own. Suddenly the cane gave way, right in the middle of the bridge. The man stood: stood there extraordinarily still and rigid and didn't move. Now he was waiting; but it was as if the enemy inside him didn't yet trust this surrender. He hesitated—but only for a moment. Then he erupted like a fire . . . [*letter*]

One can understand how Lou would be struck by writing of this caliber. Yet "Rilke's" version cannot compete with "Malte's" later telling:

But the cane was still in its place, and the expression of his hands was stern and unrelenting. So as we stepped onto the bridge, it was all right. It was all right. But now an unmistakable faltering entered his stride: he ran two steps, then stood still. Stood still. His left hand gently pulled away from the cane and rose so slowly that I could see it trembling against the sky; he pushed his hat back a little and drew his hand across his brow. He turned his head just enough, and his gaze loosened as it swept past sky, past houses, past water, without fixing on anything. Then he gave in. The cane was gone, he stretched out his arms as if he would take flight, and it broke out of him like a force of nature . . . [*book*]

In the early passage, the distance between the two men is closing, but only because of the pull of a fear that "Rilke" is unable to resist.

The book's version, conversely, turns the "he/I" structure into a "we"—to tremendous and almost unnoticed effect—and keeps the physical distance between the two men constant. More impactful is the *feeling* of the prose. The passage seems to float. Everything slows down. For a moment the St. Vitus dancer stands quiet and alone against the sky, a tragic hero and a Rilkean thing. Malte does not presume to say what is going on inside the man. Instead the language "ensouls" him. One wonders how much time had passed when Rilke wrote this version. It was surely during a period of "great changes."

Maman

On December 19, 1908, Rilke, still working on *Malte* but feeling a great confidence about his medium, wrote a letter to Auguste Rodin thanking him for "that long patience you taught me":

> Now indeed I feel that all my efforts would be in vain without it. In writing poetry one is always aided and even swept along by the rhythm of exterior things; for the lyric cadence is that of nature: the waters, the wind, the night. But to give rhythm to prose one must go deep inside oneself and find the anonymous and multifarious rhythm of the blood. Prose must be built like a cathedral; there one is truly nameless, without ambition, without help: there amid the scaffolding with only one's conscience.
>
> And to think: that in this prose I now know how to make men and women, children and old men. Above all I have evoked the women by carefully crafting all those things at their perimeter,

leaving a blank [*un blanc*] which might be only a void but which, since all around it there is tenderness and profusion, becomes vibrant and luminous, almost like one of your marbles.*

The claims about prose in the first part of this excerpt are, to be sure, entirely metaphoric, and in that quintessential "Rilkean" manner. But they do seem earned. Everything they name is *there* on the sudden first page of *The Notebooks*. Anyone who can write prose that edged and alive deserves to have their metaphors taken seriously.

But what of those in the next paragraph? So many of the book's pages are in praise of women, but are any of its actual female characters "evoked" in the way Rilke describes here? Abelone would be the logical exemplar, since she is the love interest of the story. But the prose's disinterest in her seems to me the book's gravest flaw. No tenderness or profusion shapes the contours of her white space. (One doesn't know whether to blame Malte or Rilke for this . . .) She does occupy a special place in Malte's consciousness once she has exited the narrative, but in the scenes they share together no feeling filters through to her—though her irritation with Malte can flare convincingly. Where passion is attempted, the prose becomes cloying and conventional: "Did it not grow milder around Ulsgaard from all our warmth? Do not stray roses bloom longer now in the park . . . ?" The end of the affair (i.e., the end of the telling of the affair) comes quickly, with two false-hearted sentences: "I won't tell anything about you, Abelone. Not because we deceived each other—since even then you loved someone else, whom you never forgot, and since I loved all women—but because only wrong is done in the telling." A seasoned

---

* Quoted from Hartmut Engelhardt, *Materialien*, 55.

novel reader might suspect that the narrative material withheld here will eventually return and be fleshed out—not realizing that a radical surgery has been performed.

The only other major female character in the book is Malte's mother—"Maman" as he calls her, the prose artfully sidestepping any situation where we might learn her actual name.* And how differently the prose relates to her! Here is Malte's memory of the time Maman came rushing back to him from a fancy dress ball when word was sent to his parents that he had wakened from a nightmare screaming and wouldn't stop:

> And I suddenly heard the carriage driving up into the courtyard, and I stopped screaming, sat up, and looked toward the door. And then there was a rustling in the adjoining rooms, and Maman rushed in wearing her beautiful court gown, paying it no attention at all, and was almost running and let her white fur fall to the floor behind her and took me in her bare arms. And I, with an astonishment and rapture I had never felt before, touched her hair and her delicate, beautifully made-up face and the cold jewels at her ears and the silk at the slope of her shoulders, which were fragrant like flowers. And we remained like that and wept tenderly together and kissed each other, until we sensed that Father was standing there and knew we had to separate.

---

* Count Brahe refers to the deceased Maman as "Countess Sibylle" whenever he speaks of her to Malte's father ("as if inquiring after her health"), but this is perhaps his own punning coinage, both honorific and ironic.

The moment of course is in the past, the experience of a very young boy; but the feeling of the prose is all present tense, completely uncensored by the disapproving perspective of the father or the embarrassment of a grown-up son. Indeed, Malte and Maman are the book's single intimate pair, and Malte the narrator keeps Maman almost entirely to his younger self, surrounding her with tenderness. In their times together, they seem most often like two intensely bonded, same-minded children at ease only with each other.* She tells him the story of Ingeborg whenever he asks for it, he worries about the effect his story of "the hand" would have on her; alone together, they unroll with granular attention a spool of different strips of lace, and wonder when they reach the end about the afterlife of the women who made them; they huddle on the Schulins' couch, the only two who know that outside a ghostly house is vanishing, while the rest of those inside search out a fugitive smell.

At the same time, "words of wisdom" keep popping out of Maman during her times with Malte, and though they may be spoken in a quasi-childhood language, they often sound more oracular than naïve: "No one pays proper attention when we pass away. As if a shooting star fell and no one saw it and no wish was made. Never forget, Malte, to make a wish. You should never give up wishing. I don't believe

---

* The book is careful *not* to orient the reader to Malte and Maman (nor the two of them to each other) by specifying their ages. The one partial exception occurs in the first "Danish" episode, when Malte tells us that he must have been twelve at the time or at most thirteen, and that he could scarcely picture anymore the face of his mother, who had been dead "for years." Thus all the interactions between the two of them that are narrated in the book occur within a very narrow span—though Maman seems to age in the episodes (but not sequentially) over a much longer course of time.

there's such a thing as fulfillment, but there are wishes that last a long time, some even for a whole lifetime, so that you wouldn't have time enough anyway to wait for them to come true." And again: "There are no classes in life for beginners, what's most difficult is always the first thing assigned." There is more in Rilke's "evoking" of her than at first appears. We are never quite sure how deep she goes.

The feeling of depth is especially strong and elusive when Maman and Malte remember together how he pretended as a very young child to be her imaginary daughter "Sophie." The episode is almost Shakespearean in the way it brings fraught themes and oblique motivations so lightly into play. It also collides head-on with primal "facts" about Rilke's early life, and this has created divergent opinions about how to read the resulting palimpsest of truth and fiction. The passage needs to be quoted in full, since so much of what happens in it depends entirely on tone:

Only when we were completely sure of not being disturbed, and when it was growing dark outside, we would sometimes give ourselves over to memories, shared memories that seemed old [*alt*] to both of us and made us smile, for we had both grown up since then. We remembered that there was a time when Maman wished I had been a little girl and not this boy I turned out to be. Somehow I had guessed this, and had come up with the idea of sometimes in the afternoon knocking on Maman's door. When she asked who was there, with barely suppressed delight [*glücklich*] I would answer from the outside "Sophie," making my little voice so dainty that it tickled my throat. And then when I entered (in the small, girlish house frock that I always wore anyway, with its sleeves rolled all the way up), I was Sophie pure and simple, Maman's little Sophie, who busied herself about the house and whose hair Maman had to braid for her so that Sophie wouldn't be mistaken for that wicked Malte if he ever came back. This was emphatically *not* to be desired; it was as agreeable to Maman as to Sophie that he was gone, and their conversations (which Sophie always continued in the same high-pitched voice) consisted mostly of listing Malte's transgressions and complaining about him. "Ah yes, that Malte," Maman would sigh. And Sophie could go on and on about the wickedness of boys in general, as if she had dealt with a whole crowd of the worst examples.

"I should very much like to know what has become of Sophie," Maman would say suddenly in the midst of our remembering. About that of course Malte could provide no information. But when Maman ventured that she must certainly be dead, he argued against that stubbornly and pleaded with her not to believe it, however little proof he could offer to the contrary.

I can't feel any darkness in this passage. The phrasings construct such an affectionate mutuality (how lavish Malte is with "we") across such delicate temporal boundaries—not "Maman wished I had been a little girl" but "We remembered that there was a time when Maman wished I had been a little girl." The Sophie story, which might on its own evoke strong feelings of abjectness, is told at a remove, and there is pleasure in the frame. Maman and Malte are reveling in "shared memories" that now are "old" to them, and as such quaint and theirs alone. It's clear that this is something special that they often do, and they go to great lengths to keep it private. They *smile* at the thought of him becoming Sophie—they have both "grown up" since then. In his telling, the charade is *his* brainstorm, not something forced on him by a fundamentally unhappy mother. Why does the child think to play this game with her? To materialize her wish? To make a game of her regret? To create another way of being close? Simply to surprise her with himself? And what does the charade allow him in return? To play at being what he's not? (The staff at Ulsgaard seem to take this quirk of Malte's for granted.) To give voice to a loquacious girl inside him? To confess those bad things (many no doubt fabricated) that reassure him he is a boy? How can we say for certain? All we know is that when Malte answers "Sophie" from the other side of Maman's door, he is brimming with happiness.

The Maman of the memory plays along—she even braids Sophie's hair so she won't be mistaken for Malte if he ever reappears. But surely it is love and not delusion or perversion that is at work here, whatever secondary fantasies Maman may be playing out. As she and Sophie are enumerating Malte's faults, Maman sighs (*does she do so from inside or outside the charade?*), "Ah yes, that [or "this"] Malte" (*Ach ja, dieser Malte*)—and the reader is left to choose the feeling that her sigh expresses.

The narration transitions back to the "grown-up" reminiscing in the fiction's remembered present with a trick of syntax that makes Maman's free-floating remark seem for a moment still to be coming from the time of the charade: "'I should very much like to know what has become of Sophie,' Maman would say suddenly in the midst of our remembering . . ." Does she direct this to Malte (teasing him, testing him), or say it out loud to herself? Does the spirit of the game wistfully rekindle, or does Maman wonder why the playfulness of psyches, in which Malte once so easily changed into Sophie and back again, can only survive as memory in the stricter divisions of grown-up time? Malte is never more like Rilke than when he desperately begs Maman *not* to believe that Sophie must be dead.

A reader familiar with the details of Rilke's childhood (but how many such readers can there have been at the time of publication?) will be struck immediately by the biographical elements in the Sophie story. Indeed, Rilke deploys them as if to *make sure* they are recognized—even if logically he would be the only one who could detect them. Here are the important "facts" that form the underlayer of the fiction:

1. Rilke's mother was named "Sophia," though she called herself "Phia."

2. A year before Rilke was born, Phia had given birth to a daughter, who only survived for a week. It is unclear what her name was; she was probably not given one. (Occasionally a critic will refer to her too as "Sophia.") Rilke commemorated her in the delicate concluding poem of *From a Stormy Night*, an otherwise unremarkable poem cycle in *The Book of Images*:

> *In nights like these, my little sister grows,*
> *who was here and died before me, so small.*
> *Many such nights have passed since then.*
> *She must be beautiful by now. Soon someone*
> > *will marry her.*

3. Rilke was christened "René Karl Wilhelm Johann Joseph Maria"; he stayed René Maria until he was twenty-one, when

Andreas-Salomé persuaded him in 1897 to change his name to the more manly and German-sounding "Rainer." Phia would dress him as a girl, brush and braid his long hair, play with him "like a big doll" (Rilke remembers) and show him off in exquisite new dresses to her friends. At times (if one trusts the testimony of his son-in-law) he became *Ismene*: "According to a family anecdote, on one occasion when he was expecting to be punished the seven-year-old boy made himself into a girl to placate his mother. His long hair done up in braids, his sleeves rolled up to bare his thin, girlish arms, he appeared in his mother's room. 'Ismene is staying with dear Mama,' he is quoted as saying. 'René is a no-good. I sent him away. Girls are so much nicer anyway.'"*

4. As an adult Rilke expressed a phobic aversion to Phia, including the fear that her treatment of him as a child had irrevocably harmed him. In an April 15, 1904, letter to Andreas-Salomé he wrote:

> Every meeting with her is a kind of relapse . . . I feel how even as a child I struggled to escape her, and I fear deep inside that after years and years of running and walking I am still not far away from her, that somewhere inwardly I still make movements that are supplements of her stunted gestures, small broken-off pieces of memories she carries around inside her; then I feel a horror of her mindless piety, of her obstinate religiosity, of all those distorted and deformed things to which she has clung, herself an empty dress, ghostly and terrible. And that still I am her

---

* Freedman, *Life of a Poet*, 10; citing Carl Sieber, *René Rilke: Die Jugend Rainer Maria Rilkes* (Leipzig, 1932).

child; that some scarcely discernible concealed door in this faded wall that is not part of any structure was my entrance into the world—(if indeed such an entrance can lead into the world at all . . .)!

Yet Rilke continued to meet with Phia throughout his life, and carried on a voluminous correspondence with her. She outlived him by four years.

Given this factual background, one can imagine the degree of broad psychoanalytic commentary that has accrued around this fictional episode in *Malte*. Maman is a projection of Phia, and the charade transposes Phia's attempt to turn her unwanted son into her lost daughter; Maman is the fantasized good mother; Maman's sympathetic depiction is reparation for Rilke's animus toward Phia; Maman is evidence of a wholesale problematizing of maternal love in *The Notebooks*.* And of course there's more. But all of it seems to lead down the same wrong path. It's not so much the approaches as the blunt instruments employed. A passage from *Malte* comes to mind: "Everything is made up of countless incredible details that cannot be foreseen. In imagination we hasten past them and never notice what's been missed. But realities are slow and infinitely specific." What gets overlooked in this case is precisely the *specificity* of the episode—the sense of intricate deliberateness with which elements in the dysfunctional field of the truth are carried over into the "*glücklich*" space of the fiction, situationally refigured and ton-

---

* For this literature, see Robert Vilain's introduction to his translation of *The Notebooks*, xxxvi–xxxix.

ally altered—but rarely discarded. (Malte's braided hair is a prime
example.) It's as if Rilke is playing a game of revision with himself,
in which the challenge is to reverse the valence of each dispiriting
"fact" while allowing it to survive ghostlike in the fictive alteration.
It's fun, and yet the stakes are high. And there are extra points for
cross-reference. Malte's choice of "Sophie" is fictionally indifferent,
but it is Rilke's mother's name, and perhaps his sister's; Maman's suspicion that the imaginary Sophie must be dead has its own complexities, but it also hauntingly invokes Phia's dead child, who in Rilke's
young imagination is still alive.*

Aftermath

One would like to think that to effect such transformations in an
"autobiographic" fiction would have consequences in the field of the
existential—that to take those worst isolating memories and turn
them into figures of intensely shared affection would be a powerful
therapy for the soul. As if the gnomic couplet in the last of the *Son-*

---

* The name "Sophie" has the feeling of a leitmotif in *The Notebooks*. The
old woman who accompanies Malte's paternal grandmother is introduced as
"Countess Oxe," but after the grandmother breaks off relations with the fam-
ily, she becomes "Sophie Oxe." More intriguing are the details surrounding
Count Brahe's references to Maman, long deceased: "He called her Countess
Sibylle, and all his sentences ended as if he were inquiring after her health.
It also seemed to me, I don't know why, that braided into these words was
something about a very young girl in white who might walk in to join us at
any moment. I would hear him speak in the same tone about 'our little Anna
Sophie' . . . for whom the count seemed to have a special affection."

nets to Orpheus had been prematurely understood: "What experience remains your deepest shame? / If drinking is bitter to you, become wine." But it didn't work that way for Rilke. (Maybe it never works that way—what happens in fiction remains in the fiction.) He experiences a brief period of exhilaration at the sheer fact of having completed the book, but then his old anxious self comes to the fore. It becomes important for him after publication to keep insisting on an intimate connection between himself and Malte ("He had accompanied me to Venice, he had wandered the streets of Paris as I had . . ."), but in terms that fend off an anxiety that they are (or might be perceived as) the same. A generally positive early review by his friend Ellen Key so distressed him that he had to write immediately to Andreas-Salomé in a plea for understanding:

I don't need responses to my books, you know that,—but now I need fervently to know what impression this book made on you. Our good Ellen Key, of course, promptly misidentified me with Malte and had nothing further to say; yet no one but you, dear Lou, can make the distinction and judge whether and to what extent he resembles me. Whether he, who doubtless *is* in part created from my perils, is destroyed by them in order to save me, as it were, from destruction, or whether with these journals I have finally gone all the way out into the current that will sweep me away and plunge me over the edge.*

* Letter of December 28, 1911. Andreas-Salomé responded promptly in January, and a substantial correspondence ensued. Tragically, none of her letters survive.

Later in the same paragraph Rilke will again refer to his protagonist as "the other one, the one who is destroyed." This idea of Malte's "destruction"—that he somehow fails at a fundamental task, that the outcome of the book is his downfall or perdition or even his death—is pure delusion: and yet it becomes increasingly dominant in Rilke's extended comments on the book. It's almost as if *Malte* has become in his mind another *Sorrows of Young Werther*, with its linearity, its protagonist's suicide, and its stable framing by a fictional editor. *The Notebooks* is none of those things, and all the more interesting for it. Malte doesn't die or fail, he simply fades, along with his author.

The book's last three entries constitute a kind of paradigm of the Malte-Rilke amalgam, and in the process enact its dissolution. After several gradually weakening pages about Sappho, the worldview of ancient Greek culture, "girls in my homeland," and an aging recluse's off-key involvement with those girls, an entry break catapults us into contemporary Venice. Immediately the narrative voice sharpens and interest heightens. The new episode opens with Malte addressing the lost beloved ("Once, Abelone, during these last years, I felt your presence again . . ."). But as the prose quickly comes to life, the personality of the narrative "I" transforms aurally into pure *Rilke*, praising Venice and loathing tourists as only Rilke can. Even a passing reference to things Danish doesn't dispel the sensation of "reading Rilke." Only when, near the entry's end, the narrative voice responds to the sudden rise of emotion in a woman's singing (even her lyrics are pure Rilke) by twice thinking to itself "Abelone," are we reminded that the speaker has always officially been *Malte*. The book's penultimate entry then provides Malte with a brief last chance to ruminate about Abelone, but again his thoughts are opaque and phlegmatic, and the entry winds up feeling out of place and almost dispensable. The one exception is a set of powerful aphorisms, and they are marked as *writing* retrieved anonymously from the margin of the manuscript.* Then, with the last entry, a *new* narration takes over, and there is a long, crystalline exit through the saga of the Prodigal Son, with its perfect omniscient storytelling voice (somehow neither "Rilke" nor "Malte") relating a perfect linear life-story (everything must be perfect for the writing to succeed here) with a beginning, a middle, and an end—whose last two words are nevertheless "not yet."†

Edward Snow
Rice University

---

* "To be loved is to be consumed in flames. To love is to give light with inexhaustible oil. To be loved is to perish; to love is to endure." One of nine passages that Rilke enclosed in parentheses and footnoted with "*Written in the margin of the manuscript.*" The intention is obviously to gesture toward the discrete entries in *The Notebooks* as "found documents" being brought together by a nameless editor. Rilke may have originally planned to create such an "editorial" frame around the book's entries, but as it stands, the sprinkling of these anonymous footnotes serves to ambiguate the "genre" we are reading. The diary-like heading of the opening entry works similarly: it creates reading expectations that are disconfirmed when only one other entry is similarly headed, many pages later.

† For "not yet," see the final note to the main text.

THE NOTEBOOKS OF
MALTE LAURIDS BRIGGE

11th September, rue Toullier

So people do come here to live; I would have thought they came to die. I have been out. I saw: hospitals. I saw a man who stopped and swayed and dropped to the ground. People crowded around him—so I was spared the rest. I saw a pregnant woman. She was dragging herself heavily along a high, warm wall, reaching out to it now and then as if to assure herself it was still there. Yes, it was still there. And behind it? I looked on my map: Maison d'accouchement. Good. They will deliver her child—they can do that. Farther on, rue Saint-Jacques, a large building with a cupola. The map said: Val-de-Grâce, Hôpital militaire. The information was useless, but it did no harm. The street began to smell from all sides. It smelled, so far as I could tell, of iodoform, the grease of *pommes frites*, and fear. In the summer all cities smell. Then I saw a queer old house that looked blind, as if from cataracts; it wasn't on my map, but above the door and still fairly legible was: Asyle de nuit. By the entrance were the prices. I read them. It was not expensive.

And what else? A child by itself in a baby carriage. It was fat, green-ish, and a bright rash had broken out on its forehead. Apparently it was healing and didn't hurt. The child was asleep, its mouth wide open, breathing in iodoform, *pommes frites*, fear. It was all like that. The main thing was staying alive. That was the main thing.

In spite of everything I can't give up sleeping with my window open. Electric trains speed madly through my room. Automobiles drive over me. A door slams shut. Somewhere a pane of glass shatters, I hear the large shards laughing and the small splinters snickering as they hit the ground. Then suddenly from the other direction a dull, muffled sound inside the house. Someone is climbing the stairs. Approaching, ceaselessly approaching. Reaches my door, stands there for a long time, moves on. And again the street. A girl screeches: *Ah tais-toi, je ne veux plus.* The trolley races up excitedly, slides to a stop, is off and away. Someone shouts. People run, overtake one another. A dog barks. What a relief: a dog. Toward morning a cock even crows, and it is an infinite blessing. Then suddenly I fall asleep.

Those are the noises. But there's something even more fearful here: the silence. I've heard that during large fires sometimes there's a moment of such extreme suspense that the jets of water fall back, the firemen cease climbing, no one moves. Soundlessly a black cornice inches forward overhead, and a high wall, behind which flames are leaping, tilts outward, soundlessly. Everyone stands and waits, their shoulders raised, their faces tightened around their eyes, for the terrible crash. That's how all the silence is here.

~

I am learning to see. I don't know how it's happened, but everything enters me more deeply now and keeps on going where it used to stop. I have an inner realm of which I was completely unaware. Everything goes there now. I don't know what happens there.

I wrote a letter today, and as I did so, it struck me that I've only been here three weeks. Three weeks elsewhere, in the country for instance, could be like one day; here they are years. I'm going to stop writing letters. Why should I tell someone I'm changing? If I change I'm no longer who I was, and if I'm something different from what I used to be, then certainly I have no acquaintances. And to strangers, to people who don't know me, it would make no sense to write.

~

Have I already said this? I am learning to see. Yes, I'm beginning. It still goes badly. But I want to make the most of my time.

For example: it had never occurred to me how many faces there are. There are multitudes of people, of course, but even more faces, since each person has several. There are people who wear the same face for years; naturally it wears through, it becomes soiled, its seams split, it stretches like gloves worn on long journeys. These are frugal, simple people; they don't change it, they never once have it cleaned. It's good enough, they maintain, and who's to say they're wrong? But the question arises: Since they have several faces, what do they do with the others? They put them away. Their children can wear them. But it can also happen that when their dogs go out, *they* have them on. And why not? Faces are faces.

Other people put on their faces and wear them out with uncanny speed, one after the other. At first it seems to them that they have enough for more than a lifetime; but they scarcely reach forty when they come to their last. There is obviously something tragic in this. It never occurs to them to take care of a face, their last one is used up in a week, has holes in it, is in many places thin as paper, and then little by little the underlayer shows through, the not-face, and for the rest of their lives they go about in that.

But the woman, the woman: she had fallen all the way into herself, forward into her hands. It was at the corner of rue Notre-Dame-des-Champs. The moment I saw her sitting there I started walking softly. When poor people are searching for an answer you shouldn't disturb them. Perhaps it will come to them yet.

The street was too empty, its emptiness was bored and pulled my step out from under my feet and banged around with it as if it were a wooden clog. The woman was startled and pulled up out of herself too sharply, so that her face remained in her two hands. I could see it lying there, its hollow form. It took unbelievable effort to keep focused on those two hands and not look up at what had torn itself out of them. It was horrible to see a face from the inside, but I was even more terrified of the naked flayed head that was waiting there without a face.

⁓

I am afraid. Once you contract fear you have to take some action against it. It would be very nasty to fall ill here, and if it occurred to anyone to move me into the Hôtel-Dieu, I would certainly die there.

This hôtel is a pleasant building, always bustling and hugely popular. You can scarcely pause to admire the façade of the Cathedral of Paris without risking being run over by one of the many vehicles that speed across the open square on their way inside. These vehicles are little omnibuses constantly clanging their bells, and even the Duke of Sagan would be forced to order his coach to halt if some lowly dying person had gotten it into their brain to rush pell-mell straight into God's Hôtel. The dying are headstrong, and all Paris comes to a stop when Madame Legrand, *brocanteuse* from the rue des Martyrs, is being sped toward a certain square in the Cité. One feature of these fiendish little vehicles is their unduly enticing frosted-glass windows, behind which you can imagine the most baroque agonies—the fancy of a concierge would suffice. And if your imagination is more highly developed and runs along more wayward tracks, the possibilities are truly endless. But I have also watched open carriages arriving, hired cabs with their tops folded back, transporting their passengers at the usual rate: two francs per hour en route to your death.

This excellent hôtel is very old. In the days of King Clovis people were already dying in a handful of beds here. Now there are 559 for them to die in. A kind of assembly-line dying, of course. And with such an enormous rate of production, the quality of individual deaths may suffer a bit, but never mind about that. It's quantity that counts. Who cares anymore today about a lovingly crafted death? No one. Even the rich, who can still afford to die in full, are beginning to grow neglectful and indifferent. The desire to die your own death is becoming more and more rare. A while longer, and it will be as rare as living your own life. God, it's all there waiting for you. You arrive on the scene, you find a ready-made life, all you have to do is put it on. You wish to go, or you're forced to leave: no problem: *Voilà votre mort, monsieur*: you take your death as it comes; you die the death that goes with your illness (for now that we're becoming familiar with all diseases, we understand that their various fatal outcomes belong to the disease itself and not to the person; the ill in a sense have nothing at all to do with it).

In the sanatoriums, where people die so readily and with so much gratitude toward their doctors and nurses, you die one of the deaths attached to the institution; that only seems right. But if you die at home, it's natural to want to choose that genteel death the better classes die, which is really just the initial act, as it were, of a first-class funeral, with its whole sequence of exquisite formalities. Outside the house the poor stand and watch it all unfold. *Their* death is of course banal, with no frills attached. They feel lucky if they find one that more or less fits. And if it's too big? One can always grow a little. But if it won't button around the chest or if it chokes—then there's a problem.

~

When I think of home, where no one remains now, I'm convinced that at one time it must have been different. Previously you knew (or you sensed) that you had your own death within you, as the fruit contains its seed. Children had a small one in them and adults a big one. Women bore theirs in their womb, and men theirs in their breast. It was *yours*, and that gave you a singular pride and a quiet dignity.

My grandfather, old Chamberlain Brigge: one saw immediately

that he still carried a death inside him. And what a death it was: two months long and so loud that they had to endure its screams all the way out in the distant farmsteads.

The long, old manor house was too small for this death; it seemed that wings would have to be added on, for the chamberlain's body kept growing, and he continually demanded to be carried from one room into another and fell into furious rages if the day had not ended and there were no rooms left which he had not yet occupied. At such times he would be carried upstairs, followed by the retinue of maids, manservants, and dogs that he always had around him; then, with the majordomo leading the way, they would all enter the room where his saintly mother had died twenty-three years before, and which had been kept exactly as she had left it and in which no one since had been allowed to set foot. Now the whole pack burst in. The curtains were thrown back, and the robust light of a summer afternoon examined all the shy, startled objects and swiveled awkwardly in the wide-eyed mirrors. And the people behaved similarly. Chambermaids were so curious that they didn't know what their hands were fumbling with, young servants gawked at everything, and elderly retainers wandered about trying to recall what they had been told about this locked room in which they now, by some stroke of fortune, suddenly found themselves.

But it was the dogs especially who seemed to find exciting their intrusion into this room where everything had its own special smell. The tall, lean Russian wolfhounds paced busily back and forth behind the armchairs, crossed the room with long, swinging dance steps, reared up like heraldic animals, rested their slender paws on the white-and-gold windowsill, and with sharp, observant faces and expectant brows scanned right, then left, down into the courtyard. Little glove-yellow dachshunds sat in the broad, silk-upholstered easy chair by the window, warmed by the feeling that everything was exactly as it should be. A wire-haired, sour-faced pointer rubbed his back along the edge of a gilt-legged table, while on its painted top the Sèvres cups trembled.

Yes, for these unmindful, half-awake objects it was a terrible time. From books some hasty hand had opened carelessly, rose leaves would come fluttering down and be trampled underfoot; small fragile things were seized, immediately broken, and hurriedly put back in their places, while many of the badly bent, dented things were shoved beneath curtains or even thrown behind the fire screen's golden mesh. And from time to time something would fall, fall with a thud on the carpet, fall with a sharp crack on the hard parquet, but when it fell it broke, shattering loudly or fracturing almost silently; for these things, pampered throughout their lives, could not withstand any kind of fall.

And had someone thought to ask what the cause of all this was, what had called down upon this exquisitely safeguarded room such waves of destruction, there could have been only one reply: Death.

The death of Chamberlain Christoph Detlev Brigge at Ulsgaard. For there he was, bulging more and more grotesquely out of his dark blue uniform, in the middle of the floor, not moving at all. In his large strange face that no one recognized any longer, the eyes had fallen shut: he saw nothing of what was happening. They'd tried first to lay him on the bed, but he'd fought against being put there, for ever since those first nights in which his sickness had taken hold he'd hated beds. And the bed upstairs had in any case proved too small, so there was nothing else to do but put him down on the carpet; for he would not hear of going back downstairs.

So there he lay now, looking for all the world like he was dead. As dusk slowly fell, the dogs had slipped out through the partly open door, one after another, and only the wire-haired terrier with the sour face remained beside his master, one broad shaggy paw resting on Christoph Detlev's large gray hand. Most of the servants, too, now stood outside in the white hallway, which was brighter than the room; but those who had remained inside would glance furtively toward the large darkening heap in the middle of the floor, wishing it were only a giant cloak thrown over something that had gone bad.

But it was more than that. It was a voice, the voice that until seven weeks ago no one had heard before: for it was not the voice of the chamberlain. This voice belonged not to Christoph Detlev but to Christoph Detlev's death.

Christoph Detlev's death had been living at Ulsgaard many, many days now and had spoken to everyone. Issuing demands. Demanding to be carried, demanding the blue room, demanding the small salon, demanding the great hall. Demanding the dogs, demanding that people laugh, talk, play, hush, and all at the same time. Demanding to see friends, women, people who had died, and demanding its own death: demanding. Demanding and screaming.

For when night had come and the members of the exhausted serving staff who were not on watch tried to get some sleep, Christoph Detlev's death would scream, scream and groan, howl so long and unremittingly that the dogs, which at first howled with it, fell silent and didn't dare lie down, but stood on their long, thin, trembling legs and were afraid. And when in the village they heard it howling across the wide, silvery Danish summer night, they rose from their beds as they do in a great storm, got dressed and sat around the lamp together without a word, until it had passed. And the women whose hour was near were moved into the most remote rooms and the most

protected bedchambers; but they could still hear it, they could hear
it as if it were howling inside their own bodies, and they begged to
be allowed to get up too, and they came, pale and heavy with child,
and sat among the others with their blurred faces. And the cows that
were calving had helplessly closed up, and the dead fruit had to be
torn from one of them, along with all the entrails, since it wouldn't
come out on its own. And everyone's work went badly and they forgot
to bring in the hay because all through the day they were dreading
the night and because they were so exhausted from the long hours of
lying sleepless and from the sudden terrified moments of waking that
they couldn't concentrate on anything. And on Sundays, in the white,
peaceful church, they prayed for an end to the lords of Ulsgaard; for
this last one was a horrible lord. And the thing they were all thinking
and praying the pastor himself finally said out loud from his pulpit, for he too no longer slept at night and had ceased to understand
God. And the church bell said it also, having found a frightening rival
which boomed out all night long and against which, even when the
bell pealed with every atom of its metal, it was completely powerless.
Indeed, they all said it; and among the young men there was one who
dreamed that he'd entered the castle and killed the kind master with
his pitchfork; and all of them had become so crazed, so desperate, so
sick from it, that as they listened to him tell his dream they looked at
him and wondered, unconsciously taking his measure, if this might
be the man to do the deed. People talked and felt this way throughout
the district—where only a few weeks earlier the chamberlain had been
loved and pitied. But for all their talking, nothing changed. Christoph Detlev's death, which now resided at Ulsgaard, was not to be
rushed. It had come to stay for ten weeks, and for ten weeks it would

stay. And during this time it was more the master than Christoph Detlev Brigge had ever been. It was like a king who is known forever afterward as The Terrible.

This was not the death of some dropsical nobody, it was the wicked, princely death that the chamberlain had borne with him his entire life, nourishing it from within. All the excess of pride, will, and lordly power that he himself had not been able to employ during his peaceful, conscientious days was channeled into his death, into that death which now sat at Ulsgaard and lavishly squandered every ounce of itself.

With what a look the Chamberlain Brigge would have answered someone who asked of him that he die some more peaceful way than this. He was dying his own hard death.

And when I think of the others I have seen or heard about: it is always the same. They all had their own singular death. Those men who bore theirs in their armor, inside, like a prisoner; those women who became very old and shrunken and then in an enormous bed, as on a stage, with all the family and the servants and the dogs assembled, mindful of them all, calmly and with a magisterial dignity passed away. Even the children—indeed, even the very smallest ones—died not just any child's death; with a final coalescence they died both as what they already were and what they would have become.

And what a melancholy beauty it gave to women when they were pregnant and stood there silently, with their two hands resting quietly on their large bellies, in which there were *two* fruits: a child and a death. Could not that haunting, almost nourishing smile on their inscrutable faces have come from their sometimes feeling that inside them *both* were growing?

~

I have taken action against fear. All night long I've been sitting here writing; and now I'm exhausted in a good way, as after a long walk across the fields at Ulsgaard. Still, it's painful to think that all of that no longer exists, that complete strangers now live in the broad old manor house. Perhaps at this very moment the maids are asleep up in the white room under the gable, sleeping their deep, humid sleep from evening till morning.

And you have no one and nothing and you roam the world with a trunk and a crate of books and, to speak truly, without curiosity. What kind of life is that really: without a house, without inherited things, without dogs. If you at least had your memories. But who among us does? You *may* have your childhood, but if so, it is as if interred. Perhaps you have to be old before you can reach down that far. I think it must be good to be old.

~

Today there was a beautiful fall morning. I walked through the Tuileries. Everything toward the east that caught the sun was dazzlingly bright, and where the sunlight fell, the mist hung like a gray curtain of light. Gray amid gray, the statues warmed themselves in gardens that had yet to be unveiled. Solitary flowers stood up in the long beds and said "Red" with a startled voice. Then a very tall, slender man

came around the corner from the Champs-Élysées; he was carrying a
crutch, but no longer thrust it up under his shoulder,—he held it out
in front of him, lightly, and from time to time he brought it down
firm and loud, as if it were a herald's staff. He could not suppress a
smile of intense happiness, and as he passed he smiled at everything,
at the trees, at the sun itself. His stride was shy like a child's, but
uncommonly light, full of the memory of previous walking.

How much a touch of moon can do. There are days when everything
around you is light, luminous, scarcely outlined in the bright air and
yet clear, distinct. Even the nearest things have an aura of distance
about them, have been pulled back and are only being shown to you,
not proffered; while the things that really do recede—the river, the
bridges, the long streets and the huge, profligate squares—have stood
their distance up behind them, and are painted on it as if on silk. It is
impossible to say then what a bright green vehicle on the Pont-Neuf
might be, or some red that can't be held in, or even a simple poster on
the wall adjoining a row of pearl-gray houses. Everything is simpli-
fied, refigured in a few bright, sharp planes like the face in a Manet
portrait. And nothing is trifling or superfluous. The booksellers along
the quai open up their crates, and the fresh or faded yellow of the
books, the violet-brown of the bindings, the more commanding green
of a portfolio: everything harmonizes, has value, takes part, and creates a fullness where nothing is lacking.

In the street below there's the following composition: a small hand-cart, pushed by a woman; at the front of it, lengthwise, a barrel organ. Behind that, at an angle, a portable crib, in which a tiny child is standing up on firm legs, happy in its bonnet, and refusing over and over to be sat down. From time to time the woman turns the organ handle. Then immediately the tiny child stands up again, stamping its feet in its crib, while a little girl in a green Sunday dress dances and shakes a tambourine up toward the windows.

~

I feel I must begin working on something, now that I'm learning to see. I'm twenty-eight and have accomplished close to nothing. To be specific: I have written a study of Carpaccio, which is bad, a play called "Marriage," which tries to prove something that is false by employing dubious precepts, and some poems. Ah, but with poems so little is achieved when you write them early in life. You should wait, and gather meaning and sweetness throughout a life—a long one if possible—and then, at the very end, you might perhaps be able to write ten good lines. For poems are not, as people imagine, feelings (you have those early enough),—they are experiences. For the sake of a few lines you must see many cities, see many things and people, you must understand animals, you must feel how birds fly, and know the gestures with which small flowers open in the morning. You must be able to think back to roads through unfamiliar regions, to unexpected encounters and to partings you had long seen coming, to certain days of your childhood when what happened is still a mystery, to parents who presented you with a thing of happiness and whom you had to disappoint because you couldn't grasp how it was supposed to make you happy (it was a happiness for someone else), to childhood illness, which arose so strangely and with so many deep and weighty transformations, to days in silent, pent-up rooms and to mornings by the sea, to the sea itself, to the many different seas, to nights of travel that rushed by on high and flew with all the stars,—and if you have access to all that, it is *still* not enough. You must have memories of many nights of love and none of them alike, of the screams of women in labor and of soft, tender, sleeping women who have given birth and are closing up again. But you must have also been with the dying, must have sat with the dead in the room with the open window and the sporadic noises. And it is still not enough to *have* memories. You must be able to forget them as they multiply, and you must have the great patience to wait for their return. For the memories themselves are not the thing. Only when they turn to blood in you, to glance and gesture, nameless and no longer distinguishable from your present self—only then can it happen that in a very rare hour the first word of a poem rises up in their midst and issues forth from them.

But all my poems originated differently—and are thus not poems at all. And when I wrote my play, how badly I erred. Was I such a follower and a fool that I required a third person to relate the fate of two people who were making life hard for each other? How easily I fell into the trap. And yet I *must* have known that this third person who infests all lives and literature, this ghost of a third person who never existed, has no meaning at all and must be disavowed. He is one of Nature's pretexts, for she is always careful to divert us from her deepest secrets. He is the screen behind which a drama unfolds. He is the noise at the threshold of the voiceless quiet of a true conflict. One might suppose that it has proved too difficult so far to speak directly of those two souls who are the real issue. The third person, precisely because he is so unreal, is so much easier; they can all write him. From the first moment of their plays you can feel their impatience to have this third person enter; they can hardly wait. As soon as he appears, all is well. But how tedious if he is late. Absolutely nothing can take place without him; everything stands there, stagnates, waits. Yes, and what if this waiting and blockage were all there was? What to do, Sir Dramatist, and you, wise audience who knows about life, what to do, if he were declared missing, this well-liked man about town or that ingratiating young fellow who fits into every marriage like a skeleton key? What to do, for instance, if the devil had taken him? Let's suppose he did. You'd suddenly notice the unnatural emptiness of the theaters, which have been walled up like dangerous holes; only the moths that live in the cushioned edges of the loges whirr through those baseless cavities. The playwrights no longer enjoy the poshest districts. All the best-known detective agencies are probing every corner of the earth on their behalf, looking for that irreplaceable third person who was himself the plot.

And all the time they are living in our midst—not these "third persons," but the *two alone*, about whom so incredibly much might be said, about whom nothing has ever yet been said—though they suffer and act and try to help themselves and each other but can't.

It's laughable. I sit here in my little room, I, Brigge, who have reached the age of twenty-eight and about whom no one knows anything. I sit here and am nothing. And yet this nothing begins to think, and, five flights up, on a gray Paris afternoon, thinks these thoughts:

Is it possible, it thinks, that we have not yet seen, known, or said anything real and significant? Is it possible that we have had thousands of years to observe, reflect, and record, and that we have allowed these thousands of years to slip by like a school recess during which we eat our sandwich and an apple?

Yes, it is possible.

Is it possible that despite inventions and progress, despite culture, religion, and philosophy, we have remained on the surface of life? Is it possible that even this surface, which might at least have amounted to *something*, we have covered over with unbelievably drab stuff that makes it look like drawing room furniture during the summer holidays?

Yes, it is possible.

Is it possible that the whole history of the world has been misunderstood? Is it possible that we have the past all wrong, because we have always spoken of its crowds, as if we were describing a convergence of many people while ignoring the single person they were standing around because he was a stranger and was dying?

Yes, it is possible.

Is it possible that we believed we had to retrieve all that happened before we were born? Is it possible that all of us would have to be reminded that we *issued* from those who preceded us, that we *contain* this past, and thus should be impervious to those who claim to know a different one?

Yes, it is possible.

Is it possible that all these people know, in the greatest detail, a past that never existed? Is it possible that all realities are nothing for them; that their life is slowly winding down, unconnected to anything, like a clock in an empty room—?

Yes, it is possible.

Is it possible to know nothing of girls who nevertheless have lives?

Is it possible to say "women," "children," "boys," not sensing (despite all our culture, not sensing) that these words have long since had no plural but only countless singulars?

Yes, it is possible.

Is it possible that there are people who say "God" and think they refer to something shared by all? Consider two schoolboys: one buys himself a knife, and his best friend buys one exactly like it on the same day. And after a week they show each other these two knives, and they hardly resemble each other at all—so differently have they been used in different hands. (Oh, says one mother, can't you own anything for even a day without wearing it out—) And then: Is it possible to believe that one could have a God *without* using him?

Yes, it is possible.

But if all this is possible, if there's even the slightest chance that it's possible, then something must be done, for God's sake! *Someone* down the line who has had these troubling thoughts must step up and do something about this neglect; even if they're just anybody, not at all the right person for the job—there's no one else in sight. This young foreigner of no consequence, Brigge, will have to sit himself down five flights up and write, day and night: yes, he'll have to write, that's how it will turn out.

⌒〜

I must have been twelve or at most thirteen at the time. My father had taken me with him to Urnekloster. I don't know what prompted him to call on his father-in-law. The two hadn't seen each other since the death of my mother, many years before, and my father had never been inside the old manor house to which Count Brahe had retired quite late in life. After this one time I myself never saw again that remarkable house, which at my grandfather's death passed into foreign hands. So when I think back on it now, I see not a complete building but something pieced together by childhood memories. It has been fragmented crazily inside me: over here a room, over there another room, and here a length of hallway, which however doesn't connect these two rooms but has been preserved as something with its own mysterious rationale. In this same way, everything is scattered throughout me—the rooms, the stairs that descended with such ceremonious grace, and other thin, twisting stairs whose darkness one climbed through like blood passing through veins; the tower rooms, the high, suspended balconies, the unexpected galleries onto which you were thrust when you opened a little door:—all this is still in me and will always be in me. It's as if the image of this house had fallen down into me from an infinite height and shattered on my ground.

The only part that has survived intact in my heart—this is how it feels to me, at least—is the banquet hall where we used to assemble for dinner every evening at seven o'clock. I never saw this room by day. I can't even remember if it had windows, or if it did, what they looked out on; always, by the time the family entered, the candles would already be burning in the heavy branching candelabra, and in a few minutes you forgot the time of day and everything you might have seen outside. This high room (vaulted, as I picture it now) was overwhelming; with its ceiling lost in deepening darkness, with its never-quite-clarified corners, it sucked all images out of you, and left you nothing definite in exchange. You sat there as if void, totally without will, without thought, without desire, without defense. You were like a blank space. I remember that at first this nullifying state almost brought on nausea, a kind of seasickness that I only overcame by stretching out my leg until my foot touched my father's knee, just opposite me at the table. Only later did I come to feel that he understood or at least sanctioned this odd behavior, even though between us there existed an almost cool relationship which would not have permitted such a gesture. It was nevertheless this slight contact that gave me the strength to make it through these long meals. And after a few weeks of willed endurance I had become, with a child's almost boundless adaptability, so accustomed to the eeriness of these gatherings that it no longer required effort to sit politely at the dinner table for two hours straight; now, in fact, time tended to pass quickly, for I busied myself with observing those present.

My grandfather called them the family, and I heard the others also use this term, which was completely arbitrary. For although these four people were distantly related, in no real sense did they belong together. The uncle who sat next to me was an old man whose hard, charred face was marred by several black spots—the result, I learned, of an exploded powder charge; sullen and resentful, he had retired from the army with the rank of major, and now conducted alchemical experiments in some room in the manor house whose location was unknown to me. He was also, I heard a servant say, in contact with a prison that supplied him with corpses once or twice a year, at which time he would lock himself away for days and nights together, dissecting them and preparing them by some mysterious process to resist decomposition. Opposite him at the table was the place of Fraülein Mathilde Brahe. She was a person of uncertain age, one of my mother's distant cousins, about whom nothing was known except that she maintained an intense correspondence with an Austrian spiritualist who called himself Baron Nolde; she was so completely in thrall to him that she wouldn't undertake the slightest action without first receiving his approval—or, better yet, his blessing. At that time she was exceptionally plump, of a soft, languid fullness that seemed to have been carelessly poured, as it were, into her bright, loose-fitting dresses; her movements were weary and uncertain, and tears constantly ran from her eyes. And yet: there was something in her that reminded me of my slender and delicate mother. The longer I looked at her, the more I began to find in her face all those refined and nuanced features that I'd not been able to remember except vaguely since my mother's death; only now, seeing Mathilde Brahe every day, did I know again what my mother had looked like; indeed, perhaps I even came to know it for the first time. Only now did the hundreds and hundreds of details coalesce inside me to create an image of this dead mother, the image that ever since has accompanied me wherever I go. I later realized that in the face of Fraülein Brahe all the qualities of my mother's features were indeed present; it was just that they had been forced apart, distorted and no longer in contact with one another—as if some stranger's face had crowded its way in among them.

Next to this lady sat the young son of a female cousin, a boy about my own age but smaller and frailer. His thin, pale neck reached up from a pleated ruff and disappeared beneath a long chin. His lips were thin and tightly pursed, his nostrils trembled slightly, and only one of his beautiful dark brown eyes could move. From time to time this eye would look across to me calmly and sadly, while the other always remained pointed toward the same corner, as if it had been sold and no longer had any stake in our proceedings.

At the head of the table stood my grandfather's enormous armchair, which a manservant (whose single task this was) pushed in beneath him when he sat down, and in which the old man took up very little room. There were people who called this peremptory and almost deaf old gentleman Your Excellency or Lord Chamberlain, while others addressed him as General. And undoubtedly he had earned the distinction that all these titles implied, but it had been so long since he had held office that they scarcely made sense anymore. And besides, it seemed to me that no one name could capture his personality, which at certain moments was razor sharp and yet time and again became vague and unfocused. I couldn't make myself call him Grandfather, although at times he was quite friendly toward me and would call me over to him, trying to give my name a humorous intonation. For the rest, the whole family displayed an attitude toward the count that was a mix of timidity and awe. Only little Erik shared a certain intimacy with the old master of the house; his one movable eye sometimes cast quick glances of accord toward him, which his grandfather would just as fleetingly return. Occasionally during the long afternoons you would see them appear together at the end of the long gallery, walking hand in hand past the old, darkened portraits, not speaking, apparently communicating in some other way.

I spent nearly the whole day in the park or out in the beech forests or on the heath. Luckily there were dogs at Urnekloster to keep me company, and there would always be a tenant's house or a farmstead where I could get milk and bread and fruit. I think my pleasure in this freedom was real and almost unshadowed—at least for the first few weeks—by thoughts of the evening suppers to come. I spoke with almost no one, for I was happiest alone. Only with the dogs did I sometimes have short conversations: we seemed to understand each other perfectly. Reticence was, moreover, a kind of family trait; I was accustomed to it in my father, and wasn't surprised when during the evening meal scarcely a word was spoken.

In the first days after our arrival, however, Mathilde Brahe was talkative in the extreme. She asked my father about old friends in foreign cities, she reminisced about long-ago impressions, she moved herself to tears by recalling friends who had died and a certain young man who, she intimated, had been in love with her, though she had chosen not to reciprocate his heartfelt and hopeless affection. My father listened politely, nodding sympathetically here and there and answering only when absolutely necessary. The count, at the head of the table, wore an unchanging smile on his thin, tight, downturned lips; his face seemed even larger than usual, as if he were wearing a mask. Occasionally he would enter the conversation, but without addressing anyone in particular. His voice was very soft, but it could be heard through the whole length of the hall. It had something of the steady, uninvolved sound of a clock's pendulum; the silence around it seemed to have its own empty resonance, creating equal spaces between each successive syllable.

Count Brahe considered it a special courtesy to my father to speak of his deceased wife, my mother. He called her Countess Sibylle, and all his sentences ended as if he were inquiring after her health. It also seemed to me, I don't know why, that entwined in these words was something about a very young girl in white who might walk in to join us at any moment. I would hear him speak in the same tone about "our little Anna Sophie." And when one day I asked about this young lady, for whom the count seemed to have a special affection, I learned that he was referring to the daughter of High Chancellor Conrad Reventlow, the second, morganatic wife of Frederick IV, who had been resting in one of the tombs at Roskilde for nearly a century and a half. The passage of time had no meaning at all for him; death was a minor incident that he totally ignored. People he had deigned to admit into his memory *existed*, and their mere dying could in no way subvert that. Several years later, after the old gentleman's death, people talked about how he treated the future with the same strange willfulness. Supposedly he had spoken on one occasion to a certain young woman about her sons, and about the travels of one of them in particular, while the young lady, who was only in the third month of her first pregnancy, sat there almost senseless with fear and distress as the old man talked on and on.

But the whole business began with my laughing. Yes, I laughed out loud and couldn't make myself stop. One evening Mathilde Brahe was not there for dinner. When the old, almost stone-blind servant came to her vacant place, he nonetheless stopped and held out the serving dish as always. He persisted in that stance for a time, and then moved on, maintaining perfect dignity and satisfied that all was in order. I had observed this scene, and while I was watching, nothing about it struck me as funny. But a little later, just as I had taken a mouthful of food, a fit of laughter sprang to my head so swiftly that I swallowed the wrong way and caused a great stir. And though I was horribly embarrassed, and made every possible effort to stop and be serious, the laughing kept coming back in waves and maintained its absolute hold on me.

My father, as if to draw attention away from my behavior, asked in his broad, subdued voice: "Is Mathilde ill?" Grandfather smiled that smile of his and then answered with words to which I, wrestling with my own dilemma, paid no attention, but were something like: No, she merely wishes not to encounter Christine. Nor did I register that it was in response to these words that my neighbor, the brown-faced major, abruptly stood up and, with muttered apologies and a bow in the direction of the count, left the room. But I did notice when he turned around once more in the far doorway and began nodding and beckoning to little Erick behind the count's back—and then, to my even greater astonishment, began gesturing to me also, as if he were urging us both to follow him. I was so surprised that my laughter abandoned me. But after that, I paid no more attention to the major; I found him unpleasant, and I noticed that little Erik ignored him too.

The meal dragged on as always, and we had just come to dessert when my eye was caught and held by a movement in the half-darkness at the far end of the hall. A door there, which I had thought was always kept locked, and which I had been told led to the mezzanine, had been opening little by little, and now, as I looked on with a mixture of curiosity and dread that was entirely new to me, a slender woman in a white dress stepped into the shadows of the doorway and slowly made her way toward us. I don't know if I stirred or made a sound; the noise of a chair being overturned forced me to tear my eyes away from that strange shape, and I saw my father, who had sprung to his feet and now, his face pale as death, his hands clenched at his sides, was walking toward the lady. She herself, quite untouched by this scene, kept moving toward us, step by step, and she was already not far from the count's seat when he abruptly stood up, seized my father by the arm, pulled him back to the table and held him there, while the strange woman moved on, step by step, slowly and inattentively, through the space they had cleared, traversing indescribable silence in which the clink of a trembling glass was the only sound, finally to vanish through a door in the opposite wall. I noticed then that it was little Erick who, with a deep bow, closed the door behind this stranger.

I was the only one who had remained seated at the table. I was so weighted down in my chair that I felt I would never be able to get up again without help. For a while I saw without seeing. Then I thought

of my father, and turned to see that the old man was still holding him
tightly by the arm. My father's face was angry and blood red now, but
Grandfather, whose fingers were gripping my father's arm like a white
claw, was smiling his mask-like smile. Then I heard him say something, syllable by syllable, without being able to construe his words.
But they must have lodged in my hearing, because some two years ago
I came across them deep in my memory, and now I know them verbatim. He said: "You are impulsive, Chamberlain, and ill-mannered.
Why don't you let people go about their business?" "Who is that?" my
father interrupted loudly. "Someone who has every right to be here.
Someone who is not a stranger. Christine Brahe." Again the strangely
attenuated silence arose, and again the glass began to tremble. But
then my father tore himself away and stormed out of the hall.

All night long I heard him pacing up and down in his room; for I
too was unable to sleep. But suddenly toward morning I did wake out
of something resembling sleep, and, with a horror that froze me to the
core, saw something white sitting on my bed. My desperation finally
gave me the strength to hide my head under the covers, and there,
from fear and helplessness, I began to cry. Suddenly it became bright
and cool above my weeping eyes; I pressed them shut over my tears
so I wouldn't have to see anything. But the voice that now spoke to
me from very close caressed my face with warmish, saccharine tones,
and I recognized it: it was Fräulein Mathilde's voice. I calmed down
at once, but let her go on comforting me, even though I was no longer
frightened at all. I felt, admittedly, that such sickly-sweet kindness
belittled me, but I enjoyed it nonetheless, and I somehow convinced
myself that I deserved it. "Auntie," I said finally, trying all the while
to assemble in her blurry face my mother's features: "Auntie, who was
that lady?"

"Ah," answered Fräulein Brahe with a sigh that seemed to me almost comically melodramatic, "an unfortunate woman, my child, a very unfortunate woman."

That morning I noticed in one of the rooms several servants busily packing. I assumed we were going to leave; it seemed to me completely logical that we should do so now. Perhaps that was even my father's intention. I never learned what moved him to stay on at Urnekloster after that evening. But we didn't leave. We held out in that house for eight or nine weeks more, we put up with its continual quirks, and we saw Christine Brahe three more times.

Back then I knew nothing of her story. I didn't know that she had died a long, long time before while giving birth to her second child, a son who grew up to a fearful and cruel fate. I didn't know that she herself was dead. But my father knew. Had he, a passionate man who above all valued reason and clarity, willed himself to see this adventure through to its end, unprejudiced and with all the equanimity he could muster? I saw, without understanding, how he struggled with himself; I watched, without comprehending, as he finally mastered himself.

It happened when we saw Christine Brahe for the last time. This time Fräulein Mathilde had joined us at the table; but she was not her usual self. As in the first days after our arrival, she talked incessantly, jumping from one topic to another and continually becoming confused; at the same time she seemed possessed by a physical unease that caused her to play constantly with a lock of her hair or a frill of her dress,—until finally she leapt to her feet with a high plaintive cry and disappeared.

At the same moment my gaze turned instinctively to that notorious door, and sure enough: Christine Brahe was walking through. My neighbor, the major, made a sharp, violent movement that reverberated through my own body, but he apparently lacked the strength to rise. His old, brown, spotted face turned from one of us to another, his mouth hung open, and his tongue tried to work behind his ruined teeth; then suddenly this face was gone and his gray head lay on the table, his arms under and over it like separate pieces, while a withered, spotted hand jutted out from somewhere, trembling.

And now Christine Brahe walked past, step by step, slowly, like someone sick, through indescribable silence, in which there was only a single whimpering sound like that of an old dog. But then, to the left of the large silver swan filled with narcissus, the great mask of the old man thrust forward with its gray smile. He raised his wineglass to my father. And now I watched as my father, just as Christine Brahe passed behind his chair, reached for *his* glass and lifted it, as if it were extremely heavy, a hand's breadth above the table.

And that same night we left.

Bibliothèque Nationale.

I am sitting here reading a poet. There are many people in the room, but none stand out. They are in their books. Sometimes they turn pages, like sleepers turning between two dreams. Ah, how good it is to be among people who are reading. Why aren't they always like this? You can cross over and brush past them gently: they won't feel anything. And if, when you're getting up, you accidentally bump into the people next to you and offer your apologies, they will nod in the direction of your voice, their faces will turn toward you and not see you, and their hair will be like the hair of someone sleeping. How wonderful that is. And I am sitting here and have a poet. What providence. There are perhaps three hundred people in the room now, reading; but it is impossible that each one of them should have a poet. (God knows what they have.) There aren't three hundred poets. But think what a good fortune it is that I, a foreigner, perhaps of all these readers the most wretched: I have a poet. Although I am poor. Although my suit, which I wear every day, is beginning to wear through in certain places, although my shoes are increasingly open to reproach. To be sure, my collar is clean, my underwear also, and I could, just as I am, walk into any pâtisserie, perhaps even one of those on the great boulevards, and confidently reach my hand out to a platter of pastries and help myself. No one would find that scandalous and lecture me and show me the door, for it is after all a hand of the better classes, a hand washed four or five times a day. There is no dirt under my fingernails, no ink stains on my pen finger, and my wrists, especially, are beyond reproach. Poor people don't wash that far up—it's a well-known fact. So there are certain conclusions to be drawn from the cleanliness of these wrists. And people do indeed draw them. They draw them in the best shops. But it must be said that there are a scattering of characters, out on the Boulevard Saint-Michel, for instance, or on the rue Racine, who aren't fooled at all, and who could not care less about wrists. They look at me and they know. They know that I'm really one of them, that I'm only staging a little farce. After all, it's carnival time. And they don't want to spoil my charade: they just grin the tiniest grin and wink. No one sees it. Otherwise, they pretend to treat me like a gentleman. There only has to be someone nearby and they will even begin to act servile toward me, act as if I am wearing a fur coat and my carriage is following along behind me. Sometimes I give them two sous, trembling lest they refuse; but they always take them. And all would

be well, if they hadn't once again grinned just slightly and winked.
Who are these people? What do they want from me? Do they wait for
me? How do they recognize me? My beard does look a little neglected,
and it very, very slightly calls to mind their own sickly, old, deathly
pale beards, which have always made an impression on me. But don't
I have the right to neglect my beard? Many busy, important men do
so, and it would never occur to anyone to count them among the
outcast because of that. For it is clear to me that these people are the
outcast, not merely beggars; no, not beggars at all in fact—one must
make distinctions. They are thrown-away scraps, husks of people spit
out by fate. Moist with fate's spittle, they stick to a wall, to a lamppost,
to an advertising pillar, or they dribble slowly down the street, leaving a dark, dirty trail behind them. What in the world did *she* want
from me, that old woman who had crawled out of a hole somewhere
and held out a drawer from a nightstand with a few buttons and pins
rolling around inside it? Why did she keep walking at my side, view-
ing me intently? As if she knew me and was trying to see who I was
through her bleary eyes, which looked as if some horribly ill person
had spit green phlegm under their bloody lids. And that little gray
woman: What made her stand at my side before a shop window for a
full quarter of an hour while she gradually showed me one old, long
pencil that came pushing up slowly, ever so slowly, out of her insidious
clenched hands? I pretended to be looking at the window display and
not paying attention to anything else. But she knew I had seen her,
she knew I was standing there wondering what she was really up to.
For I understood perfectly that the pencil itself was of no importance;
I felt it was a sign, a sign to the initiated, a sign the outcast recognize;
I sensed she was indicating to me that I must proceed somewhere or
carry out some assignment. And the strangest thing was that I could

not rid myself of the feeling that there actually *was* some conspiracy of which this object was the secret sign, and that this scene was in truth something that I must have long been expecting.

That was two weeks ago. But now practically no day goes by without such an encounter. Not only at dusk: in broad daylight, on the busiest streets, suddenly a little man or an old woman will be there to nod at me, show me something, and then vanish again, as if all that needed doing were now done. It's possible that one day they may come all the way up to my room; they certainly know where I live, and they'll have a plan for getting past the concierge. But here, my dears, here I am safe from you. One must have a special card to get into this room. This card is my warranty against you. I walk through the streets a bit warily, as you can imagine, but eventually I am standing before a glass door, I open it, just as if I were home, I show my card at the next door (exactly the way you show me your things, except here they understand me and know what my card means—), and then I am among these books, taken away from you as if I'd died, and I sit and read a poet.

You don't know what that is, a poet?—Verlaine . . . Nothing? No recollection? No? He didn't stand out for you among those you knew? You don't make distinctions, I know. But I am reading a different poet, one who doesn't live in Paris, someone completely different. Someone who has a quiet house in the mountains. Who rings like a bell in clean air. A happy poet who writes of his window and of the glass doors of his bookcase, which pensively reflect a dear, solitary distance. This is exactly the poet I would have liked to become; for he knows so very much about girls, and I too would have known a lot about girls. He knows about girls who lived a hundred years ago; it doesn't matter that they're dead, for he knows everything. And that's what's essential. He pronounces their names, those soft, slimly written names with the old-fashioned loops in the tall letters, and their older friends' grown-up names, which already resonate with the smallest bit of fate, the smallest bit of death and disappointment. Perhaps hidden away in a compartment of his mahogany writing desk are their faded letters and pages from their diaries that revel in birthdays, summer parties, then birthdays all over again. It might be that in the potbellied bureau at the very back of his bedroom there is a drawer in which he keeps their spring dresses: white dresses that were worn at Easter for the first time, dresses of tufted tulle which were really summer dresses, but which they couldn't wait to wear. Oh, what a happy fate, to sit in the quiet room of an ancestral house among endless calm, settled things and hear outside in the airy, light green garden the first wrens tuning up and in the distance the village clock. To sit and gaze out on a warm streak of afternoon sun and know many things about dead girls and be a poet. And to think that I too might have become such a poet if I could have lived somewhere, anywhere on earth, in one of those boarded-up country houses about which no one cares. I would only have needed one room (the bright room in the gable). There I would have lived with my old things, my family portraits, my books. And I would have had an armchair and flowers and dogs and a strong staff for the stony paths. And nothing else. Only a book bound in yellowish, ivory-toned leather with those old-style floral-patterned endpapers: and in this book I would have written. And I would have written a great many things, for I would have had many thoughts and memories of many people.

But things have turned out otherwise, and God will know why. My old furniture rots in a barn where I was permitted to store it, while

I myself, my God yes, I have no roof over my head, and it is raining into my eyes.

~

Occasionally I walk past little shops, in the rue de Seine for instance. Dealers in antiques or modest secondhand booksellers or vendors of engravings with crowded display windows. No one ever enters their shops; they apparently do no business. But if you look in, there they are, sitting and reading, unconcerned; they don't plan for tomorrow or fret about the day's sales, they have a dog that sits contentedly at their feet or a cat that is making the stillness even deeper by gliding over the rows of books as if erasing the names from their spines.

Ah, if only that sufficed: sometimes I dream of buying a full window like that and sitting behind it with a dog for twenty years.

~

It's good to say it out loud: "Nothing happened." Once more: "Nothing happened." Did that help?

That my stove began to smoke again and I had to go out is really no misfortune. That I feel faint and chilled is of no importance. That I have been rushing about from street to street all day long is my own fault. I could just as well have been sitting in the Louvre. Well, no—I couldn't have done that. There are certain people who go there to get warm. They sit on the velvet benches, and their feet stand in a row on the hot-air vents like big empty boots. They are extremely deferential men who are grateful when the guards in their dark uniforms and their many medals allow them to stay. But when I enter, they grin. Grin and nod slightly. And then, when I make a show of walking back and forth before the paintings, they keep me in their eyes, always in their eyes, always in that one skeptical look that is the sum of all their eyes. So it was just as well that I didn't go to the Louvre. I kept continually on the move. Heaven knows how many towns, districts, graveyards, bridges, and passageways I traversed. In one place I saw a man who was pushing a vegetable cart before him. He was calling out "*Chou-fleur, Chou-fleur,*" giving the "eu" in *fleur* a strangely doleful accent. An ugly, angular woman walked beside him, prodding him now and then. And when she did prod him, he would call out his call. Occasionally he would call out on his own, but that always proved fruitless, and immediately afterward he would be prodded again, for now they would be in front of a house that did make purchases. Have I already said he was blind? No? Well, he was blind. He was blind and he called out. I falsify when I say that, I'm eliding the cart he pushed, I'm acting as if I didn't know that he was calling out cauliflower. But is that important? And even if it were, doesn't it come down to what the whole thing was for me? I saw an old man who was blind and called out. I saw that. Saw.

Will people believe there are houses like this? No, they'll say I'm falsifying. But this time it's the truth, nothing left out—and certainly nothing added. Where would I get it from? People know that I'm poor. Yes, they know. Houses? But to be precise, they were houses that were no longer there. Houses that had been torn down from top to bottom. What *was* there were the other houses, the ones that had stood adjacent to them, the tall neighboring houses. Apparently these were in danger of falling too, since everything adjoining them had been removed; an entire scaffolding of long, tarred poles had been

wedged slantwise between the debris-littered ground and the exposed
wall. Have I already explained that this is the wall I'm dealing with?
Not the first wall of the existing houses (as you might have supposed),
but the last wall of those that were gone. You could see its insides.
You could see, at its successive stories, the walls of rooms to which
the paper still clung, and here and there a piece of floor or ceiling.
Next to these room-walls you could see, running down the length
of the entire wall, a dirty-white space through which there crawled,
in unspeakably sickening, worm-soft, almost intestinal twisting, the
open, rust-spotted channel of the toilet plumbing. You could see
where the gas pipes for the lighting had run along the edge of the
ceiling and then bent suddenly down the colorful walls and plunged
into a black hole that had been crassly punched open for them. But
most unforgettable were the walls themselves. The stubborn life of
these rooms had refused to be snuffed out. It was still there; it clung
to the few nails that protruded, it stood on the last sliver of flooring,
it crouched tightly under the corner joints where a slight bit of inner
space survived. You could see it in the paint, which year by year it
had slowly changed: blue into moldy green, green into gray, yellow
into a stale, putrid white. But it was also in the places that had kept
fresher, behind mirrors, paintings, and wardrobes; for it had traced
and retraced their outlines, and had kept company with cobwebs and
dust even in these hidden places that now lay bared. It was in every
strip of flayed surface, it was in the damp blisters on the edges of the
wallpapers, it flapped in the hanging shreds, and it sweated from the
foul stains that had been made long ago. And from these walls once
blue and green and yellow, framed now by the fracture tracks of the
demolished partitions, the breath of these lives came toward you—
the stubborn, sluggish, heavy breath no wind had yet dispersed. In it

lingered the midday meals and the illnesses and the exhalations and
the smoke of many years and the armpit-sweat that stains clothes and
makes them heavy and the stale breath of mouths and the oily smell
of blistered feet. In it persisted the reek of urine and the bitterness of
soot and the gray half-smell of potatoes and the slick, heavy stench
of rancid fat. The sweetish, insistent smell of neglected infants was
there, and the smell of fear in children dreading school, and the stiff
sheets of pubescent boys' beds. And mixed in were vapors risen from
the street's cauldron and odors fallen with the unclean urban rain.
And still more funneled in by the tame house winds that never leave
their single street. And many other things of unknown origin. I did
mention, didn't I, that all the walls had been torn down except for the
last—? It's this last one I've been speaking of all this time. You'd think
I had stood there looking at it for hours; but I swear that I broke into a
run the moment I recognized that wall. For that's the terrible thing: I
recognized it. I recognize everything here, and that's why it enters me
so easily: it is at home in me.

I was feeling exhausted after all that, almost assaulted as it were,
and thus it was just too much when on top of everything *he* should
be waiting for me. He was sitting in the little crémerie where I was
planning to have two fried eggs; I was hungry, I had gone the whole
day without eating. But even now I couldn't stay long enough to eat;
before the eggs were ready something compelled me out again into
the streets, which were thick with people flooding toward me. It was
carnival, and evening, and the people all had time on their hands
and were drifting to and fro and rubbing up against each other. And
their faces were full of the light coming from the carnival grounds,
and laughter welled from their mouths like pus from an open sore.
The more frantically I tried to force my way forward, the more loudly

they laughed and the more densely they crowded together. A woman's shawl had somehow gotten caught on me; I dragged her along in my wake, and people stopped me and laughed, and I felt that I ought to laugh too, but I couldn't. Someone threw a handful of confetti in my eyes, and it stung like a whip. At the corners people were tightly wedged together, one jammed into another, so that no movement forward was possible, only a soft, gentle back-and-forth motion, as if they were all copulating while standing up. But even though they were stationary and I was running like a madman along the roadside wherever I found gaps in the crowd, somehow it was they who were moving while I remained stationary. For nothing changed; when I looked up, I always saw the same houses on one side and the same carnival booths on the other. Perhaps indeed nothing moved, and it was only a vertigo in me and in them that made everything seem to whirl around. I had no time to reflect on this, I was drenched in sweat, and a numbing pain was coursing through me, as though something too big were being borne on my blood, distending the veins wherever it went. And I felt that the air had long since run out and that I was only breathing in exhalations that my lungs rejected.

But it's over now; I have survived it. I am sitting in my room by the lamp; it's a little cold, for I don't dare try the stove; what if it smoked and I had to go out again? I am sitting and thinking: if I weren't poor, I'd rent a different room, a room with furniture that isn't so worn out, so full of prior occupants, as the furniture here. At first I had to will myself to lean my head back on this armchair; for in its green upholstery there's a greasy-gray depression that seems to fit everyone's head. For the longest time I was careful to put a handkerchief behind my head, but now I'm too tired for that; I've discovered that it's all right the way it is, and that in fact the small hollow fits the back of my head perfectly, as if made to order. But if I were not poor I would first of all buy a new stove, and I would burn the clean strong wood that comes from the mountains, and not these miserable *têtes-de-moineau*, whose fumes frighten your breath so badly and make your head so confused. And then there would have to be someone to tidy up without making loud noises, and to keep the fire the way I like it; for often when I have to kneel before the stove and poke at it for a quarter of an hour, with the skin on my brow stretched tight by the heat and the fire right up in my open eyes, I exhaust all the energy in me that has to last for the whole day, so that when I finally go out among people, they naturally have an easy time with me. Sometimes, when the crush was really bad, I'd take a carriage and drive by; I'd eat in a Duval every day . . . and no longer slink into the crémeries . . . Would *he* have been sitting in a Duval? No. He wouldn't have been allowed to wait for me there. They don't permit the dying inside. The dying? But I am sitting now in my room; I can try to reflect calmly on what happened to me. It's good to leave nothing unclarified. I went in, then, and saw at first only that the table where I usually sit had been taken by someone else. I nodded in the direction of the little counter, ordered, and sat down at the next table. But I felt him there, even though he didn't move. It was in fact his very immobility that I felt, and all in an instant I understood it. The bond between us was forged, and I realized that he was stiff with terror. I knew that terror had paralyzed him, terror at something that was happening inside him. Perhaps one of his blood vessels had burst, perhaps a poison, whose effect he has long been dreading, was finally entering a chamber of his heart, perhaps a large tumor was rising in his brain like a sun and was transforming the world for him. With indescribable effort I forced myself to look over at him, for I was still hoping that it was all in my imagination. But already I was on my feet and rushing out; for I had not been wrong. He was sitting there in a thick, black winter coat, and his gray, tensed face sat deep in a woolen scarf. His mouth was closed as if it had slammed shut with great force, but it wasn't possible to say whether his eyes still saw anything: they were hidden behind smeared, smoke-gray glasses that trembled slightly. His nostrils were flared, and the long hair over his emptied temples was wilting as from too great a heat. His ears were long and yellow, with large shadows behind them. Yes, he knew that now he was withdrawing: not just from people but from everything. A moment more and all of it will have lost its meaning, and this table and the cup and the chair he was clinging to, everything quotidian and close at hand will have become incomprehensible—something merely strange, something merely heavy. So he sat there and waited as it happened. And no longer resisted.

And I am still resisting. I am resisting, even though I know that my heart is already hanging out of me and that I couldn't live even if my torturers were to walk away and leave me alone now. I say to myself: "Nothing happened," and yet I was only able to understand that man because something is happening within me as well, something that is starting to distance me and cut my ties with everything. How horrified I always was when I heard it said that someone dying "could no longer recognize anyone." I would imagine a solitary face lifting itself up from pillows and looking around everywhere, everywhere, searching for something familiar, something seen before, but finding nothing, nothing at all. If my fear were less great, I would console myself with the thought that one can see everything differently and still go on living. But I am afraid, I have a nameless fear of this change. I've scarcely begun to feel at home in *this* world, which seems to me a goodly one. How should I fare in another? I would so gladly remain among the meanings I've grown fond of here, and if this change must happen, may I at least live among dogs, whose world is related to ours and whose things are the same.

For the time being, I can write all this down and say it. But there will come a day when my hand will be far from me, and when I tell it to write, it will write words that are not mine at all. The time of the other interpretation will dawn, and not one word will be left upon another, and every meaning will dissolve like clouds and fall like rain. But for all my fear, I am yet like someone standing before something great, and I recall that it was often like this in me before I began to write. But this time I will be written. I am the impression to be transformed. Ah, except for a distance that is so short, I could understand all this and see that it was good. Only a small step, and my deep misery would become blessedness. But I cannot take this step, I have fallen and can no longer pick myself up, because I am broken. I have always believed that some help might come. There they lie before me, in my own handwriting: the words I've pronounced, evening after evening, like prayer. I copied them out of the books in which I found them, so that they might be very close to me, sprung from my hand as if they were my own. And now I want to write them out once more, kneeling here at my table I want to write them down; that way they will remain with me longer than when I read them, and each word will last and have time to fade.

Mécontent de tous et mécontent de moi, je voudrais bien me racheter et m'enorgueillir un peu dans le silence et la solitude de la nuit. Âmes de ceux que j'ai aimés, âmes de ceux que j'ai chantés, fortifiez-moi, soutenez-

moi, éloignez de moi le mensonge et les vapeurs corruptrices du monde;
et vous, Seigneur mon Dieu! accordez-moi la grâce de produire quelques
beaux vers qui me prouvent à moi-même que je ne suis pas le dernier des
hommes, que je ne suis pas inférieur à ceux que je méprise.

~

"They were the children of fools—yea, the children of villains who were viler than the earth. And now I am their song and their byword . . .

. . . they have made of me the road of their destruction . . .

. . . they delighted in my crippling, and they needed no helper.

And now my soul pours out over me; the days of affliction have arrived.

My bones are bored through in the night, and my tormentors sleep not.

Through the whims of their power my clothes are changed: I am hung up as by the collar of my coat . . .

My intestines boil ceaselessly; the days of affliction are upon me . . .

My harp has become a lament, and my flute a weeping."

~

The doctor didn't understand me. Not any of it. And it is, admittedly, hard to describe. They wanted to try electrotherapy. All right. I received a slip of paper: I was to be at the Salpêtrière at one o'clock. I was there. I had to maneuver past various small buildings and across several courtyards where here and there people in white caps were standing around under the bare trees, looking like convicts. At last I came to a long, dark corridor-like room, one side of which had four windows of opaque, greenish glass, each separated from the next by a stretch of black wall. A wooden bench ran the length of this wall, and on this bench sat those who knew me, waiting. Yes, they were all there. When I'd gotten accustomed to the half-light of the room, I could see that among all those who sat there shoulder to shoulder on that endless bench, there were probably also a few regular people, functioning people—manual laborers, housemaids, carters. Down at the narrow end of the corridor two fat women—concierges probably—had spread out on special chairs and were talking. I looked at the clock. It was five minutes to one. So in five minutes, say ten at the most, my turn would come; that wasn't so bad. The air was foul, heavy, full of clothes and breath. At one particular spot the strong, heady cold of ether blew in through a door left ajar. I began to pace up and down. It dawned on me that I had specifically been directed *here*, among *these* people, for this overcrowded, all-purpose consulting hour. It was, as it were, the first official confirmation that I was one of the outcast. Had the doctor known just by looking? Yet I'd gone to see him in a reasonably decent suit; I had sent in my card. Nevertheless he must have sensed it. Perhaps I'd somehow given myself away. In any event, now that it was a matter of record, I didn't find it so bad after all. The people were sitting there quietly and paid no attention to me. Some were in pain and swung one leg a little to help endure it. Different men had laid their heads in their hands; others were sleeping soundly with heavy, submerged faces. A fat man with a red, swollen neck sat bent forward, staring at the floor, and from time to time spitting crassly at a spot he'd picked out. A child sobbed in a corner; it had drawn its long, thin legs up onto the bench, and held them to its body in a tight embrace, as if bidding them a desperate farewell.

A short, pale woman in a crepe hat with round black flowers that sat crookedly on her hair was forcing onto her thin lips a smile that was like a grimace, while tears ran from her chafed lids. Next to her they had placed a girl with a round, smooth face and protruding eyes that lacked all expression; her mouth hung open, so that you could see her white, viscid gums with their prematurely old, decayed teeth. And there were endless bandages. Bandages that wrapped around an entire head, layer after layer, until there remained only a single eye that no longer belonged to anyone. Bandages that concealed, and bandages that revealed what lay beneath. Bandages that had come open and in which now, as on a soiled bed, a hand lay that no longer was a hand; and a bandaged leg that jutted out from the row on the bench, as big as a whole person. I paced up and down and tried my best to remain calm. I studied the opposite wall. I observed that it contained a number of single doors and did not reach all the way to the ceiling, so that this corridor was not completely sealed off from the rooms that must be on the other side. I looked at the clock; I had been pacing back and forth for an hour. A while later the doctors arrived. First a few young men who walked by with impassive faces, then finally the one I had been to see, in light gloves, *chapeau à huit reflets*, and impeccable topcoat. When he saw me, he lifted his hat a little and smiled distractedly. I hoped now I'd be called right away, but another hour passed. I can't remember how I spent it. It passed. An old man in a dirty apron came out, some sort of attendant, and tapped me on the shoulder. I stepped into one of the adjoining rooms. The doctor and the young men were sitting around a table and looked at me; someone offered me a chair. Good. And now I was to tell them what was wrong with me. As briefly as possible, *s'il vous plait*. For these gentlemen were pressed for time. I felt strange. The young men sat and looked at me with that superior, professional curiosity they had learned so well. The doctor I knew stroked his black goatee and smiled absently. I thought I would break out in tears, but I heard myself say in French: "I have already had the honor, monsieur, of giving you all the information I can give. If you think it necessary that these gentlemen share it, you can certainly, given our prior conversation, do that in a few words; whereas I myself would find it extremely difficult." The doctor rose with a polite smile, stepped to the window with his underlings, and said a few words, which he accompanied with a vague, back-and-forth movement of his hand. After three minutes one of the young men, short-sighted and fidgety, came back to the table and said, trying to seem as if he were peering deeply into me, "Do you sleep well, monsieur?" "No, badly." Whereupon he hurried back to the group. They conferred a while longer, then the doctor turned to me and informed me that I would be called. I reminded him that I had been scheduled for one o'clock. He smiled and made a few swift, flapping gestures with his small white hands, trying to communicate to me how uncommonly busy he was. So I returned to my corridor, in which the air had grown much more oppressive, and began to pace up and down once more, although I felt dead on my feet. Finally the thick, dank smell started making me dizzy; I stopped by the entrance door and cracked it open. I saw that outside it was still afternoon and there was a little sunshine, and that helped me more than words can say. But I had scarcely been standing there for a minute when I heard someone call me. A woman sitting at a little table two steps away hissed something at me. Who had told me to open that door? I said I couldn't tolerate the air inside. Well, that was my problem, but the door must remain closed. Was it permissible, then, to open a window? No, that was forbidden. I decided to resume pacing up and down, since it had a kind of numbing effect and, after all, hurt no one. But now this too displeased the woman at the little table. Did I not have a place to sit? No, I didn't. But walking about was not permitted; I would have to find myself a seat. Surely there must be one. The woman was right. A place was quickly found next to the girl with the protuberant eyes. So I sat there now with the feeling that this arrangement must be the prelude to something terrible. On my left was the girl with the rotting gums; it took me a while to make out what was on my right. It was some huge, immovable mass, with a face and one large, lifeless hand. The side of the face I could see was empty, completely without features and without memories, and it was uncanny how closely his suit resembled that of a corpse dressed for the coffin. The narrow black tie was fastened around the collar in the same slack, impersonal way, and it was obvious that the coat had been pulled onto this will-less body by other people. The hand had been placed on the trousers exactly where it now lay. Even the hair looked as if had been combed by those women who wash corpses, and it now stood stiffly and suitably, like the hair of stuffed animals. I observed all this very carefully, and it suddenly came to me that this was the seat that fate had chosen for me—that I had finally arrived at the place in my life where I would remain forever. Yes, fate takes strange paths.

Suddenly, from somewhere close to me, I heard the terrified screams of a child trying to ward something off. They kept coming rapidly, one after another, before finally subsiding into a soft, muffled weeping. While I strained to discover where this could have come from, a small suppressed cry began trembling again, and I heard voices asking questions, another voice almost whispering commands, and then some sort of relentless machine was activated, and it hummed on indifferently. Now I remembered that partial wall, and I understood that everything was coming from beyond the doors and that the doctors were at work in there. The attendant with the dirty apron actually appeared from time to time and signaled. I had almost given up thinking that he might mean me. *Did* he? No. Two men appeared with a wheelchair; they lifted the mass beside me into it, and I saw now that it was an old paralytic who had another, smaller side to him, used up by life, and an open, clouded, melancholy eye. They wheeled him inside, and now suddenly there was a large place beside me. And I sat and wondered what they planned to do to the empty girl beside me and whether she would scream too. The mechanical hum of the machines in the back was so sedating that there was nothing disturbing about the thought at all.

But suddenly everything fell silent, and into the silence a haughty, self-satisfied voice I thought I recognized said: *"Riez!"* A pause. *"Mais riez, riez!"* Already I was laughing. I couldn't understand why the person on the other side didn't want to laugh. Another machine started up, but then quickly went silent. Words were exchanged, the same assertive voice rose again and commanded: *"Dites-nous le mot: avant."* Spelling: *"A-v-a-n-t."* Silence. *"On n'entend rien. Encore une fois . . ."*

And then, amid the warm, spongy babble leaking in from the other side: it was *here* again, for the first time in many, many years: that nightmare which had struck terror into me—my first, my deepest terror—when as a child I lay in bed sick with fever: the Big Thing. Yes, that was what I had always said when they all stood around my bed and took my pulse and asked me what was frightening me: the Big Thing. And when they fetched the doctor and he was there and tried to talk to me, I would just keep begging him to make the Big Thing go away; nothing else mattered. But he was like all the others. He could not remove it, although back then I was still little and it would have been so easy to help me. And now it was back again. Later, it had simply stayed away of its own accord; even on nights when I lay with fever it had not come back. But now it was here, and I was awake and had no fever. Now it was here. Now it grew out of me like a tumor, like a second head, and was a part of me, even though it was far too big to belong to me. It was there like a big dead animal that once, when it was still alive, had been my hand or my arm. And my blood flowed through me and through it, as through a single body. And my heart had to work extra hard to pump blood into the Big Thing; there was almost not enough blood for the task. And the blood entered the Big Thing unwillingly and came back sick and tainted. But the Big Thing swelled and spread over my face like a warm bluish boil and spread over my mouth, and already it was casting its shadows over my last eye.

I can't remember how I escaped through all those courtyards. It was evening, and I lost my way in that foreign district and walked up boulevards with long walls and then, when I saw there was no end to those walls, I walked back down again until I came to some random square. There I chose a street and began to walk down it, and came to other streets I had never seen before, and then still others. From time to time electric trolleys came rushing up and past, impossibly bright and with harsh, incessant clanging. But their destination panels displayed names I didn't recognize. I didn't know what city I was in and whether somewhere here I had a place to stay and what I had to do in order to stop walking.

~

And now, on top of everything, this illness again, which has always affected me so strangely. I am sure that it is underrated. Just as the seriousness of certain other illnesses is exaggerated. This illness has no defining characteristics; it takes on those of the people it attacks. With a sleepwalker's unerring instinct, it draws out their deepest danger, which seemed long past, and confronts them with it again, so that it seems right there before them, less than a stride or a moment away. Grown men, who back in their school days practiced that compulsive vice whose duped partners were their own poor boyhood hands, find themselves at it again; or an illness they overcame as children takes hold again; or a lost habit reappears—a certain hesitant turn of the head, for instance, that had marked them years before. And attached to what comes back, a long tangle of errant memories arises, like wet seaweed clinging to some sunken thing. Lives you would never have recognized surge to the surface, mingle with the life you actually lived, displace the past you thought you knew: for what rises from the depths has a fresh new strength, while what has always occupied the surface is wearied from too much remembering.

I am lying in my bed, five flights up, and my day, which nothing interrupts, is like a dial without hands. Just as one morning something that went missing long ago is suddenly there again, resting mysteriously in its old place, safe and sound, looking almost newer than when it disappeared, as if someone had been caring for it the whole time—: in just that way things lost from my childhood are scattered before me on my blanket, and they are like new. All the lost fears are back again.

The fear that a small woolen thread jutting from the hem of my blanket is hard, hard and sharp like a steel needle; the fear that this small button on my nightshirt is bigger than my head, bigger and heavier; the fear that the bread crumb now falling from my bed will shatter like glass when it hits the floor, and the feverish anxiety that when that happens, everything will be shattered along with it, every-thing forever; the fear that the edge of a letter that was torn open may be something forbidden that no one should see, something indescrib-ably secret for which no hiding place in my room is safe enough; the fear that if I fell asleep I would swallow the piece of coal that lies in front of the stove; the fear that some number in my brain will begin to increase until it occupies all the space in my inner being; the fear that I am lying on granite, on gray granite; the fear that I will start screaming and people will come running to my door and finally break it open, and the fear that when that happens I will betray myself and start confessing all my fears, and the opposite fear that in fact I will say nothing because everything is unsayable; and still the fears go on, all the other fears.

Well, I prayed for my childhood, and it has returned, and I feel that it is just as difficult now as it was then, and that growing older has done me no good at all.

~

Yesterday my fever was better, and today is starting out like spring, like the springtime in paintings. I'm going to try to go out to the Bib-liothèque Nationale to visit my poet, whom I haven't read for such a very long time, and perhaps later I can take a slow walk through the gardens. Perhaps there will be wind over the big pond that has such real water, and children will come to launch their boats with red sails and watch them as they float off.

Today I didn't expect it; I went out with such a full heart, as if doing so was the simplest, most natural thing in the world. And yet once again something happened that snatched me up like a piece of paper and crumpled me and tossed me away: something scarcely to be believed.

The Boulevard Saint-Michel was broad and empty, and walking along its gentle slope was effortless. Overhead casement windows opened with a glassy sound, casting their reflections over the street like white birds. A carriage with bright red wheels rolled past, and farther down someone was carrying something that was light green. Horses in shimmering harness trotted along the dark, freshly sprinkled boulevard. The new wind was brisk and mild, and everything was rising: smells, shouts, bells.

I passed one of those cafés where in the evenings fake red gypsies perform. Sleepless night air crept guiltily out of the opened windows. Sleek-haired waiters were busy scrubbing the pavement in front of the doors. One of them stood bent over, throwing handfuls of yellowish sand under the tables. A passerby stopped, nudged him, and pointed down the street. The waiter, whose face was deep red, gazed intently in that direction for a few moments, and then a laugh spread over his beardless cheeks, as if it had been spilled on them. He gestured to the other waiters, swiveling his laughing face rapidly from left to right, trying to direct their attention without missing anything of the spectacle himself. Now they all stood there gazing or searching the street, smiling or growing frustrated at not being able to find what it was that was so amusing.

I felt a slight fear starting up in me. Something told me to cross over to the other side of the street; but I only began to walk faster while scanning instinctively the few people in front of me, about whom I could find nothing unusual. But I did see that one of them, an errand boy wearing a blue apron and with an empty basket slung over his shoulder, was gazing after someone. When he'd looked long enough, he pivoted toward the houses and gestured to a laughing clerk across the street with that finger at the forehead that everyone understands. Then his dark eyes flashed and he came toward me with a knowing swagger.

I expected that as soon as my eyes had an opening I would see someone who was strikingly unusual; but it turned out that there was no one in front of me except a tall, lean man in a dark overcoat and with a soft black hat over his short, light blond hair. I made sure there was nothing comical about this man's clothing or comportment, and was already trying to look past him down the boulevard when he tripped over something. Since I was following close behind him, that put me on my guard, but when the place in question arrived, there was no obstacle there, absolutely nothing. We both continued on, he and I, the distance between us remaining the same. Now we came to a crossing, and the man ahead of me raised one leg and hopped down the steps to the street, much the way children, when they are happy, will sometimes hop or skip as they walk. The steps on the other side he managed easily with one long stride. But he was scarcely on his way again when he lifted one leg slightly and hopped high on the other foot, then did it quickly once more and then again. This time too you might quite easily have taken this sudden motion to be a stumble, and assumed that some commonplace object lay there in his path— the core or slick skin of a fruit, for instance, or anything similar; and the strange thing was that the man himself seemed to believe in the reality of such an obstacle; for each time, he turned and looked back at the offending place, with that half-annoyed, half-reproachful look people have at such moments. Once again something warned me to cross to the other side of the street, but I didn't heed it and continued on behind this man, fixing my whole attention on his legs. I must

confess that I felt oddly relieved when for some twenty steps the hopping movement did not recur, but now when I looked up, I saw that
something new had begun to harass the man. The collar of his overcoat had flipped up, and try as he would, now using one hand, now
taking elaborate pains with both, he could not get it to lie flat again.
Such things happen. It didn't really worry me. But just then I saw
with openmouthed astonishment that there were *two* motions at work
in his busy hands: a swift, secret movement with which he covertly
flipped the collar up, and a more deliberate, prolonged, almost exaggeratedly explicit movement that was meant to accomplish the work
of smoothing the collar back down. This observation so disconcerted
me that two minutes passed before I recognized that in his neck,
behind the upturned overcoat and the desperate playacting of his
hands, there was the same fearful, bipolar hopping motion that had
just left his legs. From that moment I was bound to him. I understood
that this hopping was searching around in his body, attempting in
various places to break out. I understood now why he was afraid of
people, and I myself began to observe cautiously whether those who
passed by noticed anything peculiar. A cold stab sliced down my spine
when his legs suddenly made a small, convulsive leap, but no one had
seen it, and I decided that I too would stumble a little when he did, in
case anyone began to notice. That would certainly be a way of making
the curious believe that there really had been some small, inconspicuous obstacle lying in the way, and that we both had tripped on it. But
while I had been thinking of ways to help, he himself had hit upon a
new, ingenious solution. I forgot to mention that he carried a cane; it
was an ordinary cane, made of dark wood with a plain curved handle.
And in his desperation, it had occurred to him that he could hold this
cane, at first in one hand (for who knew what the other might yet be

needed for?), at his back, against his spine, pressing it firmly into the small of his back and thrusting the crook under his coat collar, where he could feel it as something hard, like a brace behind the neck and the first dorsal vertebra. This resulted in a posture that was inconspicuous, at most a bit excessively high-spirited; but the unexpected spring day could easily account for that. No one thought of turning around to look, and now all went well. Blessedly well. True, at the next crossing two hops escaped, two tiny, half-suppressed hops, but they didn't amount to anything; and the one really visible leap was so cunningly timed (just at that point a hose lay across his path) that there was no cause for alarm. Yes, things were still going well; from time to time his other hand would grip the cane and press it more firmly against his back, and the danger was quickly survived again. But I couldn't keep my anxiety from growing. I knew that while he was walking along and expending infinite effort to appear casual and unconcerned, the terrible convulsions were accumulating in his body; I too felt the fear with which he felt them growing and growing, and I saw how he clamped down on his cane when the spasms began inside him. The expression of those hands would then be so fierce and unyielding that I placed all my hope in his will, which must be huge. But what good was a will. The moment would inevitably come when his strength was used up; it couldn't be far off. And I, who was following along behind him with my heart pounding, I gathered together all my bits of strength like coins, and, with my eyes still fixed on his hands, I begged him to please take it if he needed it.

I think he did take it; there was so little, but how could I help that?

The Place Saint-Michel was busy with many vehicles and people hurrying here and there; several times we were caught between two carriages, and then he would take a breath and relax his hold on himself just a little, as if to rest, and then he would hop a bit and his head would twitch. Perhaps this was the trick by which his caged malady planned to break out of him. His will had been breached in two places, and the act of yielding had left behind in his restive muscles a gentle, seductive quivering and that continual two-beat rhythm. But the cane was still in its place, and the expression of his hands was stern and unrelenting. So as we stepped onto the bridge, it was all right. It was all right. But now an unmistakable faltering entered his stride: he took two steps, then stood still. Stood still. His left hand gently pulled away from the cane and rose so slowly that I could see it trembling against the sky; he pushed his hat back a little and drew his hand across his brow. He turned his head just enough, and his gaze loosened as it swept past sky, past houses, past water, without fixing on anything. Then he gave in. The cane was gone, he stretched out his arms as if he would take flight, and it broke out of him like a force of nature and bent him forward and ripped him backward and set him to nodding and bowing and flung pure dance-mania out of him and into the crowd. For by now many people had gathered around him, and I could no longer see him.

What sense would it make to go somewhere now. I was drained. Like a blank sheet of paper I drifted along past the houses and back up the boulevard again.

~

*I am trying to write to you now, although there is really nothing to say after a necessary farewell. I am trying anyway; I think I must,

---

*   *The draft of a letter.* [Rilke's note]

because I have seen the saint in the Panthéon, the solitary saintly woman and the ceiling and the door and the lamp inside with its modest circle of light and, beyond, the sleeping city and the river and the moonlit distance. The saint watches over the sleeping city. I wept. I wept because it was all so suddenly and unexpectedly there. I wept standing before it; I couldn't help myself.

I am in Paris. The people who hear this are glad; most of them envy me. They are right. It is a great city, great and filled with strange, remarkable temptations. For my part, I must admit that I have, in a certain sense, succumbed to them. There is no other way of putting it. I have succumbed to these temptations, and doing so has brought about certain changes, if not in my character, then at least in my view of the world, and, in any case, in my life. Under these influences a completely different conception of all things has gradually formed in me; certain distinctions now mark me off from other people more sharply than anything previously. A world transformed. A new life filled with new meanings. For the moment I am finding it a bit difficult, because it is all too new. I am a beginner in the circumstances of my own life.

Might it not be possible, just for once, to see the sea?

Yes, but just think, I'd imagined that you might come. Perhaps you could have told me if there was a doctor? I forgot to inquire. But it doesn't really matter anymore.

Do you remember Baudelaire's incredible poem "Une Charogne"? Perhaps now I understand it. Except for the last stanza, he was in the right. What should he have done after encountering that? It was his task to perceive in this terrible thing, which seemed only a repulsive anomaly, the Being that validates all existence. Beyond choice, beyond refusal. Do you think it was by chance that Flaubert wrote his "Saint Julien l'Hospitalier"? Here, it seems to me, is the crux: Can one bring oneself to lie down at the side of a leper and warm him with the heat that the heart puts forth? Only good could come from such an action.

But don't imagine that I am suffering disappointments here—quite the contrary. It amazes me sometimes how readily I relinquish all my expectations in favor of what turns out to be real, even when what is real is terrible.

My God, if only something of this could be shared. But would it *exist* then, would it *exist*? No, it *is* only at the price of solitude.

~

The existence of the horrific in every particle of the air. It's invisible when you breathe it in; but inside you it precipitates out, hardens, forms needle-sharp, geometric structures in the spaces between your organs; because all the torment and horror undergone at places of execution, in torture chambers, in madhouses and operating rooms, under the arches of bridges in late autumn: it all has a tenacious staying power, it persists in itself and, jealous of what has material existence, clings to its own frightful reality. People would like to forget as much of this as possible; sleep gently files down these ridges in the brain, but dream drives sleep off and re-engraves the patterns. And they wake up gasping and melt an entire candle's length in the darkness and drink the pale reassurance as if it were sugared water. But alas, on how thin a ledge this security stands. Only the slightest shift, and the gaze is once again looking out beyond the known and the friendly, and the gentle contour that was so comforting a moment ago comes into focus as the edge of terror. Beware of the light, for it hollows out space. Don't look round when you sit up: a shadow may have risen up behind you as your master. It would have been better, perhaps, if you had remained in the dark, and your unexplored heart had persisted as the heavy heart of a presence that cannot be distinguished. But now you know your outlines, you can see where you come to an end at your hands that are right there in front of you; from time to time you trace with an uncertain gesture the contours of your face. And inside you there is scarcely any room; and it almost calms you to think that nothing very large could possibly lodge in this narrow space; that even the monstrous, to become an inner thing, would have to accommodate itself to these cramped dimensions. But outside—nothing limits it outside. And when its level rises out there, it also starts to fill in you; not in your veins and arteries, which are partly subject to your will, nor in the phlegm of your more impassive organs: it rises in your capillaries, sucked up through their tubes into the outermost branch-work of your infinitely traversed being. There it mounts, there it floods you, rising higher than your breath, toward which you have fled as to your last refuge. Ah, where then, where then? Your heart is driving you out of yourself, it's pursuing you, and already you're almost standing outside yourself and can't get back in. Like a beetle that's been stepped on, you spurt from yourself, and your shards of outer hardness and adaptability count for nothing.

O night without objects. O window inured to the outside, O dutifully locked doors; devices from olden times, inherited, accredited, never fully utilized. O silence in the stairwell, silence from adjoining rooms, silence high up against the ceiling. O mother: Only you stood between your child and all this silence. You took it all upon yourself, saying: Don't be afraid, it's me. You had the courage deep in night to *be* this silence for this child who was afraid, who was perishing from fear. You light a lamp, and already that sound is you. And you hold it out before you and say: It's me, don't be afraid. And you put it down slowly, and there is no doubt: it *is* you, you are the light around all these familiar intimate things that rest where they are without deeper meaning—simple, unambiguous, good. And if something moves restlessly in the wall, or a step creaks in the floor: you simply smile, smile transparently against the bright background of your visage, into the anxious face that is searching yours; as if you shared the secret of every half-sound, and whatever occurred had already been agreed on and approved by you. Does any power equal yours in the realm of earthly rule? Look, kings lie and stare, and the storyteller cannot distract them. Though they lie at the blessed breast of their beloved, dread suddenly creeps over them and makes them sick and impotent. But you are the first to come and you keep the monstrous behind you and you truly are a barrier it cannot breach; not just some curtain that ripples open here or there. As if you had arrived far ahead of anything dark that might be on its way, and had behind you only your own rush to be here, your eternal path, the flight of your love.

~

[On Beethoven] The *mouleur* whose shop I pass every day has hung two masks beside his door. The face of the young drowned woman, which they took a cast of in the morgue: because it was beautiful, because it smiled, because its smile was so mysterious, as if it *knew*. And beneath it, *his* knowing face. That hard knot of tightly contracted thinking. That relentless compression of a music always about to evaporate. The visage of one whose hearing a god had closed, so there would be no sounds other than his own. So he would not be misled by what is murky and ephemeral in the realm of sounds—he who had within him their clarity and permanence. So that only the mute senses might carry the world in to him, silently, an unfinished, waiting world, tense with the anticipation of sound.

World-consummator: as what falls as rain over the earth and onto the waters falls without purpose, falls carelessly: and as it then rises again out of everything, invisible now, joyous, its actions following a law, and ascends and floats and forms the heavens: just so did all our fallings rise out of you and vault the world with music.

Your music: perhaps it was for the universe to hear, not for us. Perhaps a *Hammerklavier* was to have been built for you in the Theban desert, and an angel was to have led you to that solitary instrument, out through the mountains of the wilderness, where kings rest and courtesans and anchorites. And then he would have swooped up and away, fearful that your first chords would slay him.

And you would have streamed forth torrents of sound, unheard; giving back to the universe what only the universe can endure. The Bedouins would have raced by in the distance, superstitious; the merchants would have flung themselves to the ground at the far edge of your music, thinking you were the storm. Only a few solitary lions would have prowled around you at night in wide circles, frightened of themselves, alarmed by the increase of passion in their blood.

And who will rescue you now from lascivious ears? Who will drive from the concert halls these venal ones whose sterile hearing copulates and never conceives? The semen irrupts, and they lie beneath it like whores and play with it, or it falls on the ground like the seed of Onan, while they writhe in their fruitless consummations.

But Master: If an innocent youth whose ear was virgin lay with your sound, he would die of bliss—or else become pregnant with the infinite, and his inseminated brain would burst with sheer birth.

~

I don't underestimate it. I know it takes courage. But let's assume for a moment that someone had it, this *courage de luxe* to follow them, and discover once and for all (for who could forget it again or remember it wrongly?) what impossible place they creep into afterward and what they do with the rest of their slowly passing day and whether they sleep at night. That especially needs to be ascertained: whether they sleep. But it will take more than courage. For they don't come and go like other people, whom it would be a simple matter to follow. They are here and then gone, set down and taken away like lead soldiers. You find them in places that are slightly out-of-the-way but by no means hidden. The bushes clear, the path bends a little around the lawn: and there they are, with a large transparent space around them, as if they were standing under a bell jar. You might take them for strollers who've been arrested by some thought, these nondescript little men with their modest, completely unassuming bodies. But you'd be wrong. Do you see the left hand, how it reaches for something in the slanted pocket of the old overcoat; how it finds it and pulls it out and takes the small object and awkwardly lifts it up into the air, as if for everyone to see? In less than a minute, two, three birds have appeared, sparrows, hopping up inquisitively. And if the man satisfies their very strict perception of stillness, there is no reason why they shouldn't hop a bit closer. Eventually one of them flies up and for a while flutters warily in the space around that hand, which holds out God knows what crumbs of dry sweet bread in its undemanding, expressly self-abjuring fingers. And the more people collect around him—at an appropriate distance, of course—the less he has in common with them. He stands there like a candle that is burning down and gives light with the remainder of its wick and is all warm from it and has never moved. And his power of attraction, his ability to lure, remains a complete mystery to those many small, witless birds. If there were no onlookers and he was allowed to stand there long enough, I am certain that an angel would suddenly appear and, overcoming an aversion, swoop down and eat the stale, sweetish morsel from that ravaged hand. But now, as always, humans block the way. They make sure that only birds come; they find that sufficient, and they maintain that he expects nothing more. What else should it expect, this old, weather-beaten doll, stuck in the ground at a slight angle like those ships' figureheads in the small gardens back home? Is he leaning like that because once he stood somewhere on the forward curve of life, where the force of motion is greatest? Is he now so faded because he was once so bright? Will you ask him?

Only don't ask the women anything when you see them feeding the birds. You could even follow them; they do it as they walk; it would be easy. But let them be. They don't know how it happens. Suddenly they have bread in their bag, and they hold big pieces out from under their thin shawls, pieces that are slightly chewed and moist. It helps them to think that their saliva is getting out into the world a little, that the small birds will fly around with that taste in their mouths—though of course they immediately forget it.

[On Ibsen] There I sat at your books, obstinate man, trying to consume them in the manner of the others, who don't confront them as one great work, but take a small piece for themselves and go away satisfied with that. For I didn't yet understand fame, that public demolition of one still evolving, whose building site the mob overruns, scattering its stones.

Young man (wherever you may be) in whom something is taking shape that makes you tremble; use to your advantage the fact that no one knows you. And if those who think you are worthless contradict you, and if those whom you call your friends abandon you, and if they want to destroy you on account of your tender thoughts—what is this obvious danger, which concentrates your inner strength, compared to that later, more cunning enmity of fame, which renders you harmless by spreading you everywhere?

Ask no one to speak of you, not even with contempt. And when time passes and you hear your name beginning to circulate among people, take it no more seriously than anything else you might find in their mouths. Think: This name's gone bad; I must dispose of it. Take another one, *any* other one, so that God can call you in the night. And conceal it from everyone.

Loneliest of men, remotest of men, how they've used your fame to expropriate you. Not so long ago they were bitterly against you, and now they treat you like one of their own. And they carry your words around with them in the cages of their conceit and display them in the public squares and poke at them a little from their own safe distance. All your terrible wild beasts.

That time I first read you, those desperate beasts broke free in me and fell upon me in my own desert. Desperate, as you yourself were in the end, you whose course has been plotted wrongly on every chart.

Like a crack, it runs through the heavens, this hopeless hyperbola of your trajectory, which bends toward us once only and shears away in horror. What did it matter if a woman stays or leaves, if someone is seized by vertigo and someone else by madness, if the dead are alive and the living seem dead: What did it matter? For you that was all so banal. You passed through as one might pass through a vestibule, not even pausing at the threshold. But on the far side you lingered, stooping for a closer look: there where our life's real events come to a boil and precipitate out and change color: within. Farther in than anyone had ever ventured; a door had sprung open for you, and now you were among the retorts in the fiery light. And there, where you never took anyone with you, mistrustful man—there you sat and observed transitions. And there, since *showing* was in your blood, more so than shaping or relating, you made a huge decision: to concentrate solely on these minute events (which you yourself had first observed only through lenses), and magnify them in such a way that they'd be plainly visible, revealed in their enormity to thousands, observed by everyone. Thus your theater was born. You couldn't wait for this life almost without spatial substance, condensed by the centuries into drops, to be discovered by the other arts, to become slowly intuited by those few who, feeling their own way through their own forms toward this same inner life, would rejoice to *see* its illustrious rumors confirmed in those scenes of yours played out before their eyes. You couldn't wait for that, you were there, you had to weigh and note down things that were scarcely measurable—the increase of half of a degree in a feeling; the angle of deflection (which you could only read off from very close) of a will that was being resisted by an almost infinitesimal weight; the slight cloudiness in a drop of longing; and that barest trace of color change in an atom of trust: all this you had to capture and record. For in such phenomena life now resided—*our* life, which had slipped inside us, and had continued to withdraw there, to so deep a place that one could scarcely conjecture about it anymore.

Since, as a timeless tragic poet, it was in your nature to make visible, you had to translate with single strokes this capillary action into the most convincing gestures, the most commonplace things. So you embarked on that unparalleled act of violence that is your work, which ever more impatiently, ever more desperately, sought in the visible world equivalents for what you had seen within. There was a rabbit, an attic, a room in which a man paces up and down; there was a clatter of glass in the next room, a fire outside the windows, there was the sun. There was a church and a rocky valley that was like a church. But that was not enough; finally towers had to be brought in, and whole mountain ranges; and the avalanches that bury landscapes covered a stage piled high with tangible things—all so that the intangible might be grasped. But then your powers failed. The two ends, which you'd bent around toward one another till they touched, sprang apart; your mad strength escaped the flexible wand, and it was as if your work had never existed.

How else to understand why, in the end, you wouldn't come away from the window, obstinate as always? You wanted to continue watching the people passing by. For it had occurred to you that if someday you decided to write, it might be worth giving them a try.

~

There was a certain moment when I first realized how nothing could be said about a woman. I noticed when they spoke of her, how much they left blank, how they named and described the other people, the surroundings, the places, the various objects, right up to a certain point where all that stopped, gently and almost cautiously stopped, at the very edge of the faint, untraced contour that enclosed her. What was *she* like? I'd then ask. "Fair, much like you," they would answer, and then recite all sorts of other things that had stuck in their minds; but in the process, she would become more and more indistinct, until I couldn't picture anything at all. I could really only *see* her when Maman told me the story, which I asked for again and again—.

—And each time she came to the scene with the dog, she would close her eyes and with a strange urgency spread her fingers over her face, masking it coldly as it shone through everywhere. "I saw it, Malte," she insisted, "I saw it." It was in the last years of her life that I heard her say this—in those times when she no longer cared to see anyone, and when she always, even on trips, carried with her that small, fine-meshed silver strainer through which she filtered every drink. She no longer took food in solid form, except for some cake or bread, which she would break into tiny pieces when she was alone and then eat one at a time, the way children eat crumbs. By that time her fear of needles already held complete sway over her. To others she would simply excuse herself by saying: "I can't really digest anything anymore, but you mustn't let that worry you, I'm perfectly fine." But to me she might suddenly turn (I was fairly grown up by then) and say, with a smile she struggled to maintain, "What a lot of needles there are, Malte, and they stick out everywhere, and when you think about how easily they can come loose . . ." She tried to say this playfully; but terror shook her at the thought of all those badly fastened needles that might anywhere, at any moment, drop into anything.

But when she talked about Ingeborg, she was safe from all harm, she gave freely of herself, she spoke more loudly, she laughed recalling Ingeborg's laugh, she strove to make everyone see how beautiful Ingeborg had been. "She made us all happy," she said, "your father too, Malte, *actually* happy. But then, when it turned out that she was going to die, even though she only seemed a little bit sick, and we all were going around carefully avoiding it, she sat up in bed one day and pronounced to herself, like someone who wants to hear how something will sound out loud: 'You mustn't all tiptoe around this; we know what's happening, and I can assure you, it's fine this way; I've had enough.' Just imagine, she said 'I've had enough'—she who made us all so happy. Do you think you will understand that, Malte, when you are grown up? Think about it later on; perhaps the answer will come to you. It would be good if there were someone who understood such things."

"Such things" preoccupied Maman when she was solitary, and she was always solitary in those last years.

"I shall never understand it, Malte," she would sometimes say with her strangely intrepid smile, which wasn't meant to be seen by anyone and fulfilled its whole purpose just in being smiled. "But to think that no one bothers to look into it! If I were a man, yes, certainly if I were a man, I'd reflect on it, step by step, in the proper sequence, starting at the beginning. For there must be a beginning, and it would at least be something to lay hold of that! Oh Malte, our lives are so short, and it seems to me that people become distracted and preoccupied and no one pays proper attention when we pass away. As if a shooting star fell and no one saw it and no wish was made. Never forget, Malte, to make a wish. You should never give up wishing. I don't believe there's such a thing as fulfillment, but there are wishes that last a long time, some even for a whole lifetime, so that you wouldn't have time enough anyway to wait for them to come true."

Maman had arranged for Ingeborg's little secretaire to be brought up to her room, and I often found her sitting at it, since I was allowed to go in without knocking. My footsteps were completely absorbed by the carpet, but she could feel me enter and would hold one of her hands out to me over her opposite shoulder. This hand was practically weightless, and kissing it was almost like kissing the ivory crucifix held out to me each evening when I went to bed. At this low writing desk, whose leaf folded out toward her, she would sit as at a musical instrument. "There is so much sunlight in it," she would say, and truly, the inside *was* remarkably bright, with its old yellow lacquer on which flowers were painted, a red and a blue one always touching. And wherever there were three, the third was always a violet one, keeping them apart. These colors, and the green of the slim horizontal arabesques, had darkened to the same degree that the ground, without being completely clear, had remained luminous. The result was a strangely muted interplay of tones that existed in some silent, almost intimate relation.

Maman pulled open the little drawers, all of which were empty.

"Ah, roses," she said, and bent forward a little into the faint scent that had not completely disappeared. She always imagined when she did this that she might yet find something suddenly in a secret drawer that no one knew about, and that would only yield to the pressure of some hidden spring. "It will shoot open all of a sudden, you'll see," she would say gravely and anxiously as she pulled open all the drawers. But in reality any papers that had been left in the compartments she had carefully folded up and locked away without reading them. "I wouldn't understand anyway, Malte, it would doubtless be too difficult for me." She was always insisting that everything was too difficult for her. "There are no classes in life for beginners, what's most difficult is always the first thing assigned." I was told that she had only been this way since the terrible fate of her sister, the Countess Ollegaard Skeel, who had burned to death just before a ball as she stood in front of a candlelit mirror trying to rearrange the flowers in her hair. But more recently it was Ingeborg who seemed to present the greatest challenge to her understanding.

And now here is the story just as Maman told it when I asked.

It was in the middle of summer, on the Thursday after Ingeborg's funeral. From the place on the terrace where we were having tea, you could see the gable of the family vault amid the giant elms. The table had been set as if there had never been one additional person at it, and indeed we were all spread evenly around it. Each one of us, moreover, had brought something with us—a book or a work basket—so that we were actually a bit cramped. Abelone (Maman's youngest sister) was pouring the tea, and everyone was busy passing things around, except for your grandfather, who was looking from his armchair toward the house. It was the hour when the mail was expected, and it was usually Ingeborg who brought it, since she had to stay inside longer, making the arrangements for dinner. During the weeks of her illness we had had plenty of time to get used to her not coming; for we knew, of course, that she was too sick to come. But on that afternoon, Malte, when she could *truly* come no longer—: she came. Perhaps it was our fault; perhaps we had conjured her. For I remember that all at once I was sitting there trying so hard to grasp what was so different now. Suddenly it had become impossible for me to say what it was;

my mind had gone completely blank. When I looked up I saw all the others turned toward the house, not in any alarmed or unusual way, but quite calmly and perfectly relaxed, as if they were waiting for the most routine, everyday occurrence. And I was about to—(it makes me icy cold to think about it, Malte)—but, God help me, I was about to say: "Wherever is—" when Cavalier bolted from under the table, as he always did, and ran to meet her. I saw it, Malte; I saw it. He ran toward her, even though she wasn't coming; for him, she was coming. We realized that he was running to meet her. Twice he turned around toward us, as if asking something. Then he raced up to her the way he always did, Malte, just the way he always did, and he reached her; because he began to dance all around her, Malte, all around something that wasn't there, and then he leapt up to lick her face, leapt right up, deliriously happy. And from the way he leapt up high, over and over again, as fast as he could leap—you might almost have thought that he was trying to hide her from us with his leaping. But suddenly there was a howl and he twisted around in the air from the force of his leaping and fell back with a strange gracelessness and lay there completely flat and didn't move. From the other side a servant came out of the house with the mail. He stopped for a moment: it was obviously not easy to approach our faces. And your father motioned to him to stay where he was. Your father, Malte, wasn't fond of animals; but now he walked over, slowly, it seemed to me, and bent down to the dog. He said something to the servant, something brief, monosyllabic. I saw the servant start forward to pick Cavalier up. But your father took the animal himself and went into the house with him, as if he knew exactly where he was heading.

Once, when it had almost grown dark during this story, I was on the verge of telling Maman about "the hand": at that moment I could have done it. I had taken a deep breath before beginning, but then I remembered how well I had understood the servant when he had been unable to approach all their faces. And I was afraid, despite the dark, of what Maman's face would look like as I brought her to see what I had seen. I quickly took another big breath, to make it look like that was all I had wanted to do. A few years later, after that strange night in the gallery at Urnekloster, I went about for days resolving to share the story with little Erik. But after our conversation that night he had completely shut me out again; he avoided me; I think he despised me. And precisely for that reason I wanted to tell him about "the hand." I imagined that his opinion of me would change for the better (and for some reason I desperately wanted that to happen) if I could make him understand that it was something I had really experienced. But Erik was so clever at avoiding me that I never got the chance. And then in any case we left shortly afterward. So, oddly enough, this is my very first time relating (and even now, only to myself) an occurrence that lies far back in my childhood.

I can tell how small I must have been back then by the way I had to kneel on the chair to reach up to the table I was drawing at. It was evening, in winter, if I'm not mistaken, in our apartment in town. The table stood in my room, between the windows, and there was no lamp in the room except for the one that shone on my sheets of paper and on Mademoiselle's book; for Mademoiselle sat beside me, pushed back a little from the table, reading. She was far away when she read, and I don't know if she was even in her book; she could read for hours, hardly ever turning the pages, and I imagined that the pages grew fuller and fuller beneath her eyes, as if her gaze were adding words, particular words that she required and that were not there. That's how it felt to me while I was drawing next to her. I always started out drawing slowly, without any precise goal in mind, and when I didn't know how to proceed, I would stop and survey the whole, with my head tilted slightly to the right; from that angle what was needed always came to me most quickly. It was soldiers on horseback, riding into battle—or no, they were already in the thick of it, and that made things much easier, since then almost all I had to draw was the enveloping smoke. Maman always claimed that I was painting islands; islands with big trees and a castle and a flight of steps and flowers along the edge that were reflected in the water. But I think she was making that up—or else it had to be later.

It is certain that on that particular evening I was drawing a knight, a single, very clearly distinguishable knight on a strikingly caparisoned horse. He was becoming so multicolored that I had to change pencils constantly, but most often I needed the red one, which I was having to reach for time and again. Now I needed it yet once more; but it rolled (I can still see it) right across the brightly lit sheet at the edge of the table and, before I could stop it, dropped to the floor and was gone. I needed it desperately, and it was maddening to have to clamber down after it now. Clumsy as I was, I had to go through all sorts of contortions to get down; my legs seemed much too long, I couldn't pull them out from under me; kneeling for so long without moving had numbed them; I didn't know what belonged to me and what was the chair's. Finally I did manage to arrive, somewhat confused, down below, and found myself on an animal-skin rug that stretched under the table all the way back to the wall. But here a new difficulty arose. My eyes, attuned to the brightness up above and still dazzled by the colors on the white paper, could not distinguish anything at all beneath the table, where the blackness seemed so solid and unyielding that I was afraid of bumping into it. So I relied on my sense of touch, and, down on my knees, supported on my left hand, I groped about with the other one in the cool, long-haired rug, which felt quite welcoming to my touch; but there was no pencil. I was afraid I was using up too much time, and was about to call up to Mademoiselle and ask her to come hold the lamp for me, when I noticed that the darkness was gradually becoming penetrable to my slowly adapting eyes. I could already make out the wall in back, which ended in a blond molding; I navigated by the table legs; above all I recognized my own outspread hand as it moved around down there all alone, a little like some strange aquatic creature exploring the floor. I still remember how I watched it with an almost distanced curiosity; it seemed to me that it knew things I had never taught it, as it groped about down there all by itself with movements I had never seen it make before. I followed it as it made its way, I was fascinated by it, I was prepared for almost anything. But how could I have been prepared to see another hand suddenly emerge from the base of the wall—a larger, impossibly gaunt hand, unlike any hand I had ever seen before. It came groping about in similar fashion from the opposite side, and the two outspread hands were moving blindly toward each other. My curiosity intensified, but then suddenly it evaporated and there was only terror. One of those hands belonged to me, and I felt that it was about to enter into some terrible pact from which it would never be able to extricate itself. With all the authority I still had over it, I brought it to a stop and pulled it slowly back, flat against the rug, never taking my eyes off the other hand, which went on groping. I realized that it would never cease; how I got back up again, I don't recall. I sat as deep and as far back in the chair as I could, my teeth chattering, and with so little blood in my face that I thought all the blue in my eyes must be gone. "Mademoiselle—," I wanted to say and couldn't, but she became alarmed all on her own and flung her book away and knelt beside my chair and called my name; I think she shook me. But I was perfectly conscious. I swallowed a few times; for now I wanted to tell her about it.

But how? Almost impossibly I regained control, but there was no way I could relate what had happened so that someone else could understand. If there were words for this experience, I was too small to find them. And all at once I was seized by the fear that, at some point, in spite of my years, those words would suddenly be there, and then— it seemed the most terrible thing of all—I would have to say them. To undergo once more the reality of what had happened down there, but differently, verbalized, beginning coherently at the beginning and hearing myself narrate it—for that I lacked the strength.

It is of course imagination on my part to maintain now that back then I already felt something had entered my life, entered directly into *mine*, and that I would have to carry it about with me alone, always and always. I see myself lying in my little bed and not sleeping and somehow vaguely foreseeing that this is how life would be: full of amazing experiences that are meant for one person only and can never be told. But it is a fact that gradually a sorrowful and heavy pride took hold of me. I imagined how it would feel to go about full of inward things about which one kept absolutely silent. I felt an impetuous sympathy for grown-ups; I admired them, I resolved to tell them that I admired them. I resolved to tell Mademoiselle at the very next opportunity.

And then came one of those illnesses bent on demonstrating to me that this was *not* my first occulted adventure. The fever burrowed into me and from deep down unearthed experiences, images, and facts that I had been completely unaware of; I lay there, with my unpacked self strewn all around me, waiting for the moment when I would be ordered to pack all these scattered things back inside me where they belonged, neatly and properly arranged. I began the task, but it grew under my hands, it resisted, it was much too much. Then rage seized me and I threw everything back inside me in random heaps and pressed down on the top of it as hard as I could. But I wouldn't close back up. And then I screamed, partly open as I was, I screamed and screamed. And when I began to look out beyond myself, they had all been standing around my bed for a long time, holding my hands, and there was a candle, and their huge shadows were moving behind them. And my father commanded me to say what was wrong. It was a friendly, muted command, but a command nonetheless. And he grew impatient when I didn't answer.

Maman never came to me at night—well, yes, she did come that once. I had been screaming and screaming, and Mademoiselle had come with Sieversen, the housekeeper, and Georg, the coachman; but that hadn't helped at all. Then finally they sent the carriage for my parents, who were at a great ball—at the crown prince's, I think. And I suddenly heard the carriage driving up into the courtyard, and I stopped screaming, sat up, and looked toward the door. And then there was a rustling in the adjoining rooms, and Maman rushed in wearing her beautiful court gown, paying it no attention at all, and was almost running and let her white fur fall to the floor behind her and took me in her bare arms. And I, with an astonishment and rapture I had never felt before, touched her hair and her delicate, beau-

tifully made-up face and the cold jewels at her ears and the silk at
the slope of her shoulders, which were fragrant like flowers. And we
remained like that and wept tenderly together and kissed each other,
until we sensed that Father was standing there and knew we had to
separate. "He has a very high fever," I heard Maman say timidly, and
Father seized my hand and took my pulse. He was in the uniform
of the Grand Master of the Hunt, with its wonderful broad, blue
watered-silk sash of the Order of the Elephant. "What nonsense to
call us away," he said, speaking into the room. They had promised to
return to the ball if it was nothing serious. And something serious it
certainly was not. But on my blanket I found Maman's dance card
and white camellias, which I had never seen before and which I laid
on my eyes when I felt how cool they were.

～

But it was the afternoons that were long during such illnesses. In the
early hours sleep always came after a night of tossing and turning,
and then when you woke up again and thought it was morning, it
was really afternoon and remained afternoon and wouldn't stop being
afternoon. So you lay there in your freshly made bed and felt your
joints might have grown a bit larger and were much too tired to think
of anything at all. The taste of applesauce lasted a long time, and it
was a great accomplishment if you could draw it out somehow and
let it spread, so that the clean tartness circulated in you in place of
thought. Later, as your strength returned, they stacked the pillows
behind you, and you could sit up and play with lead soldiers; but they
fell over so easily on the unsteady bed tray, and then always whole
rows at once; and you weren't yet sufficiently reconciled to the way

life worked that you could simply start all over again, time after time, endlessly. Suddenly it was more than you could take, and you would plead to have the whole thing removed posthaste, and it felt good to see in front of you only your two hands again, a little ways away on the empty blanket.

When Maman sometimes came for half an hour and read me fairy tales (Sieversen was responsible for the long, serious reading), it was not for the sake of the stories. For we were agreed that we didn't care for fairy tales. We had a different conception of the marvelous. For us the things that happened in a completely natural way were always the most marvelous. We scoffed at flying through the air, fairies disappointed us, and when people underwent transformations we expected only very superficial changes. But we did read a little, in order to appear occupied; if someone came in, we didn't like having to confess what we were actually doing. Especially when Father looked in on us, we became exaggeratedly absorbed readers.

Only when we were completely sure of not being disturbed, and when it was growing dark outside, we would sometimes give ourselves over to memories, shared memories that seemed old to both of us and made us smile; for we had both grown up since then. We remembered that there was a time when Maman wished I had been a little girl and not this boy I had turned out to be. Somehow I had guessed this, and had come up with the idea of occasionally in the afternoon knocking on Maman's door. When she asked who was there, with barely suppressed delight I would answer from outside "Sophie," making my little voice so dainty that it tickled my throat. And then when I entered (in the small, girlish house frock that I always wore anyway, with its sleeves rolled all the way up), I was Sophie pure and simple, Maman's little Sophie, who busied herself about the house and whose hair Maman had to braid so that Sophie wouldn't be mistaken for that wicked Malte if he ever came back. This was emphatically *not* to be desired; it was as agreeable to Maman as to Sophie that he was gone, and their conversations (which Sophie always continued in the same high-pitched voice) consisted mostly of listing Malte's transgressions and complaining about him. "Ah yes, that Malte," Maman would sigh. And Sophie could go on and on about the wickedness of boys in general, as if she had dealt with a whole crowd of the worst examples.

"I should very much like to know what has become of Sophie," Maman would say suddenly in the midst of these reminiscences. About that of course Malte could provide no information. But when Maman suggested that she must certainly be dead, he argued against that stubbornly and begged her not to believe it, however little proof he could offer to the contrary.

When I think about it now, I can only marvel at how I managed again and again to come back completely from the world of these fevers and readjust to that life we held in common, where everyone needed to feel assured of existing among beings like themselves and all the shared familiar things, and where people maneuvered so carefully in the realm of the understandable. There was an expectation, and it was either fulfilled or it was not; there was no third option. There were things that were sad, and that was that; there were happy things, and a whole host of completely neutral things. But if someone arranged a happiness for you, then it *was* a happiness, and you were obliged to respond accordingly. At heart it was all quite simple, and once you had it down, it went on functioning almost of its own accord. Within the agreed-upon boundaries, even the worst things fitted in: the long, monotonous hours in school, when outside it was summer; the walks you had to report on afterward in French; the visitors whom you were called in to meet, and who thought you were amusing at the very moment you were feeling sad, and who laughed at you the way people laugh at the melancholy visage of certain birds who have only that one face. And of course the birthdays, to which children had been invited whom you scarcely knew, awkward girls who made *you* feel awkward, or brazen boys who scratched your face and broke your gifts and then left when all the empty boxes and wrappings lay scattered in heaps on the floor. But when you played alone, which was most of the time, there were moments when you inadvertently stepped outside this agreed-on and for the most part predictable world, and found yourself amid circumstances that were completely different and unforeseeable.

Occasionally Mademoiselle had her migraine, which came on with sudden and uncommon violence; and those were the days when I was hard to find. I know that the coachman would be sent to search the grounds of the estate if Father thought to ask for me and I wasn't there. From one of the guest rooms upstairs I could see him running out and calling to me from the opening of the long avenue. These guest rooms were side by side in the gable of Ulsgaard, and since we scarcely ever had houseguests in those days, they were almost always empty. But adjoining them was the great corner room that was a place of such fascination for me. There was nothing in it but an old bust, which I think was of Admiral Juel; but the walls were lined all the way around with deep, gray wardrobes, in such a way that even the window had to be framed in the bare whitewashed space above them. I had found the key in one of the wardrobe doors, and it unlocked all the others. So in a short time I had examined everything: chamberlains' dress coats from the eighteenth century, cold with their inwoven silver threads, and the beautiful embroidered vests that went with them; ceremonial costumes of the Order of the Dannebrog and the Order of the Elephant, which were so rich and elaborate, and whose linings were so soft that at first I mistook them for women's expensive gowns. Then real gowns, which, outspread on their frames, hung there stiffly like the marionettes from some oversized puppet play, now so terminally outmoded that their heads had been removed and put to newer uses. Next to these, however, were wardrobes that were dark when they were opened, dark from the high-buttoned uniforms inside, which looked much more worn than the others and seemed to wish not to be preserved any longer.

No one will find it surprising that I pulled all these things out and held them up to the light; that I pressed this one up to me and wrapped that one around me; that I hastily pulled on a costume that more or less fit and ran into the nearest guest room wearing it, curious and excited to stand before the slender pier mirror made of individual pieces of unevenly green glass. Ah, how I trembled to be taken into that mirror realm, and how riveting when I *was*—when something approached from out of its gloomy depths, more slowly than myself— for the mirror was not, so to speak, convinced by my reflection, and was reluctant, still sleepy as it was, to repeat back instantaneously what I recited to it. But finally it had to, of course. And what I beheld took me very much by surprise—something strange, completely different from what I had imagined, something with a suddenness, a life of its own, all of which I took in with a quick glance before realizing in the next moment that it was myself I was looking at—not without a certain irony, which came within a hair's breadth of spoiling the whole adventure. But if I immediately began to talk, to bow, if I made gestures, if I walked away, continually looking back, and then returned, brisk and resolute,—then I had imagination on my side, for as long as I pleased.

That was when I first came to know the influence that can directly emanate from a costume. Scarcely had I donned one of them when I had to admit that it had me in its power; that it was dictating my movements, the expression on my face, yes, even my thoughts; my hand, over which the lace cuff would fall and fall again, was not at all my everyday hand; it moved like an actor, indeed I'm tempted to say that it observed its own movements, however exaggerated that might sound. But these disguises never had the effect of estranging me from myself; on the contrary, the more elaborately I transformed myself, the more confident I became in my own identity. I grew more and more reckless, I flung myself higher and higher— for I never doubted my ability to catch myself. I didn't register the danger lurking in this rapidly increasing self-confidence. The moment of my undoing came when one day the last wardrobe, which up till then had refused to budge, suddenly opened, and yielded up not specific costumes but all sorts of random trappings for masquerades, whose fantastic possibilities drove the blood into my cheeks. I can't possibly list all the things that were in there. In addition to a Venetian carnival mask that I remember, there were dominoes of various colors, there were women's skirts that tinkled from the coins sewn onto them; there were Pierrot costumes that seemed silly to me; there were pleated Turkish pants, and Persian fezzes from which little sacks of camphor slipped out, and coronets with stupid, expressionless stones. All these I rather scorned; their unreality was so shallow and explicit, and they hung there bodiless and pitiable and collapsed unresistingly when I pulled them out into the light. But what sent me into a kind

of frenzy were the flowing cloaks, the scarves, the shawls, the veils, all
the wide, compliant, unused fabrics that were so soft and caressing,
or so smooth that you could barely grasp them, or so light that they
flew past you like a breeze, or simply heavy with their own weight. In
them I first truly saw possibilities that were free and endlessly trans-
formable: you could be a slave girl at auction, or Joan of Arc, or an old
king, or a wizard; all this I now had at my disposal—especially since
there were also masks, enormous menacing or astonished faces with
real beards and thick or upraised eyebrows. I had never seen masks
before, but I understood immediately now that it was imperative that
masks exist. I had to laugh when I remembered that we had a dog who
looked as if he wore one. I pictured his affectionate eyes, which always
seemed to be inside his skull, peering out through his hairy face. I was
still laughing as I dressed up, and in the process I forgot completely
what I had intended to represent. All right then, it would be new and
exciting to decide that afterward, in front of the mirror. The face that
I tied on had a strange hollow smell; it fitted tightly over my own
face, but I could see through it comfortably, and not until the mask
was on did I choose a variety of scarves, which I wound around my
head as a sort of turban, so that the edge of the mask, which extended
down into an enormous yellow cloak, was also almost entirely covered
above and on the sides. Finally, when there was nothing more to add,
I declared myself sufficiently disguised. As a last effect I took a large
staff and walked it along beside me at arm's length, and in this way,
not without difficulty, but, as it seemed to me, with great dignity, I
shuffled into the guest room and up to the mirror.

It was truly spectacular, beyond all expectation. And the mirror
gave it back instantly: it was *too* convincing. It wouldn't have been
necessary to move much; this apparition was perfect, even in doing

nothing. But it was important for me to find out what I actually was, so I turned a little and finally raised both arms: great, almost conjuring gestures, which were, I saw at once, exactly the right ones. But just at this solemn moment I heard very close to me, muffled by my disguise, a confused noise of things breaking. Much frightened, I broke off contact with the shape in the mirror and was dismayed to see that I had overturned a small round table with heaven knows what on it, probably very fragile objects. I bent down as well as I could and found my worst fears confirmed: it appeared that everything that had been on it was in pieces. The two useless green-violet porcelain parrots were of course broken, each in a differently malicious way. A jar spilling out bonbons that looked like insects wrapped in silk cocoons had cast its lid far away; only half of it was visible, the other was completely out of sight. But the worst thing was a flacon that had shattered into a thousand tiny fragments; the remnant of some ancient essence had spurted out of it and spread, and had now formed a spot with a most repellent physiognomy on the clean parquet. I scrubbed at it furiously with some fabric that was hanging down from me, but that only made the spot blacker and more repulsive. I was truly desperate now. I got up and looked for some object with which I could make things right again. But nothing was to be found. On top of that, my vision and my every movement were so hampered that rage surged up in me at my ridiculous state, which no longer made sense to me. I pulled at everything, but it only clung more tightly to me. The cords of the cloak were strangling me, and the stuff on my head pressed down as if more and more of it were being added. Meanwhile the air had grown thick, as if misted by the stale vapor of the spilled perfume.

Hot and angry, I rushed to the mirror and with difficulty looked through the mask at what my hands were trying to undo. But that was just what the mirror had been waiting for. Its moment of revenge had come. As I was struggling, with wildly mounting anxiety, to extricate myself from my disguise, the mirror compelled me, I don't know how, to look up, and dictated to me an image—no, a reality, a strange, inexplicable, monstrous reality that captured me against my will: for now *he* was the empowered one, and I was the mirror. I stared at this huge, terrifying stranger before me, and felt the danger of being alone with him. But at the moment I was thinking this, the worst happened: I lost all sense of myself, I simply ceased to be. For a single second I felt a painful and futile longing for myself—and then only *he* remained; there was nothing except him.

I ran away, but now it was he who ran. He collided with everything, he wasn't familiar with the house, he had no idea which way to go; he managed to get down a flight of stairs, in a corridor he stumbled over someone who screamed and struggled free. A door opened, several people came out: Ah, ah, what a relief it was to recognize them. There was Sieversen, dear Sieversen, and the housemaid and the butler: now it would be over. But they didn't spring to my rescue; their cruelty knew no bounds. They stood there and laughed; my God, they could stand there and laugh. I was weeping, but the mask kept the tears in, they ran down inside over my face and dried at once and ran again and dried. And finally I was kneeling before them, as no human being ever knelt; I knelt and lifted my hands to them and implored them: "Get me out, if you still can, and hold me," but they didn't hear; I no longer had a voice.

To her dying day Sieversen would tell the story of how I sank to the floor and how they went on laughing, thinking it was all part of my charade. They were so used to that sort of thing from me. But then I went on lying there and didn't respond. And their horror then, when they finally realized that I was unconscious and lay there like a scrap in that heap of fabric, yes, just like a scrap of cloth.

~

Time went by with incredible speed, and suddenly the pastor, Dr. Jespersen, was due to be invited again. That meant a long breakfast, tiresome and difficult for all concerned. Accustomed to the deeply pious country people who fawned over his every word, Dr. Jespersen was completely out of his element when he visited us; he lay, so to speak, on dry land, gasping for breath. The gills he had developed scarcely functioned; bubbles were forming, the whole system was in danger of shutting down. As far as topics of conversation were concerned, strictly speaking there were none; remainders were being disposed of at unbelievable discounts, all holdings were being liquidated. In our house Dr. Jespersen had to restrict himself to being a species of private person; but that was exactly what he had never been. As far back as he could remember, he had been employed in the department of souls. The soul was for him a public institution that he represented, and he saw to it that he was never off duty, not even in his relations with his wife, "his modest, faithful Rebecca, whom childbirth was gradually leading toward heaven," as Lavater expressed it on another occasion.

*(As for my father, his attitude toward God was scrupulously correct and irreproachably civil. In church it sometimes seemed to me that he was God's own Master of the Hunt, as he stood there and waited patiently with bowed head. To Maman, on the contrary, it

---

* *Written in the margin of the manuscript.* [Rilke's note]

seemed almost traitorous to assume a civil relationship to God. Had
she been born into a religion with bold and elaborate observances, she
would have thought it bliss to kneel for hours and prostrate herself
and with great dramatic gestures make the sign of the cross on her
breast and across her shoulders. She didn't really teach me to pray,
but it cheered her that I seemed to enjoy kneeling and holding my
palms together with my fingers sometimes interlocked and sometimes
straight, depending on which seemed more expressive. Left mostly to
my own devices, I passed early on through several stages that I did
not until much later, during a period of despair, associate with God,
and then with such violence that he took shape and shattered almost
in the same moment. It was clear to me afterward that I would have
to start over with him from scratch. And for this new beginning I
often thought that I would need Maman, though of course it was
only right that I undergo it alone. And besides, by that time she had
long been dead.)

With Dr. Jespersen Maman could be almost teasingly playful. She
would initiate conversations with him about subjects she knew he took
very seriously, and then, when he had worked up a full head of steam,
she would decide that she had done her duty and promptly forget him,
as if he had already left. "How," she sometimes said of him, "can he
bear to go around dropping in on people just when they're dying."

He came to see her also on that occasion, but she most certainly
did not see him. Her senses were failing, one by one, and the first to
go had been sight. It was in the autumn; we were preparing to move
back to the city, but just then she fell ill, or rather began to die, slowly
and hopelessly, over the whole surface of her body. The doctors began
arriving, and there was a day when they were all there together and
took control of the entire house. For a few hours it seemed to belong

to the privy councilor and his assistants, as if we had no say in the matter. But shortly after that they lost all interest, and began coming only one at a time, and then as if merely out of sociality, to have a cigar and drink a glass of port. And meanwhile Maman died.

Now we were just waiting for Maman's only brother, Count Christian Brahe, who, it will be recalled, had served for a time in the Turkish army, where, everyone always said, he had been highly decorated. He arrived one morning accompanied by a strange-looking servant, and I was surprised to see that he was taller than Father: and apparently older as well. The two gentlemen exchanged a few quick sentences which I assumed had to do with Maman. There was a pause. Then my father said: "She looks very bad." The words made me shudder. I couldn't grasp what he meant by them, but it was obviously very hard for him to make that remark. He seemed to be fighting back very strong emotions. But it was probably his pride that was suffering most.

⁓

It wasn't until several years later that I again heard Count Christian talked about. It was at Urnekloster, where he was one of Mathilde Brahe's favorite subjects. I'm certain she embellished freely when she spoke of his various exploits, since the life of my uncle, about which only rumors reached the public and even the family (rumors, by the way, that he never bothered to deny), was open to almost boundless speculation. Urnekloster is now in his possession. But no one knows if he is living there. Perhaps he is still voyaging, as was his custom; perhaps news of his death is on its way from some far-off continent, written by the hand of the foreign servant in bad English or some unfamiliar language. Or perhaps this man will send no word at all when one day he remains behind, alone. Perhaps they both vanished long ago, and exist only on the passenger list of a lost ship, under names that aren't their own.

At any rate, if in those days at Urnekloster a coach drove up, I would always expect *him* to step out, and my heart would beat in a special way. Mathilde Brahe maintained that it was exactly how he *would* make his entrance—that it was his very essence suddenly to appear when you least thought it possible. He never did come, but for weeks he occupied my outsized imagination; I had the feeling that there ought to be some real human contact between the two of us, and I longed to know something about him that was undeniably true.

Shortly after this, however, certain events caused my interest to shift entirely to Christine Brahe. But in her case, curiously enough, my obsession had nothing to do with the particulars of her life. I became preoccupied instead with the question of whether her portrait hung among those in the gallery. The need to find out grew so insistent that for several nights I couldn't sleep, until quite unexpectedly one night I jumped up out of bed, God only knows why, and made my way upstairs with my candle, which flickered as if afraid.

As for myself, I had no thought of fear. I had no thoughts at all; I simply went. The tall doors opened easily before me and above me; the rooms I walked through kept very quiet. And finally I could tell from the hint of depth in the air around me that I had entered the gallery. On the right I sensed the windows that looked out onto the night, so the left must be where the portraits hung. I lifted my candle as high as I could. Yes: there they were.

At first I decided that I would look only at the women; but then I recognized one man and then a second, whose portraits also hung at

Ulsgaard, and when I lifted my candle toward them from below they stirred and yearned to come forward into the light, and it seemed heartless not to give them long enough at least for that. There was Christian IV, again and again, with his beautiful braided queue framing his broad, elegant face. There presumably were his wives, of whom I recognized only Kirstine Munk; and then suddenly Frau Ellen Marsvin was looking at me, suspicious in her widow's dress and with the same string of pearls on the brim of her tall hat. There were King Christian's children: always fresh ones from new wives; and the "incomparable" Eleonore on a white palfrey, in her most radiant period, before the treasons. The Gyldenloves: Hans Ulrik, who the ladies in Spain thought painted his face, so flush were his cheeks; and Ulrik Christian, whom no one ever forgot. And almost all the Ulfields. And that one, with one eye overpainted black, might well be Henrik Holck, who was made imperial count and field Marshall at the age of thirty-three, and the story went like this: on his way to the demoiselle Hilleborg Krafse, he dreamed that instead of a bride he was given a naked sword: and he took this to heart, turned back, and embarked on his short, impetuous career that was ended by the plague. I knew them all. At Ulsgaard we even had the ambassadors to the Congress of Nijmegen, all of whom resembled one another slightly, since they had been painted at the same time—each with that thin, precisely trimmed mustache above the sensual, almost watching mouth. That I recognized Duke Ulrich goes without saying, and Otto Brahe and Clara Daa and Sten Rosensparre, the last of his line; for I had seen portraits of them in the hall at Ulsgaard or found copper engravings of them in old portfolios.

But then there were many I had never seen; only a few women, but more of children. My arm had long since grown tired and was trembling, yet again and again I lifted up the candle to see these children. I understood them, these little girls who carried a bird on their hand and had become oblivious to it. Sometimes a little dog sat at their feet, a ball next to it, and on the table beside them there were fruits and flowers; and on a pillar behind them, small and provisional, hung the coat of arms of the Grubbes or the Billes or the Rosenkrantzes. So many things had been placed around them, as if to compensate them for their childhood. But they simply stood there in their dresses and waited; you could see that they were waiting. And that made me think of the women again, and of Christine Brahe, and whether I would recognize her.

My plan was to run quickly to the far end of the gallery and from there walk back looking for her, but I immediately bumped into something. I whirled around so violently that little Erik leapt back, whispering, "Watch out with your candle."

"*You* here?" I said, breathless, not sure whether that would be a good thing or something very bad. He just laughed, and I had no idea what would happen next. My candle was flickering, and I couldn't quite make out the expression on his face. It almost surely boded ill that he was present. But then, drawing closer, he said, "*Her* portrait isn't here. We're still looking for it upstairs." With his low voice and his one movable eye, he made a kind of upward gesture. And I realized that he meant the attic. But suddenly a strange thought occurred to me.

"We?" I asked. "Is she up there too?"

"Yes," he nodded, standing right next me.

"She's looking for it with you?"

"Yes. We're both looking."

"So it's been put away, the painting?"

"Yes—can you believe it!" he said, indignant. But I didn't quite understand what she wanted with it.

"She wants to see herself," he whispered, even closer to me.

"Ah yes," I returned, as if I understood. At this, he blew my candle out. I saw him stretch forward into the light, his eyebrows raised high. Then everything went dark. I took an involuntary step back.

"Why did you do that?" I said, stifling a shout, my throat gone dry. He leapt at me and caught me by the arm and giggled.

"What is it?" I snapped at him, and tried to shake him loose, but he held on tight. I couldn't keep him from putting his arm around my neck.

"Shall I tell you?" he hissed, and a bit of saliva sprayed my ear.

"Yes, yes, quickly."

I didn't know what I was saying. He held me in a full embrace now, stretching up to do so.

"I've brought her a mirror," he said, and giggled again.

"A mirror?"

"Yes, because the portrait isn't there."

"No, no," I said.

He suddenly pulled me a little closer to the window and pinched my upper arm so hard that I cried out.

"She's not in it," he breathed into my ear.

Instinctively I shoved him away from me; there was a cracking sound; I thought I'd broken him.

"Oh come on," and now I had to laugh myself. " 'Not in it'? What do you mean, not in it?"

"You're very stupid," he retorted angrily, no longer whispering. The register of his voice had changed radically, as if he were taking on a new, untried part of it. "You're either in it," he pronounced with an almost didactic sternness, "in which case you're not here; or else, if you're here, you can't be in it."

"Of course," I answered quickly, without thinking. I was afraid that otherwise he might go away and leave me alone. I even reached for him.

"Let's be friends," I proposed. He wanted to be begged. "It's all the same to me," he answered indifferently.

I tried to start up our friendship, but didn't dare put my arm around him. "Dear Erik" was all I could get out as I touched him lightly. I was suddenly very tired. I looked around; I no longer understood how I'd come here or why I hadn't been afraid. I wasn't sure anymore where the windows were and where the paintings were. And as we left, he had to lead me.

"They won't hurt you," he assured me magnanimously, and giggled again.

Dear, dear Erik; perhaps you were my only friend. For I've never really had one. It's a pity that friendship meant so little to you. I would have liked to tell you so many things. Perhaps we would have gotten along. One never knows. I remember that back then your portrait was being painted. Grandfather had arranged for someone to come and paint you. One hour every morning. I can't recall what the painter looked like; his name escapes me, although Mathilde Brahe would repeat it constantly.

Did he see you the way I see you? You wore a suit of heliotrope-colored velvet. Mathilde Brahe was wild about that suit. But that's of no importance now. I'd only like to know if he really saw you. Let's assume he was a true painter. Let's assume he never had the thought that you might die before he finished; that he didn't see things in a sentimental light; that he simply worked. That the difference between your two brown eyes intrigued him; that he wasn't the least bothered by the one that didn't move; that he had the tact not to place anything on the table by your hand, which perhaps rested on it just a little for support—. Let's assume whatever else is necessary, and embrace it all: now we have a portrait, your portrait, the last one in the gallery at Urnekloster.

(And when people will have walked through the gallery and seen them all, there will still be one boy there. Just a moment: Who is that? A Brahe. Don't you see the silver palisade on the sable field, and the peacock feathers? There's the name, too: Erik Brahe. Wasn't there an Erik Brahe who was executed? Yes, of course; almost everyone knows that story. But this can't be him. This boy died when he was still a boy, whenever that might have been. Can't you see that?)

~

Whenever there were visitors and Erik was called in, Mathilde Brahe would go on about how absolutely incredible it was that he so closely resembled the old Countess Brahe, my grandmother. They say that she was a great lady. I never knew her myself. But I do remember very clearly my father's mother, the true mistress of Ulsgaard. For mistress she had remained, however much she resented Maman for entering the house as wife to the Master of the Hunt. From that time on, she ostentatiously behaved as if she had resigned completely from that role, referring the servants to Maman about even the slightest trifles (while in crucial matters quietly reserving the decisions and their deployment to herself). And I don't think Maman really wished it any other way. She was so ill-equipped to oversee a large house, and she completely lacked the ability to distinguish what was important from what was merely incidental. Whenever someone came to her with a question, it would immediately become for her the One Thing that mattered, to the exclusion of everything else—even though so many other things required attention. She never complained about her mother-in-law. And to whom could she have complained? Father was an extremely respectful son, and Grandfather had little to say about anything.

Frau Margarete Brigge had always been, as far back as I can remember, a tall, unapproachable old woman. I can't picture her except as much older than the chamberlain. She lived her life in our midst, without showing the least regard for anyone. She was not dependent on any of us, and always had a sort of companion attending on her, the aging Countess Oxe, who seemed bound to her by a limitless obligation the old woman had placed upon her through some act of generosity. Whatever the favor, it must have been an extraordinary exception in the latter's life, since kindness to others was emphatically *not* her style. She didn't like children, and animals weren't allowed anywhere near her. I don't know if there was warmth in her heart for anything. It was told that as a very young woman she had been engaged to the dashing Prince Felix Lichnowski, who so cruelly lost his life in Frankfurt. And indeed, after her death, they found among her possessions a portrait of the prince—which, if I'm not mistaken, was returned to his family. I wonder now if perhaps, in living this rural existence at Ulsgaard that year by year had become increasingly sequestered, she had missed out on another life, a glittering, splendid life that more truly suited her. It would be hard to say whether she consciously mourned its loss. Perhaps she scorned it for not having sought her out more diligently—for having missed *its* chance to be lived with verve and brilliance. She had lodged all of this deep inside her, and had grown protective carapaces over it, one on top of the other, hard, brittle sheaths with a slight metallic sheen, so that the uppermost would always appear new and cool. At times, though, she would give herself away, as with her childish impatience at not being paid enough attention. I can recall how at table she would suddenly swallow the wrong way and choke, in a patently baroque manner which assured her the concern of everyone present, and which, for a moment at least, made her appear as arresting and dramatic as she would have liked to have been in the world at large. But I suspect that my father was the only one who took these far too frequent accidents seriously. He would watch her, politely leaning forward, and you could see how he was unconsciously offering her his own properly functioning windpipe and placing it, as it were, entirely at her disposal. Of course the chamberlain too had stopped eating; he took a little sip of wine and kept whatever he was thinking to himself.

Only once at dinner did he express his own opinion of his wife's behavior. It had happened long ago; yet the story was still being passed around maliciously; almost everywhere there would be someone who hadn't yet heard it. It seemed there had been a time when the chamberlain's wife could not endure the sight of wine stains on the tablecloth; any new stain, no matter what its occasion, she would draw attention to and expose, as it were, with a monologue of outraged censure. This even happened once when several distinguished guests were present. A few innocent flecks, which she blew out of all proportion, became the target of her sarcasm, and no matter how insistently Grandfather kept trying to warn her with oblique little signals and droll interjections, she persisted doggedly in her reproaches—until at a certain moment she broke off in mid-sentence. For something had happened at the table that was unprecedented and completely unthinkable. The chamberlain had called for the red wine, which was just then being passed around the table, and had begun, with the most exacting concentration, to fill his own glass. But then: as the wine approached the glass's rim, he kept on pouring, slowly and deliberately, amid the deepening hush—until Maman, who could never stop herself, burst out laughing, and through her laughter turned the whole incident into a pleasant diversion. For now everyone joined in to their great relief, while the chamberlain looked up and handed the bottle to the servant.

Later on, another peculiarity took hold of my grandmother. She could not bear it if anyone in the house fell ill or had to deal with pain. Once when the cook had cut herself and she chanced to see her with her hand bandaged, she claimed that the whole house reeked of iodoform, and it was difficult to convince her that the woman couldn't be dismissed for such a reason. She didn't want to be reminded of infirmity. If anyone was so incautious as to give voice even to some minor ailment in her presence, she took it as an insult to herself personally, and she went on resenting it long afterward.

In the autumn that Maman died, the chamberlain's wife closed herself off completely in her rooms with Sophie Oxe, and broke off all relations with us. Not even her son was admitted. The death did indeed come at a most inopportune time. The rooms were cold, the stoves smoked, and mice had invaded the house; there was no place where one was safe from them. But it was more than that. Frau Margarete Brigge was indignant that Maman was dying, that there was an item on the agenda about which she had not been consulted, and that the young wife had actually dared to take precedence over her, since she had herself been planning to die—at some date yet to be determined. For she often did reflect that she would have to die. But she refused to be rushed. She would die, certainly, but when she was pleased to do so, and then they could all die their own uneventful deaths after her if they were in such a hurry.

She never quite forgave us for Maman's death. But she herself aged swiftly during the following winter. She still held herself tall and straight when she walked, but in her armchair she would gradually cave in, and she grew harder and harder of hearing. You could sit and stare straight at her for hours and she wouldn't feel it. She was somewhere within; she returned only seldom (and then only for a few moments) to her empty senses, which she'd ceased to inhabit. She would say something to the countess, who would straighten her shawl, and then with her large, freshly washed hands she would pull her dress tightly around herself, as if water had been spilled or as if we were not entirely clean.

She died one night in town, at the approach of spring. Sophie Oxe, whose door stood open, had heard nothing. When they found her the following morning, she was cold as glass.

Immediately after this the chamberlain's great and terrifying illness commenced. It was as if he had been waiting patiently for her end, so that he could die his own death with the ruthlessness it demanded.

~

It was in the year after Maman's death that I first really noticed Abelone. It was an axiom that Abelone was always there. And so it was easy to overlook her. Then, too, Abelone was not the sympathetic type, as I personally had discovered on an earlier occasion, and nothing since had encouraged me to revise that opinion. To become curious about the particulars of Abelone's life, or to wonder what she was really like, would have struck me as almost nonsensical back then. Abelone was there, and we all interacted with her according to our different needs. But suddenly one day I asked myself: *Why* is Abelone there? Each one of us had a specific rationale for being there, even if it was not always as obvious as, for instance, the usefulness of Fräulein Oxe. But why was Abelone there? For a while it was said that she needed to take her mind off things. But that was soon forgotten. No one made any attempt to take Abelone's mind off things. Nor did Abelone give the least impression that she herself was trying to take her mind off anything.

All else aside, Abelone had one sublime quality: she sang. That is to say, there were times when she would sing. She had a strong, unwavering music in her. If it's true that angels are male, you could say that there was something masculine in her voice: a radiant, celestial maleness. I, who even as a child had been so mistrustful of music (not because it lifted me out of myself more powerfully than anything else, but because it always seemed to put me down someplace different—someplace deeper, where everything was still in process), I gave myself over to *this* music, on which you could rise as if standing upright, higher and higher, until you thought you must have reached something like heaven. I didn't guess then that Abelone would open still other heavens for me.

At first our relationship consisted of her telling me stories from Maman's girlhood. It was very important to her that I understood how bold and dashing Maman had been. In those days, she assured me, no one could equal her in dancing or riding. "She was so fearless and full of life—and then suddenly she married," said Abelone, still baffled after so many years. "It was so unexpected; no one could grasp why."

I was curious to know why Abelone had remained single. I thought of her as relatively old, and it never occurred to me that she still might marry.

"There wasn't anyone," she answered simply—and became beautiful in the saying of those words. Is Abelone beautiful? I asked myself, surprised. But then I left home to attend the Academy for Young Noblemen, and a dreadful period in my life began. There at Sorö, when I stood at a window, apart from the others, and they left me alone for a while, I would look out into the trees, and in such moments and at night it became clear to me that Abelone *was* beautiful. And I began to write her all those letters, long ones and short ones, many secret letters in which I thought I was talking about Ulsgaard and my unhappiness. But I now see that they were love letters. For when summer vacation finally arrived, which for so long had seemed reluctant to come at all, it was as if we had implicitly agreed that our reunion would not take place in the presence of the others.

Nothing at all had been arranged between us, but when my carriage turned into the park I could not help getting out—perhaps only because I didn't want to come driving up like some stranger. Summer was already at full height. I turned down one of the paths and walked toward a laburnum tree. And there was Abelone. Beautiful, beautiful Abelone.

I will never forget how you looked at me then. How your gaze lay on your back-tilted face, poised there, as if nothing held it down.

Has the climate there not slightly changed? Did it not grow milder

around Ulsgaard from all our warmth? Do not stray roses bloom longer now in the park, all the way into December?

I won't tell anything about you, Abelone. Not because we deceived
each other—since even then you loved someone else, whom you never
forgot, and since I loved all women—but because only wrong is done
in the telling.

~

There are tapestries here, Abelone, hanging on the walls. I am imagining that you're with me. There are six tapestries—come, let's walk
past them slowly. But first step back and take them all in. Are they
not peaceful? So little changes from one to the next. There's always
that blue oval island, floating against a background of subdued red
strewn with flowers and alive with small, busy animals. Only there, in
the last tapestry, does the island rise a little, as if it had grown lighter.
It always bears one figure, a woman, in varying dress but always the
same person. Sometimes there's a smaller figure next to her, a handmaid, and the heraldic animals are always there, large, sharing the
island, involved in the action. On the left, a lion, and on the right,
bright white, the unicorn; they hold the same pennants, which high
above them display: three silver moons, rising, in a blue band on a red
field.—Have you looked? Shall we begin now with the first?

She is feeding a falcon. How magnificent her garments are. The
bird is on her gloved hand and stirs. She watches it and reaches into
the bowl her handmaid brings, in order to feed it something. Below
and to the right, a little silken-haired dog sits on the train of her dress,
looking up and hoping she'll remember that it's there. And have you

noticed the low rose trellis that closes off the island along the back? The lion and the unicorn stand on their hind legs with heraldic pride. The coat of arms is repeated as a cloak around their shoulders. A beautiful clasp fastens it. There is a breeze.

Don't we instinctively approach the next tapestry more softly, once we see how engrossed she is? She is weaving a garland, a small round crown of flowers. Pensively she chooses the color of the next carnation from the shallow bowl the handmaid is holding out to her, as she binds in the one before. Behind her on a bench, unused, stands a basket full of roses, which a monkey has discovered. But this time she is braiding carnations. The lion has lost interest; but to the right, the unicorn understands.

Mustn't music come into this silence? Hasn't it been there all along, restrained? Gravely and silently adorned, she has approached (very slowly, don't you think?) the portable organ and now plays, standing, separated by the pipes from her handmaid, who is working the bellows on the other side. She has never been so beautiful. How wondrously her hair has been brought forward in two braids and fastened together over her headdress so that the ends rise out of the knot like a short helmet plume. Disgruntled, the lion reluctantly endures the sounds, biting back a howl. But the unicorn is blissful, as if it were afloat on waves.

The island broadens outward. A tent is erected. Of blue damask and flamed with gold. The animals draw it open and she advances, almost plain in her princely dress. For what are her pearls compared with her own presence? Her handmaid has opened a small casket, and the lady is now lifting out a chain, a heavy, magnificent treasure that has always been locked away. The little dog sits beside her, on a high place prepared for it, and looks on. Have you found yet the motto on the tent's upper edge? It reads: *"A mon seul désir."*

What has happened, what has caused that little rabbit down below to run, why can you see right away that it is running? Everything is discomposed. The lion has nothing to do. She herself holds the pennant. Or is she clinging to it? With her other hand she has reached out and grasped the unicorn's horn. Is this grief, can grief stand so erect, and can a mourning dress be as muted as this black-green velvet with its faded places?

But last to come, a festival: one to which no one has been invited. Anticipation plays no part in this. Everything is present. Everything forever. The lion is looking around, almost threateningly: no one is allowed here. We have never before seen her tired; *is* she tired, or has she only sat down because she holds a heavy object? You could mistake it for a monstrance. But she inclines her other arm toward the unicorn, and the animal arches its back and pillows its head on her lap. What she holds is a mirror. Do you see?—She is showing the unicorn its image—.

Abelone, I am imagining you are here. Do you understand, Abelone? I think you must understand.

~

Now even the tapestries of *La Dame à la licorne* no longer hang in the old château Boussac. We have entered a time when everything is leaving the houses; they can no longer retain anything. Danger has become safer than safety. No one from the Le Viste line walks beside you and has all this in his blood. They have all departed. No one speaks your name, Pierre d'Aubisson, great grand master of an ancient house, who perhaps gave the instructions for these tapestries, which praise everything and divulge nothing. (Ah, why have poets ever written otherwise about women, more "realistically," or so they thought? For surely this is all we are allowed to know.) Now we stand before these images by chance among other chance visitors and feel uneasy to be here uninvited. There are others who walk past distractedly, though never very many. Young people scarcely even pause, unless they've been assigned to look at these works, and study this or that particular quality.

But you do sometimes find young girls standing before them. For a good many young girls are drawn to the museums, young girls who have left the various houses that no longer retain things of value. They find themselves in front of these tapestries and forget themselves a little. They have always felt that this existed—this quiet life of slow, never-quite-clarified gestures, and they remember dimly that for a time they even thought this life would be their own. But then they quickly take out a sketchbook and begin to draw, anything at all, one of the flowers or a small, carefree animal. It doesn't matter, they've been told, what specifically they draw. And it really *doesn't* matter. The main thing is just to draw; for that is why they left home one day, rather forcefully: to draw. They come from good families. But now when they lift their arms as they draw, you can see that their dress is not buttoned up in back, at least not all the way. There are a few at the very top they couldn't reach. When this dress was made, there was never any thought that they might suddenly leave, in order to be on their own. And within the family there is always someone to help with such buttons. But here, dear God, who could be bothered in such a big city? The thing would be to have a girlfriend; but girlfriends suffer the same predicament, and so they would have to button up each other's dresses. But that's no good; it would remind both of the family that each is trying to keep out of mind.

But they can't help wondering sometimes, as they stand there drawing, if it still might have been possible, in spite of everything, to stay. If only they could have been religious, piously religious in the way of the others. But it seemed to make so little sense to attempt that life collectively. The path has somehow grown narrower: whole families can no longer make their way collectively to God. So there remained only a few other things that, if need be, could be shared. But if they truly shared those, equally among the others, what a small portion each would receive! And if they shared unequally, quarrels would arise. No, it really is better just to start drawing, no matter what. With time resemblance will emerge. And art that is achieved slowly and heedlessly this way truly is something to be envied.

But in their intense absorption in this work they've undertaken, these young girls no longer think to look up. They don't notice how with all their drawing they are denying in themselves the unalterable life that in these woven images opens up before them, radiant and infinitely unsayable. They don't want to believe in it. Now, when so much else is changing, they want to change also. They are very close to abandoning themselves and thinking of themselves as men might speak of them when they are absent. This seems to them their path toward progress. They are already almost convinced that one seeks out a pleasure and then another pleasure and then an even stronger one: that this is how life is to be lived, if one doesn't want to foolishly let it slip by. They have already begun to look around, to search out opportunities: they whose strength has always lain in being found.

This is because they've grown weary, I think. Throughout the centuries they have performed the whole of love, playing both parts of the dialogue. For man has only repeated after them, and done so badly. And has made their learning difficult with all his inattentiveness, his negligence, his jealousy, which is itself a kind of negligence. And still they have persevered, day and night, and have increased in love and misery. And from among them, under the pressure of endless want, there have come forth those powerful women in love who, even as they called to the man, survived his absence, and grew far beyond him when he did not return: women like Gaspara Stampa or the Portuguese nun, who didn't cease until their torment suddenly transformed into an austere, icy magnificence that could no longer be held in check. We know of these women from letters that by some miracle were saved, or from books of poems that accuse or lament, or from portraits in some gallery that look at us through a veil of weeping that the painter caught because he didn't know what he was painting. But there were so many more of them: those who burned their letters, and others who no longer had the strength to write them. Old women who had hardened around a kernel of lovingness they kept hidden within them. Formless women whom exhaustion had caused to grow thickset like their husbands, who had let themselves grow to resemble their husbands and yet were completely different inside, there in the darkness where love had been working. Childbearing women who never wanted to bear and who, when they finally died in their eighth confinement, had the gestures and lightness of girls looking forward to love. And those who stayed at the side of loudmouths and drunkards, because they had found the means to be truly alone, farther removed from them inside themselves than anywhere else; and when they mixed with people they could not disguise that fact, because they were radiant, as if they had spent their lives in the company of saints. Who can say how many or who they were. It is as if they had destroyed in advance the words by which they might be known.

But now that so much is changing, isn't it time for men to change? Couldn't we try to evolve just a little, and slowly, bit by bit, take upon ourselves our share in the task of love? We've been spared all its effort, and so it has slipped in among our diversions, the way a piece of true lace sometimes gets into a child's toy chest and delights the child and then delights no longer and finally lies there among the broken and disassembled things, the most abused of all. We have been spoiled by easily achieved pleasures, like all dilettantes, and bask in the aura of mastery. But what if we despised our successes, what if we were to begin all over again and learn, from the very first, the work of love that has always been done for us? What if we went off and became beginners, now that so much is changing?

Now I know too what it meant when Maman would take out the little pieces of lace and unroll them. She had reserved for herself one drawer in Ingeborg's secretaire.

"Shall we look at them, Malte?" she would say excitedly, as if she were about to receive as a gift everything in the small yellow-lacquered drawer. In those moments she was so full of anticipation that she couldn't unfold the tissue paper. Each time I had to do it. But I too grew excited when the lace appeared. The pieces were wound on a wooden spindle that was invisible beneath so much lace. And so we would slowly turn it and watch the patterns unspool, and we were both a bit frightened every time one of them came to an end. They stopped so suddenly.

First came strips of Italian work, knotty pieces with drawn-out threads, in which one pattern constantly repeated, plainly, as in a peasant's garden. Then suddenly our looks were latticed by long runs of Venetian needlepoint, as if we were in cloisters, or prisons. But then we were freed again, and peered deep into gardens that became more and more dreamlike and artificial, until everything was moist and warm to our eyes, as in a hothouse: luxuriant plants we couldn't identify put forth gigantic leaves, tendrils reached for one another as if they were reeling, and the large open flowers of the points d'Alençon misted everything with their pollen. All of a sudden, dazed and disoriented, we stepped out into the long path of the Valenciennes, and it was winter and early morning and there was hoarfrost. And we pushed through the snowy thicket of Binche and came to places where no one had been before; the branches hung down so strangely that there could have been a grave beneath them, but we kept that thought from each other. The cold pressed in on us more and more closely, and finally, when we came to the delicate pillow lace, Maman said, "Oh, now we'll get frost-flowers on our eyes." And so we did, since we were very warm inside.

When it was time to roll the laces back up, we both sighed; it was long, tedious work, but we wouldn't trust it to anyone else.

"Just imagine if we had to make them," said Maman, looking properly alarmed. But I couldn't imagine it at all. I caught myself envisioning tiny creatures spinning lace incessantly while humans left them in peace. No—of course it had been women.

"Those who made these must surely be in heaven," I said in awe. I remember thinking that it had been a long time since I'd asked about heaven. Maman took a deep breath: the laces were all rolled up again.

After a while, when I had already forgotten my remark, she responded, very slowly, "In heaven? I believe they are completely in these laces. If you think about it, each of these pieces may be a heaven unto itself. We know so little about such things."

~

Often when visitors came, the talk was about how the Schulins were "cutting back." The grand old manor house had burned down a few years before, and now they lived in the two narrow side wings and were cutting back. But having guests was in their blood. They couldn't give it up. Whenever visitors showed up at our house unexpectedly, they had probably come from the Schulins'; and if someone glanced up at the clock and stammered out to us a hasty farewell, it was no doubt because they were expected at Lystager.

By that time Maman didn't really go out anymore, but that was not something the Schulins could comprehend; so there was nothing to be done but drive over and see them one day. It was in December, after a few early snowfalls; the sleigh had been ordered for three o'clock; I was to come too. But at our house we never got started on time. Maman, who didn't like having the carriage announced, usually went down much too early, and when she saw that no one was there, she would always remember something that should have been taken care of long ago, and began searching for something or rearranging things upstairs, so that we would have to look for her all over again. At last we would all be standing there waiting. And when she was finally seated and bundled in the sleigh, it turned out that something had been forgotten, and Sieversen had to be fetched, for only Sieversen knew where it was. But then we would abruptly drive off before Sieversen returned.

On that day it had never really brightened. The trees stood as if lost in the mist, and there was something unfeeling about driving straight past them. From time to time it had quietly begun to snow again, and now it was as if the last writing had been erased and we were driving into a blank page. There was only the sound of the sleigh bells, and you couldn't really tell where it was coming from. There was a moment when it stopped completely, as if the last little bell had died; but then the sound rallied and returned to full strength and scattered itself gaily through the air. We might have only imagined the church steeple on the left, but suddenly the outline of the park wall appeared, high up, almost straight overhead, and we found ourselves in the long driveway. The sound of the bells didn't stop completely when we paused; it seemed to hang in clusters in the trees to our left and right. Then we swung in and drove around something, and past something else on the right, and finally came to a halt in the central court.

Georg had forgotten that the house was not there anymore, and in that moment it *was* there for us all. We climbed the flight of steps that led up to the old terrace and were surprised to find it completely dark. But then a door opened below and behind us to the left, and someone called "Over here!" and raised and swung a misty lantern. My father laughed: "Here we are wandering about like ghosts," and he helped us make our way down the steps.

"But there was a house here just now," Maman said, unable to adjust that quickly to Viera Schulin, who had come running out to us, warm and laughing. Now of course we had to hurry inside, and there was no more thinking about the house. Coats were shed in a narrow vestibule, and an instant later there we all were, in among the lamps and opposite the fire.

These Schulins were a redoubtable family of independent women. I don't know if there were any sons. I only remember three sisters: the eldest had married a marchese in Naples and was now slowly divorcing him amid countless lawsuits; then came Zoë, who was said to know everything conceivable; and above all there was Viera, this warm Viera; God knows what has become of her. The countess, a Narischkin, was really the fourth sister, and in many ways the youngest. She knew nothing and had to be continually schooled by her children. And the good Count Schulin felt as if he were married to all these women, and as he wandered about he kissed whichever one he happened to encounter.

As we entered he was laughing heartily, and he greeted each of us at length. I was passed around among the women, who squeezed me and asked me about myself. But once that was over I was determined to slip out somehow and look for the house. I was convinced it was there that day. Getting out was not so difficult; I could creep among all the dresses like a dog, and the door to the vestibule had been left ajar. But the outer door refused to budge. There were various locking devices on it that in my haste I could only fumble with. Suddenly it did open after all, but with a loud noise, and before I could get outside I was grabbed and pulled back.

"Halt! There'll be no sneaking away here," said Viera Schulin playfully. She bent down to me, and I was resolved to disclose nothing to this warm person. But when I said nothing, she immediately assumed that the call of nature had driven me to the door; she took me by the hand and set out, half conspiratorially, half imperiously, to rush me away somewhere. This intimate misunderstanding mortified me beyond all measure. I tore myself loose and looked at her angrily. "I want to see the house," I said haughtily.

She didn't understand.

"The big house outside by the steps."

"You silly boy," she said, reaching out for me, "there *is* no house there anymore." But I stood my ground.

"We'll go out sometime when it's daylight," she promised, trying to appease me. "You can't go crawling around out there now. There are holes everywhere, and right in back are Papa's fish ponds that aren't allowed to freeze. You'd fall in and turn into a fish."

With that she prodded me along in front of her, back into the brightly lit rooms. They were all sitting there talking, and I studied them one by one: of course they would only go looking when it's not there, I thought disdainfully; if Maman and I lived here, it would always be present. Maman seemed lost in thought, while everyone else talked at once. Doubtless she was thinking about the house.

Zoë sat down next to me and began to ask questions. She had a wonderfully steady face which from time to time would brighten with insight, as if she were constantly in the process of coming to some new understanding. My father sat leaning a little to the right, listening to the marchesa, who was laughing. Count Schulin stood between Maman and his wife and was telling a story. But the countess interrupted him, I noticed, right in the middle of a sentence.

"No, child, you're imagining that," the count said good-humoredly, yet suddenly he had the same worried look on his face, which he stretched out over the two ladies. The countess, meanwhile, was not to be dissuaded from her so-called "imagining." She looked to be concentrating intently, like someone who doesn't want to be interrupted. She was making small quietening gestures with her soft hands that were heavy with rings; someone said "ssh" and suddenly there was complete silence.

Behind the people in the room, the large objects from the old house were crowding in upon the scene, much too close. The heavy family silver shone and bulged as if it were being viewed through a magnifying glass. My father looked around uneasily.

"Mama smells something," Viera Schulin said behind him. "We all have to be quiet now: she smells with her ears." But she herself stood there with raised eyebrows, apprehensive and all nose.

In the matter of smells, the Schulins had grown a bit peculiar since the fire. In the narrow, overheated rooms a smell might arise at any moment, and when it did it had to be investigated, and they all had their part to play. Zoë, practical and wary, went to check the stove. The count walked around and stood for a while in each corner of the room and waited; "it's not here," he said each time. The countess had stood up and didn't know where to look. My father turned slowly in place, as if he felt the smell behind him. The marchesa, who had immediately assumed it was an offensive odor, held her handkerchief over her mouth and looked at each of us in turn to see if it was gone. "Here, here," Viera called from time to time, as if she had found it. And around each word there was a curious silence. As for me, I had been diligently sniffing along with the others. But all at once (was it the heat in the room or the closeness of so many lights?) I was overcome, for the first time in my life, by something like the fear of ghosts. It came to me like a vision that all these confident, well-defined grown-ups, who just moments before had been talking and laughing so easily, were going around bent over, occupied with something invisible; that they were conceding that something was there they couldn't see. And the terrible thing was that it was stronger than all of them.

My fear increased. It struck me that what they were searching for might suddenly break out of me like a rash; and then they would see it and point at me. In desperation I looked across at Maman. She was sitting oddly erect; I sensed that she was waiting for me. The moment I joined her and felt her trembling within, I knew that the house was starting to vanish again.

"Malte, you coward," came a voice from somewhere, laughing. It was Viera's voice. But we did not let go of one another, and endured it together; and we stayed that way, Maman and I, until the house had finished disappearing.

~

Richest in disconcerting experiences, however, were the birthdays. You already knew, of course, that life works best when it doesn't play favorites; but on this day, you woke up certain of a joy that by right was yours alone. Your conviction that you were owed this right had probably been instilled in you very early on, at that age when you reach out for the things your eyes light upon and get them all; when, with the power of an imagination that nothing can deflect, you invest whatever winds up in your hand with all the primary-color intensity of the desire that caused you to grasp it.

But then all at once come those strange birthdays, when your awareness of this right is still secure but the actions of the others become uncertain. You would like to be dressed up by someone as in earlier years and then receive everything that follows as perfectly bestowed on you. But scarcely are you awake when someone outside shouts that the cake hasn't come yet; or you hear something break as the presents are being arranged on the table in the next room; or someone comes in and leaves the door open, so that you see everything before you're supposed to. At this moment something like a surgery is being performed on you. A short, horribly painful incision. But the hand that does it is practiced and firm. It's quickly over. And a moment afterward, you're no longer thinking of yourself; all your focus is on saving the birthday, observing the others, anticipating their blunders, strengthening them in the illusion that they are managing everything splendidly. They don't make it easy for you. They turn out to be unbelievably inept, almost stupid. They manage to stumble in with random parcels addressed to other people; you rush to meet them and then have to veer off and pretend you were just running through the room for a bit of exercise, not with anything specific in mind. They plan to surprise you, and with the most ridiculous show of expectation they lift up the bottommost corner of the toy box, and lo, there's nothing there but packing material; then you have to relieve them of their embarrassment. Or if it's something mechanical, they overwind it and break it on the first try. So it's a good idea to practice beforehand, secretly nudging along with your foot an overwound mouse or some other such broken toy: in this way you'll often be able to fool them and help them over their guilt.

You did all this, finally, as the need arose; no special skill was necessary. Talent was only required when someone who was full of true fellow-feeling and anticipation went to great lengths to bring you something they really did want to delight you with, and yet even from a distance you could tell that it was a delight for someone else entirely, a totally alien delight; you couldn't even imagine the person it would have been right for—that's how alien it was.

The days of storytelling, real storytelling, must have been before my time. I've never heard it done. When Abelone used to tell me things about Maman's youth, it was clear that she was not a storyteller. The old Count Brahe, she said, still had that gift. I'll put down here what she remembered about it.

As a very young girl Abelone must have possessed an intense, almost poetic sensibility. Back then the Brahes lived in town, in Bredgade, and led quite an active social life. When she went up to her room late in the evening, she would think she was tired like the others. But suddenly she would be drawn to the window, and then, if I understood correctly, she would stand for hours facing the night and thinking: All this is calling to me. "I stood there like a prisoner," she said, "and the stars were freedom." When she did go to sleep, she could do so without making herself heavy. The expression "falling asleep" does not apply to this time of her girlhood. Sleep was something that took you and rose; from time to time you would open your eyes and see that you were lying on a higher plane and that there were many more planes above it. And then you were up before daybreak—even in winter, when the others came down sleepy and late to a late breakfast. In the evenings, when it grew dark, there were of course only household lights, lights that everyone shared. But those two candles that were lit very early in the fresh new darkness with which everything begins again—those were yours alone. They stood in their low double candlestick and shone calmly through the small oval lampshades with roses painted on them, which had to be lowered a notch from time to time. It was no bother to do so; for once, you were in no hurry at all; sometimes you'd look up and think for a while, when you were writing a letter or resuming the diary that you'd begun long ago in a quite different hand, a hand that was timid and beautiful.

Count Brahe lived quite separately from his daughters. He considered it a delusion when someone claimed to be sharing life with others. ("Ah yes," he would say, "sharing . . .") But he quite enjoyed it when people talked to him about his daughters; he would listen closely, as if they lived in a different city.

So it was extraordinary when one day after breakfast he motioned Abelone over to him: "We have the same habits, it appears; I too write very early in the morning. You can help me." Abelone recalled it as if it were yesterday.

The very next morning she was led into her father's study, which had always been considered forbidden territory. She didn't have time to look around, for she was immediately sat down opposite the count at his desk, which seemed to her to stretch between them like a plain, with books and stacks of paper dotting the space between them like scattered villages.

The count dictated. Those who maintained that Count Brahe was writing his memoirs were not completely wrong. Only these were not the political and military reminiscences that everyone was eagerly anticipating. "I forget," the old gentleman would say curtly when asked about such matters. But he didn't want to forget his childhood. He clung to that. And it seemed completely natural to him that this very distant time should occupy the foreground now, and that when

he turned his gaze inward, it lay before him as on a clear Nordic summer's night, intense and wakeful.

Sometimes he would leap to his feet and dictate into the candles
so forcefully that they flickered. Or whole sentences would have to
be crossed out, and then he would pace violently back and forth, his
Nile-green silk dressing gown billowing out behind him. During all
this, one other person was always present—Sten, the count's old Jut-
land valet, whose job it was, whenever my grandfather jumped up, to
quickly put his hands down on all the loose pages covered with notes
that lay scattered over the tabletop. His Lordship considered modern
paper worthless, thought it was much too light and would blow away
at the slightest breath. And Sten, whose long upper body was all you
saw of him, seemed to share this distrust and sat at the table with his
hands ready, eyes narrowed in the daylight and solemn as an owl.

This Sten spent his Sunday afternoons reading Swedenborg, and
the other servants were loath to enter his room, since they all believed
that he was communing with the dead. Sten's family had always traf-
ficked with spirits, and Sten especially had seemed preordained for
such commerce. Something had appeared to his mother in a vision
on the night she gave birth to him. Sten had large round eyes, and
the far end of his gaze always seemed to rest somewhere behind the
person he was looking at. Abelone's father often asked him how the
spirits were, the way you might inquire to someone after their family:
"Are they coming, Sten?" he would ask easily. "It's always good to have
them here."

For a few days the dictation proceeded without incident. But then
Abelone was unable to spell "Eckernförde." It was a proper noun,
and she had never heard it before. The count, who deep down had

long been seeking some pretext for giving up this business of writing, which always lagged behind his recollections, feigned exasperation.

"She can't write it, and others won't read it," he said peevishly. "And in any case, will anyone really be able to *see* what I am saying here?" he continued angrily, keeping his eyes fixed on Abelone. "Will they *see* him, this Saint-Germain?" he shouted at her. "Did we say Saint-Germain? Cross that out. Write: the Marquis de Belmare."

Abelone crossed out and wrote. But the count went on so rapidly that she couldn't keep up.

"He couldn't abide children, this excellent Belmare, but he took me on his knee, small as I was, and for some reason I decided to chew on his diamond buttons. That delighted him. He laughed and raised me up till we were gazing at each other face-to-face. 'You have excellent teeth,' he said, 'enterprising teeth . . .' But I was looking at his eyes. I've been many places since then, and I've seen all sorts of eyes—but believe me, never again eyes like his. For those eyes, a thing didn't need to be present to be seen; it was already in them. You've heard of Venice? Good. Let me tell you, those eyes could have looked Venice right into this room, and it would have been here as surely as this desk is here. I once sat in a corner listening as he told my father about Persia; and sometimes I think my hands still smell of Persia. My father held him in very high esteem, and His Highness the Landgrave was a sort of disciple of his. But of course there were always more than enough people who dismissed him for claiming to believe in the past only if it was *in* him. They couldn't understand that such ideas only have meaning if you're born with them.

"Books are empty," the count shouted, gesturing angrily toward the walls. "Blood, that's what counts, that's what you must be able to read. He had extraordinary tales and incredible images in his blood, this Belmare; he could open it wherever he wished, there was always some fascinating account there; not a single page was blank. And when he shut himself away occasionally and browsed through it in solitude, he would come to the passages about alchemy and precious stones and colors. Why shouldn't all those things have been there? They have to be somewhere.

"The man might have lived quite happily with a truth as his mistress, if he had been alone. But it was no small thing to be alone with a truth such as his. Nor was he so vulgar as to invite people to visit him when his truth was with him; he didn't want her to become the subject of gossip: he was too much the oriental for that. And so he said to her in loving candor: 'Adieu, madame, until another time. Perhaps in a thousand years we will be stronger and less easily disturbed. Your beauty, madame, is just beginning to bloom,' he said, and it was no mere courtesy. With that, he went off and laid out his zoo for the public, a sort of *jardin d'acclimatation* for the larger species of lies, which had never been seen in our part of the world, and a palm court of exaggerations, and a small, well-tended *figuerie* of false mysteries. And the public came from all quarters to visit it, and he walked about with diamond buckles on his shoes and was completely at his guests' disposal.

"A superficial existence, you say? But at heart it was an act of gallantry toward his lady, and in living it he was able to keep his own deeper self untouched."

For a while now the old man had ceased directing his words to Abelone, whom he had forgotten. He was pacing back and forth furiously and casting defiant glances at Sten, as if at a certain moment Sten would change into the man of his thoughts. But Sten was not yet changing.

"You had to *see* him," Count Brahe forged on, more and more obsessed. "There was a time when he was quite visible, although in many towns the letters he received weren't addressed to anyone: they simply had the name of the town written on them, nothing else. But I saw him.

"He wasn't handsome." The count gave an odd, fractured laugh. "He didn't even resemble the kind of person people recognize as important or esteemed: there were always more 'distinguished' men around him. He was rich: but he seemed to regard wealth as a kind of fickle accident, not something on which you would ever rely. He was well proportioned, but others carried themselves with more poise. Back then of course I couldn't judge if he had real wit, or whether he possessed this or that quality by which people claim to gauge the value of a man—: but he *existed*."

Trembling, the count stopped and made a gesture—as if he were placing something in the space before him that would stay there always.

At that moment he became aware of Abelone.

"Do you see him?" he demanded of her. And suddenly he snatched one of the silver candelabras and thrust it blindingly close to her face.

Abelone remembered that she could indeed see him.

In the following days Abelone was summoned regularly, and after this incident the dictation proceeded much more smoothly. With the help of all sorts of documents, the count was assembling his earliest recollections of the Bernstorff circle, in which his father had played a certain role. Abelone was now so used to the peculiarities of her task that anyone who saw the two of them together might easily have taken their steady collaboration for true intimacy.

Once, as Abelone was preparing to leave, the old gentleman walked up to her as if he were holding a surprise behind his back. "Tomorrow we shall write about Julie Reventlow," he said, and savored his words. "She was a saint."

Abelone must have looked at him in disbelief.

"Yes, yes, such things are still possible," he insisted with authority. "All things are possible, Countess Abel."

He took Abelone's hands and opened them like a book.

"She had the stigmata," he said, "here and here." And with his cold, hard finger he tapped sharply on both her palms.

Abelone didn't know the word "stigmata." I'll understand it later, she thought; she was impatient to hear about the saint her father had actually known. But she wasn't summoned again, not the next morning nor any mornings after that.

When I asked her to go on, Abelone concluded tersely: "Countess Reventlow has often been the subject of conversation in your family." She looked tired, and claimed to have forgotten the rest. "But sometimes I can still feel those two places," she said, smiling, unable to shake that thought, as she gazed almost with curiosity into her empty hands.

~

Even before my father's death everything had changed. Ulsgaard was no longer in the family's possession. My father died in the city, in an apartment that felt hostile and alien. It happened when I was living abroad, and by the time I arrived it was too late.

He lay on a bier, between two rows of tall candles in a room overlooking a courtyard. The scent of the flowers was unintelligible, like many voices all talking at once. His eyes had been closed, and his handsome face bore the look of someone politely reminiscing. He was

dressed in the uniform of the Master of the Hunt, but for some reason
they had put on the white sash instead of the blue one. His hands were
not folded, they were crossed at the wrists and looked artificial and
meaningless. They'd hastily told me that he had suffered a great deal:
but nothing of that could be seen. His features had been straightened
up like the furniture in a guest room from which someone had just
departed. I felt as though I had already seen him dead many times
before: it all seemed that familiar.

Only the surroundings were new, unpleasantly so. This oppressive
room was new, and it faced onto windows, probably somebody else's
windows. It was new that Sieversen came in from time to time and
did nothing. Sieversen had grown old. Then I was supposed to have
breakfast. Several times it was announced. I couldn't think of anything worse than having breakfast that day. I didn't see that they were
trying to get me out of the room; finally, when I didn't leave, Sieversen somehow managed to make me understand that the doctors
had arrived. I didn't see why. There was something that still had to
be done, said Sieversen, looking at me pointedly with reddened eyes.
Then two gentlemen entered as if in a rush: they were the doctors.
The one in front lowered his head abruptly, as if he had horns and was
going to butt me, but it was only to look at us over his glasses: first
Sieversen, then me.

He bowed with the stiff formality of a student. "His Excellency the
Master of the Hunt had one final wish," he said in the same way that
he'd entered the room: again I had the feeling of his almost visceral
haste. I somehow got him to look through his glasses. His colleague
was a plump blond man with skin thin as tissue paper; it occurred to
me that I could easily make him blush. A pause ensued. It was odd
that the Master of the Hunt should still have wishes.

My eyes drifted over again to the handsome, perfectly proportioned face. And at that moment I grasped that what he wanted was finality. Deep down it was what he had always wanted. Now he would have it.

"You are here for the perforation of the heart: please, proceed."

I bowed and stepped back. The two doctors both returned my bow and began at once to confer about their task. Someone was already moving the candles aside. But the older doctor again stepped toward me. At a certain point he stopped, leaned forward to spare himself the last few paces, and glared at me disapprovingly.

"It's not necessary," he said, "that is to say, I mean, perhaps it would be better . . ."

He suddenly struck me as neglectful and shabby as he stood there in his pitiful hasty stance. I bowed once more: some mechanism dictated that I should bow again.

"Thank you," I said curtly. "I won't be a disturbance . . ."

I knew that I would be up to this and that there was no reason to avoid it. This was how it had to happen. Perhaps it was even what gave meaning to it all. Besides, I had never witnessed someone's heart being pierced. It seemed perfectly legitimate not to refuse such an uncommon experience when it presented itself so freely and naturally. And since I'd long been inured to disappointments, there was nothing left to fear.

No, no, nothing in the world can be imagined in advance, not the least thing. Everything is made up of countless incredible details that cannot be foreseen. In imagination we hasten past them and never realize what's been missed. But realities are slow and infinitely specific.

Who, for example, would have imagined that resistance? Scarcely had the broad, high breast been laid bare than the hurried little man was already fixed upon the correct spot. But the speedily applied instrument would not penetrate. I felt that all time had suddenly left the room. It was as if we were in a picture. But then time rushed in again with a faint, skimming noise, and there was more than we could make use of. Suddenly there was tapping somewhere. I had never heard such a sound before: a warm, muffled double-tap. My ear transmitted it, and in the same instant my eyes saw the doctor drive his instrument home. But there was a brief space of time before the two impressions coalesced inside me. So, so, I thought, he's got through. The tapping seemed to speed up, almost as if it were gleeful.

I looked at the doctor I thought I'd seen through so completely. No, he was in complete command of himself: a gentleman working away swiftly and unemotionally, so as not to be late for his next appointment. There was no trace of pleasure or satisfaction in his manner. Only a few hairs were sticking out at his left temple, from some ancient impulse. He carefully withdrew the instrument, leaving behind a kind of mouth, from which blood spurted twice in succession, as if it were saying something with two syllables. With one quick, elegant motion, the young blond doctor dabbed it up in his wad of cotton. And now the wound lay at peace, like a closed eye.

I assume I bowed again; my mind was somewhere else entirely. At any rate, I was surprised to find myself alone. Someone had buttoned the uniform back up, and the white sash lay across it as before. But now the Master of the Hunt was dead, and not just him. Now the heart had been perforated, our heart, our family's heart. It was over. This was the shattering of the helmet. "Today Brigge and nevermore," something inside me said.

I was not thinking of my own heart. And later, when I did reflect on it, I knew for the first time with utter certainty that none of this pertained to mine. It was a single, unaffiliated heart. And it was already back at its one task: beginning from the beginning.

~

I know that I assumed I wouldn't be able to leave right away. First everything has to be put in order, I kept repeating to myself. Exactly *what* needed to be put in order was unclear to me. In truth, there was practically nothing that needed doing. I wandered through the city and saw that it had changed. It was pleasant to step out of the hotel where I was staying and see that it was now a city for grown-ups, trying to look its best for me, almost as if I were a stranger. Everything had become slightly smaller, and I walked along the Langelinie to the lighthouse and back again. When I entered the neighborhood around the Amaliegade, I would sometimes feel influences coming from something in the vicinity that years ago had always drawn me to it and that now was testing its old power over me. Certain corner windows or archways or streetlamps knew a lot about me and threatened me with that knowledge. I looked them in the eye and made it clear to them that I was staying at the Hotel Phoenix and at any moment might be leaving. But that did not satisfy my conscience. I had a growing conviction that I had not put any of these influences and connections truly behind me. I had secretly abandoned them one day, leaving them all unfinished. So in a certain sense my childhood, too, still remained to be accomplished, if I didn't want to give it up as lost forever. And even as I grasped how close I was to losing it, I sensed that there would never be anything else to which I could appeal.

Every day I spent a few hours in Dronningens Tværgade, in those small rooms that wore the affronted look of all apartments for rent in which someone has died. I went back and forth between the writing desk and the large white-tiled stove, burning the papers of the Master of the Hunt. I had begun by throwing the packets of correspondence into the fire, just as I'd found them; but the little bundles were tied too tightly, and they only charred at the edges. It was difficult to loosen them. Most of them had a strong, compelling scent that penetrated me as if they too were trying to awaken memories in me. I had none. Now and then photographs would slip out, heavier than the rest. It took them an unbelievably long time to burn. I don't know why, but suddenly I imagined that Ingeborg's picture might be among them. But each time I looked, I saw gazing back at me mature, splendid, strikingly beautiful women, who conjured in me a different train of thought. It turned out that I was not wholly without memories after all. In just such eyes I had sometimes found myself caught when, as a boy growing up, I walked along the street with my father. Gazing at me from inside a passing carriage, they would capture me in a look from which there was almost no escape. I knew now that they had only been comparing me with him, and that the comparison had not turned out in my favor. Obviously not: the Master of the Hunt had no need to fear comparisons.

It may be that I know something now that he did fear. Let me explain how I arrived at this conjecture. Deep in his wallet there was a sheet of paper, folded long ago, brittle, broken at the creases. I read it before I burned it. It was in his best hand, assured and unwavering, though I saw immediately that it was only a transcription.

"Three hours before his death," it began, and went on to describe the last moments of Christian IV. I can't of course repeat the text verbatim. Three hours before his death he desired to get up. The doc-

tor and the valet Wormius helped him to his feet. He stood a bit
unsteadily, but he stood, and they put his quilted dressing gown on
him. Then suddenly he sat down at the foot of his bed and said something they couldn't understand. The doctor held onto his left hand so
that the king would not sink back into the bed. Thus they sat, and
from time to time the king would say, thickly and with great effort,
the thing they couldn't understand. Finally the doctor began to talk
encouragingly to him: he hoped that he could gradually tease out
what it was that the king was saying. After a while the king interrupted him and said quite clearly: "Oh doctor, doctor, what is his
name?" The doctor struggled to think:

"Sperling, most gracious Majesty."

But that was not what the king meant. As soon as he realized he
could make himself heard, he opened wide his right eye, the one that
still worked, and said with his whole face that one word which his
tongue had been forming for hours, the only one that still existed:
"*Døden*," he said, "*Døden*."

There was nothing else on the sheet of paper. I read it several times
before I burned it. And I recalled that my father had suffered greatly
toward the end. So at least I had been told.

Since then I have thought a good deal about the fear of death, and not
without taking into account key experiences of my own. I think I can
honestly say that I have felt it. It has descended on me in the cities,
among all the bustling people there, often for no reason at all. Sometimes, however, the reasons were legion: when for instance someone
died on a bench and everyone stood around staring at him, and he was

already far beyond fear: then I had his fear. Or that time in Naples, when the young girl sitting opposite me in the trolley died. At first it looked like a fainting spell—we even continued on our way awhile. But finally there was no doubt that we had to stop. And the vehicles behind us stopped and were backed up as if there would never be motion in that direction ever again. The pale, fat girl might have died just like that, peacefully, leaning against the woman beside her. But her mother wouldn't allow it. She put every possible obstacle in her way. She tore at her clothes and poured something into her mouth that could no longer hold anything in. She kept rubbing on her forehead a lotion someone had handed her, and then when the girl's eyes rolled back a little, she began shaking her so that her gaze would face forward again. She screamed into those eyes that didn't hear, she jerked the body toward her and pushed and pulled it as if it were a doll and reached back and slapped the fat face with all her might so that it would not die. That time I was afraid.

But I had been afraid long before that. When my dog died, for example. The dog who bequeathed to me a guilt I could never expiate. He was very sick. I had been kneeling beside him all day long when suddenly he looked up and barked—a brief, sharp bark like the one he would give when a stranger entered the room. That bark had become a kind of signal between us, so I instinctively looked toward the door. But it had already entered him. Alarmed, I sought his eyes, and he also sought mine; but not to say goodbye. The look he gave me then was hard and incredulous. He was reproaching me for letting it in. He was convinced I could have stopped it. It was obvious now that he had always overestimated me. And there was no time left to explain. He continued to look at me, aggrieved and lonely, until it was over.

Or I was afraid when in autumn, after the first night frosts, the flies came into the rooms and revived in the warmth. They were oddly dried up, and frightened by their own buzzing; you could see that they no longer knew quite what to do. They sat there for hours, simply letting themselves go, until they realized that they were still alive; then they started flinging themselves blindly in all directions, with no notion of where they were when they collided with something; and you would hear them all falling again, here, there, everywhere. And at last they would be crawling about and slowly spreading death over the whole room.

But even when I was alone I could be afraid. Why should I deny those nights when I sat straight up in bed out of pure dread of death, clinging to the thought that at least that posture placed me among the living: the dead don't sit up. It was always in one of those chance rooms that quickly deserted me whenever things got bad, as if they were afraid of being arraigned and implicated in my sordid affairs. There I would sit, probably looking so frightful that nothing had the courage to take my side. Not even the lamp, which I had just done the favor of lighting, wanted anything to do with me. It simply stood there burning, as in an empty room. My last hope, then, was always the window. I imagined that there could still be something outside that was mine, even now, even in this sudden poverty of dying. But scarcely had I looked when I wished the window had been nailed shut, closed up like the wall. For now I knew that out there, too, things were going on with the same indifference, that out there, too, there was nothing but my own loneliness. The loneliness which I had brought upon myself and which had grown out of all proportion to my heart. People I had left came to mind, and I couldn't fathom how one could leave people.

My God, my God, if more such nights lie before me, at least leave me one of those thoughts which from time to time I've been able to think. What I'm asking is not so unreasonable; for I know that the thoughts themselves were born of fear, because my fear was so great. When I was a boy they slapped my face and told me I was a coward. That was because I was still so bad at being afraid. But since then I have learned to be afraid with real fear, which grows only as the power that engenders it grows. We have no access to this power except through our fear. For it is so utterly unthinkable, so wholly alien to how our minds work, that our brain malfunctions precisely when we strain to grasp it. And yet: for some time now I've been convinced that this power is *ours*, that it is entirely our own, even if it's still too strong for us. It's true that we don't know it, but aren't we always most ignorant about what is most vitally our own? Sometimes I reflect on how heaven came into being, and death: we pushed far away from ourselves what was most precious in us, because there were so many things that needed doing right away and it wasn't safe inside our busy selves. And now ages have passed, and we've accustomed ourselves to lesser things. We no longer recognize what is our own and are terrified by its vast dimensions. Might it not be so?

I understand very well now, by the way, how a man can carry around deep inside his wallet for many a year an account of someone's dying hour. It wouldn't even have to be an especially unusual one; they all have something quirky about them. I can imagine, for instance, someone copying out how Félix Arvers died. It was in a hospital. He was dying sweetly and serenely, and the nun might have thought he was farther along than he actually was. She called out quite loudly some instruction involving where certain things were to be found. This required reference to a corridor. But the nun was rather poorly educated, and having never seen the word "corridor" written down, she pronounced it "collidor." Jolted by that, Arvers promptly postponed his dying. It seemed to him necessary to clear this up first. He became perfectly lucid and explained to her that the word was "corridor." Then he died. He was a poet and hated imprecision; or perhaps he was only concerned with truth; or else he was loath to take with him as his last impression an instance of the world proceeding on so carelessly. There is no way of knowing which it was. But let no one think that it was pedantry. Else the same charge might be brought against the saintly Jean de Dieu, who jumped up from his deathbed just in time to cut down a man who was hanging himself in the garden, news of which had in some miraculous fashion penetrated the hermetic tension of his agony. He too was concerned only with the truth.

There is a creature that is completely harmless if your eyes alight on it; you hardly notice it and instantly forget about it. But if it should somehow get into your hearing unseen, it evolves there, it hatches, and in some cases it manages to creep all the way into your brain and flourish there, to devastating effect, like the pneumococci in dogs that enter through the nose.

That creature is your neighbor.

Now, because I move around from place to place so much, I've had countless neighbors, above and below, to the right and to the left,

sometimes all four at once. Simply to write a history of my neighbors would be a life's work. Actually, it would wind up being more
a history of the symptoms they have induced in me; but that's how
it always is with creatures of their sort—their presence can only be
detected by the disturbances they cause in certain tissues.

I have had unpredictable neighbors, and others who were like
clockwork in their habits. I have sat trying to puzzle out the law that
governed the first sort, for I was sure there was one. And if the con-
sistent ones stayed out one evening, I imagined what accident had
befallen them and left my lamp burning and fretted like a young
wife. I have had neighbors who hated passionately and neighbors who
were embroiled in a violent love; or I have been there when the one
suddenly turned into the other in the middle of the night—and then
of course there was no thought of sleep. Indeed, I've observed from
all this and more that sleep isn't nearly as frequent as people suppose. My two St. Petersburg neighbors, for instance, attached little
importance to sleep. One stood and played the violin, and I am sure
that as he played he looked out on the wide-awake houses that never
ceased to beam brightly on those improbable August nights. As for
my other neighbor on the right, I know that he lay in bed; indeed,
during the whole time I was there he never once got up. He even kept
his eyes closed, but you could not say that he slept. He lay there recit-
ing long poems, poems by Pushkin and Nekrasov, with that cadence
children use when they have to recite in class. And despite the music
of my neighbor on the left, it was this one with his poems who spun
a cocoon inside my head, and God knows what would have crawled
out of it if the student who sometimes visited him had not knocked
on the wrong door one day. He told me the story of his friend, and

it turned out to be reassuring, at least in one respect. Whatever else, it was a straightforward, unambiguous story that killed off all those maggots of my conjectures.

One Sunday, this minor official next door had hit upon a solution to a peculiar problem. He assumed that he would live for quite a long time, say another fifty years. This generosity he had shown himself put him in a glittering good mood. But now he wanted to go further. He reasoned that those years could be converted into days, into hours, into minutes, even (if you wanted to take it that far) into seconds, and he calculated, and calculated, and came up with a sum the likes of which he had never seen before. It was dizzying; he had to rest awhile. Time was money, he had always heard, and it surprised him that a man who possessed such a vast quantity of time was not under perpetual guard. How easily he could be robbed. But then his buoyant, almost jubilant mood returned, he put on his fur coat to appear a bit larger and more imposing, and made himself a gift of this fabulous amount, addressing himself a bit patronizingly:

"Nikolai Kusmitch," he said benevolently, picturing his modest self still sitting on the horsehair couch, with no fur coat, looking thin and shabby, "I do hope, Nikolai Kusmitch, that you won't puff yourself up over your wealth. Always remember that it is not the main thing; there are poor people who are perfectly respectable; there are even threadbare noblemen and generals' daughters who wander the streets selling all sorts of things to get by." And the benefactor adduced other instances that were well known in the city.

The other Nikolai Kusmitch, the one on the horsehair sofa, the recipient of the gift, didn't look at all puffed up; one could safely assume that he would continue behaving sensibly. Indeed, he changed nothing about his prudent, regular way of life, and now spent Sundays putting his accounts in order. But after only a few weeks it was clear to him that he was spending incredible amounts. I must cut back, he thought. He began getting up earlier, washing less thoroughly, drinking his tea standing up, running to the office and getting there much too early. Everywhere he saved a bit of time. But on Sunday none of these savings appeared in his calculations. Then he realized that he had been duped. I should never have converted it, he thought. How long a full, unbroken year would have lasted. But this infernal small change simply vanishes, God knows how. And so one miserable afternoon he sat himself down in a corner of the sofa and prepared to wait for the gentleman in the fur coat, determined to get his time back. He would bolt the door and not let him out until he had handed over the full amount. "In notes," he would say, "ten-year notes if you please. Four notes of ten and one of five," and the rest he could keep, the devil take him. Yes, he was willing to make him a present of the rest, if that would be the end of it. So he sat there in a pique and waited, but the man never came. And he, Nikolai Kusmitch, who only a few weeks ago had so condescendingly gazed on himself sitting there, was unable, now that he really was sitting there, to picture the other Nikolai Kusmitch, the magnanimous gentleman in the fur coat. Heaven knows what had become of him; probably his frauds had been exposed, and he was behind bars somewhere. Surely he was not the only man his benefactor had duped. Such swindlers always cast their nets wide.

It occurred to him that there must be a public authority, a sort of Time Bank, where he could exchange at least a portion of his miserable seconds. After all, they *were* genuine. He had never heard of such a place, but surely something like that must be in the directory, under *T*, or perhaps it was called "Bank of Time"—it would be easy to check under *B*. It might even be under *I*, since it would presumably be an imperial institution, given its importance.

Later, Nikolai Kusmitch would always maintain that on that Sunday evening, even though he was understandably quite dejected, he hadn't had a drop to drink. He was thus perfectly sober when the following event occurred, so far as one can be sure of what actually happened. Perhaps he had dozed off for a bit in his corner; he easily might have done that. At first this little nap brought him pure relief. I have gotten too involved in numbers, he said to himself. Granted, I understand nothing about numbers. But it's clear that you shouldn't attach so much importance to them; after all, they're only an instrument of the state for maintaining order. No one has ever seen them except on paper. It would be impossible, for instance, to meet a Seven or a Twenty-Five at a social gathering. They had no material existence. And then this slight confusion had taken hold, out of sheer mental carelessness, between time and money—as if they couldn't be kept apart. Nikolai Kusmitch almost laughed. It was good that he had found himself out, and just in time, that was the important thing, just in time. Now things would be different. Time—yes, that was a tricky affair. But did it work that way for me alone? Didn't time pass in seconds for other people too, just as he had discovered, even if they weren't aware of it?

Nikolai Kusmitch was not entirely free of schadenfreude. Just let it—he had started to think, when something peculiar happened. A current of air suddenly brushed his face, it blew past his ears, he could feel it on his hands. He opened his eyes wide. The window was tightly closed. And as he sat there in the dark room with eyes wide open, he began to understand that what he was feeling now was real time, time actually passing. He even recognized them, all those seconds, equally tepid, all exactly like each other, but how fast, how fast. Heaven knows what their goal was. That this should be happening to *him*, for whom every sort of wind became a personal crisis! Now he would sit there and it would always blow past like that, his whole life long. He foresaw all the neuralgias it would cause him, he was beside himself with rage. He leapt to his feet, but the surprises were not over. Under his feet there was something like a movement, not just one, but several curiously interrelated movements. He froze in horror: Could it be the earth? Indeed, it *was* the earth. The earth *did* move; in school they had taught us that, even if they passed over it rather hastily and later hushed it up for good. It was considered an inappropriate subject for discussion. But now, with his new sensitivity, he could feel this too. Did the others feel it? Perhaps, but they didn't show it. Apparently it didn't bother them, these good seagoing people. But it was precisely with respect to such movements that Nikolai Kusmitch's feelings were most sensitive; he even avoided streetcars. He staggered around the room as on a ship's deck and held on with his right hand and then his left. Unfortunately he then remembered something about the tilt of the earth's axis. No, he could not deal with all these motions. He felt sick. Lie down and keep still, he had read somewhere. And ever since, Nikolai Kusmitch had been in bed.

He lay there and kept his eyes closed. And there were times, the less turbulent days, so to speak, when it was quite bearable. And then he came up with the idea of using poems. It was unbelievable how much they helped. To recite a poem slowly, with a steady emphasis on the end rhymes, created a certain stability upon which you could focus, inwardly of course. It was a great stroke of luck that he knew all those poems by heart. But he had always had an enthusiasm for literature. He didn't complain about his condition, I was assured by the student

who had known him so long. In fact, he had come to feel over time
an exaggerated admiration for those who, like the student, walked
around and silently endured the motion of the earth.

I remember this story in such detail because it calmed me greatly. I
can honestly say that I have never again had so admirable a neighbor
as this Nikolai Kusmitch, who doubtless would have admired me too.

~

After this experience I resolved that in similar cases I would always
stick to the facts. I noted how simple and assuaging they were, compared with conjectures. As if I had not known that all our insights
draw a line under an account, nothing more. On the next page something completely different begins, without anything being carried forward. What use in my present circumstances were the few facts that
were so easily gathered? I'll lay them all out in a moment, once I've
specified what is revolving in my mind right now: that in this case the
facts have tended to make my situation, which was really quite difficult to begin with (I now can see), more difficult still.

Let it be said to my credit that I have written a great deal in recent
days; I have been scribbling wildly. Even so, when I went out I didn't
look forward to returning home. I even made little detours which cost
me a full half hour of writing time. I confess that this was a weakness.
But once I was in my room I had no reason to reproach myself. I was
writing, I had my life, and the life on the other side of the wall was a
completely different life which had nothing in common with mine:
the life of a medical student who was studying for his exams. I was not
facing anything like that, which was in itself a crucial difference. And
in other respects also our circumstances were as different as could be.

All that was perfectly clear to me. Right up to the moment when I would realize that *the thing* was about to happen; then I forgot that between us there was nothing in common. I listened so hard that my heart pounded. I stopped whatever I was doing and listened. And then it would happen: I was never wrong.

Almost everyone knows the noise that any round tin object makes—the lid of a can, for instance—when it slips out of your hand. Usually it's not very loud when it hits the floor. There's a sharp impact, then it rolls on its edge and only really becomes annoying when it loses momentum and starts wobbling around and around, clattering ever closer to the floor, until it finally stops and lies flat. Well, that's the whole story: some such tin object fell next door, rolled, and lay still, while at certain intervals there was a stamping on the floor. Like all repetitive noises, the sound this tin object made also had its internal organization. It went through a whole range of inflections and was never exactly the same. But precisely this argued that it was obeying its own inner laws. It could be violent or gentle or melancholy; it could rush headlong toward its conclusion or glide for the longest time before finally coming to rest. And the last wobble was always a surprise. By contrast there was something almost mechanical about the stamping that accompanied it. But it always punctuated the sound differently—indeed, that seemed to be its rationale. I have a much firmer grasp of these details now; the room next to me is empty. He has gone home, back to the provinces. He needed rest. I live on the top floor. On my right is another building, and no one has moved into the room below me: I have no neighbor.

Feeling as I do now, I'm almost surprised that I didn't regard the matter with greater equanimity. Although each time an intuition warned me it was coming. But I could have profited from that. Don't be afraid, I could have told myself, now *the thing* is about to happen; I knew that I was never wrong. But perhaps my fear in this case was a function of the very facts I had learned about him; after I found them out, I became more easily spooked than ever. There was something almost chilling in the thought that what unleashed this noise was the small, slow, soundless motion with which his eyelid drooped over his right eye and closed of its own accord as he read. This was the motive force in his story: a mere trifle. He had already had to forgo his exams more than once, his own ambition was growing increasingly impatient, and the people back home were probably hounding him each time they wrote. So what could he do except just pull himself together? But then, a few months before his deadline, this weakness had set in; this small, improbable fatigue, which was so frustratingly ridiculous, as with a window shade that won't stay up. I'm sure that for weeks he thought he should be strong enough to master it. Otherwise I would never have thought of offering him my will. For I realized one day that his own was running out. From that moment on, when I felt *the thing* coming, I would stand on my side of the wall and beg him to make use of mine. And in time it became clear to me that he was accepting my offer. Perhaps he ought not to have done so, especially when you consider that it didn't really help. Even assuming that we managed to delay *the thing* a bit, it remains doubtful whether he was well enough to make use of the few moments we gained. As for my own expenditures, I was beginning to feel their effects. I remember that I was wondering how long we could go on like that on the very afternoon someone walked up to our floor. Such ascents always caused quite a commotion, given the narrow staircase of our little hotel. After a time I had the impression that someone was entering my neighbor's room. Our doors were the last ones in the hallway; his was at an angle to mine and right next to it. I knew that occasionally he had friends over, but, as I've said, I took no interest at all in his affairs. It might even be that his door opened several times more, and people came and went. It was really no business of mine.

But that evening it was worse than ever. It was not very late, but I was tired and had already gone to bed; I thought perhaps I could get some sleep. Suddenly I sat up with a start, as if someone had touched me. Immediately after that, *the thing* began. It jumped and rolled and slammed against something and wobbled and came to a clattering close. The stamping was terrible. Meanwhile someone from the floor below was banging loudly and angrily on his ceiling. The new lodger was obviously upset. Now: that must be the lodger's door. I was so wide awake I thought I could hear it in spite of the extreme care with which he was opening it. It felt like he was coming closer. Doubtless he wanted to know which room it was coming from. What perturbed me was how exaggeratedly considerate he was being. Surely he had observed by now that quiet was not a priority in this house. Why on earth was he walking so softly? For a time I thought he had stopped at my door: but then I heard him—beyond any doubt—enter the next room. He simply walked right in.

And now (how shall I describe it?), now silence fell. Silence, as when a pain ceases. A strange palpable, prickling silence, as if a wound were healing. I could have fallen asleep instantly; I could have taken one deep breath and been asleep. Only my astonishment kept me awake. In the room next door someone was saying something, but that too was part of the silence. You had to experience this silence; it can't be conveyed in words. Even outside, everything seemed smoothed out. I sat up, I listened, it was like being in the country. Dear God, I thought, his mother is there. She was sitting next to the lamp, she was talking to him, perhaps he was resting his head on her shoulder. Soon she'd be putting him to bed. Now I understood those soft steps outside in the corridor. Ah, so it really does exist. A presence before whom doors open so differently than they do for us. Yes, now we could sleep.

~

I've already almost forgotten my neighbor. I can see that it wasn't real empathy I felt for him. Downstairs from time to time I do ask in passing if there is any news of him and what it might be. And I rejoice when the news is good. But I exaggerate. I don't really feel any great need to know. If I do sometimes feel a sudden urge to enter the room next door, it no longer has anything to do with him. It's only a single step from my room to the next, and the room is not locked. It would be interesting to see what that room actually does look like. It's easy to imagine any room, and often what you imagine is not far from the truth. The only room that is always completely different from the way you picture it is the room next door.

I tell myself that this curiosity is what draws me there. But I know full well that the real attraction is a certain tin object that is waiting for me in there. I've assumed it's the lid of a can, though of course I may be wrong. That doesn't bother me. It accords with my character to blame the whole affair on a tin lid. And it's plausible to assume he wouldn't have taken it with him. In all likelihood the room has been cleaned up and the lid placed back on its can where it belongs. And now the two together form the concept "can," a round can, to be precise—a simple, completely familiar concept. Somehow I seem to recall seeing them both on the mantelpiece, these two parts that constitute the can. Yes, they are standing in front of the mirror, so that behind them a second can appears, an illusory one that's just like it. A can to which we attach no value but which a monkey, for example, would reach for. Actually, there would be two monkeys reaching for it, since the monkey itself would be doubled as soon as it was above the edge of the mantelpiece. But I digress: it's the lid of this can that was intent on me.

Let us agree on this: the lid of a can, a healthy can whose edge is curved exactly like its own—this lid should experience no other desire than to find itself fitted perfectly on its can; this would be the utmost it could imagine, the ultimate satisfaction, the fulfillment of its desires. Indeed, it represents a kind of ideal: to have been turned patiently and gently until you come to rest evenly on the small matching protrusion and feel the two spiraling edges mesh within you, elastic and as sharp as your own edge is when you lie there by yourself. Ah, but how few lids still value this. It's a perfect example of the confusion that commerce with human beings has worked on things. For humans—if they can be fleetingly compared to lids of this kind—for the most part sit badly and grudgingly atop their occupations. Partly because in their haste they've found the wrong ones, partly because they've been put on crookedly and in a fit of anger, partly because the two rims that should fit so snugly have been bent, each in a different way. Let's be honest about this: at bottom their only thought is to leap down the moment they get the chance and roll and clatter about. Where else would all these so-called diversions come from, and the noise that they make?

The world of things has been observing this for centuries now. It's no wonder if they grow corrupted, if they lose their taste for their natural, silent purpose and desire to exploit existence in the same way they see it being exploited all around them. They devise ways to evade their proper applications, they grow listless and negligent, and people are not at all scandalized when they catch them red-handed in some licentious act. People know all that so well from the way *they* behave. They become embittered because *they* are the stronger ones, because they think *they* are the ones with the right to change, because they feel they are being aped; but they let the matter go, just as they let themselves go. But whenever there is one who steels himself, some solitary who wants to rest roundly all along his whole circumference, day and night, this person immediately provokes the enmity of those degenerate objects whose own bad consciences can't abide the thought that anything should actually hold itself together and press instinctively toward its true end. Then they join forces to distract him, to frighten him, to lead him astray, and they have no doubt they will succeed. Winking at one another, they set in motion that temptation that grows into infinity and enlists every creature and even God himself against that one solitary who may perhaps hold out: the saint.

How well I understand now those fantastic paintings in which things with practical, well-defined uses elongate irrationally and stretch toward one another lewdly, curiously, twitching with the random arousals of distraction. Those kettles that walk about steaming, those pistons with plans, and those indolent funnels that push themselves into a hole for the sheer pleasure of doing so. And then those limbs and members, thrown up by the envious void, and the faces pouring streams of warm vomit over them, and farting buttocks that present themselves for anyone's pleasuring.

And the saint cringes and shrinks; yet in his eyes there is a fugitive look that says all this is possible: he has gazed on it. And already his senses are precipitating out of the clear solution of his soul. Already his prayer is losing its leaves and protrudes from his mouth like a dead tree. His heart has tipped over and spills into the muck. His scourge lands on him as weakly as a tail flicking at flies. His sex is again in one place alone, and when a woman comes striding through the heaving mass, her bared bosom full of breasts, it points at her like a finger.

There was a time when I considered these pictures obsolete. Not that I doubted them. I could imagine that back then the saints did experience such things, given the headlong zeal with which they *started* with God, immediately, whatever the cost. We no longer expect this of ourselves. We sense that he is too difficult for us, that we must postpone him, so that we may slowly accomplish the long work that separates us from him. But I know now that this work leads to battles just as fraught as those which sainthood encountered; that such trials plague anyone who is solitary for the sake of the work, just as they plagued God's solitaries in their caves and desert shelters, long ago.

When we speak of solitaries, we always take too much for granted. We assume that people know what we are referring to. But they don't know at all. They have never encountered anyone like that, they have simply hated him. They have been his neighbors who depleted him, and the voices in the room next door that tempted him. They have incited objects to make noise and drown out his concentration. Children banded against him when he was tender and a child himself, and at every stage of his development the grown-ups saw him as a threat.

They tracked him down in his hiding places like a hunted animal, and over the course of his long youth there was never an off-season. And when they couldn't pursue him to exhaustion and he escaped, they cried out against what he had brought forth and called it ugly and cast suspicion on it. And when he didn't listen to them they grew louder and clearer and ate up his food and sucked up his air and spit on his poverty to make it repugnant to him. They warned against him as against someone carrying an infectious disease and threw stones at him to drive him off more swiftly. And what their ancient instincts told them was true: for he was indeed their enemy.

But then, when he didn't look up from his work, they reflected. It dawned on them that in all they did, they were actually doing his will; that they had been strengthening him in his solitude and helping him to cut himself off from them forever. And they changed tactics, and approached him with the ultimate weapon, that *other* means of subversion: fame. Whenever cries of fame break out, almost everyone who is absorbed in something looks up and is distracted.

~

Last night I thought again of the small green book that I must have been given as a boy. (I don't know why, but I always imagine that it once belonged to Mathilde Brahe.) It didn't interest me when I received it, and I didn't read it until several years later, during holidays at Ulsgaard, I think. But it was hugely important to me from the first. Every part of it seemed to have significance—even its externals. The green of the binding *meant* something, and you felt at once that the inside had to be just as it was. There seemed to be some plan by which the smooth endpaper, watered white on white, was followed by the

busy title page that seemed strangely mysterious. It made you think
that there might be illustrations inside, but there were none; and you
had to admit, almost against your will, that this too was as it should
be. It was compensation of a sort when you came upon the slim, brittle ribbon marking slantwise a particular place, so poignant in its
confidence that it was still bright rose, even though it had been lying
between the same two pages since God knows when. Perhaps it had
never been used, and it still rested where the bookbinder had hastily
inserted it, without regard for where. But perhaps it wasn't there by
chance. Perhaps someone had marked a stopping place there, never to
begin again; for fate may have knocked on their door just then with
a charge that took them far away from books, which after all are not
life. It was impossible to know if anyone had read past that marker. Or
it might simply be that someone wished to open to this passage again
and again, and had done so, most often very late at night. At any rate,
I felt reticent before these two pages, the way you can feel before a
mirror at which someone is standing. I never read them. Indeed, I
don't know if I read the whole book. It wasn't very thick, but there
were lots of stories in it, especially good for the afternoon; I could
always find one then that I hadn't read yet.

I remember only two: "The End of Grisha Otrepyev" and "The
Downfall of Charles the Bold."

God knows whether it made an impression on me at the time.
But now, after so many years, I remember vividly the details of how
the corpse of the false czar was tossed into the mob and lay there
three days, mutilated and covered with stab wounds, a mask on its
face. Of course there is practically no chance the little book will come
into my hands again. But this passage must have been remarkable.
I wish too that I could reread the account of his meeting with the

mother. He must have felt very confident, since he had summoned her to Moscow; I am even convinced that he believed so strongly in himself at that point that he actually believed he was summoning his own mother. And this same Maria Nagoi, arriving from her wretched convent after days of hurried travel, had, after all, everything to gain by acquiescing in his fiction. But wouldn't his confidence have been shaken at the very moment she acknowledged him? Didn't the power of his transformation reside in no longer being the son of anyone?

*(That, in the end, is the power wielded by all young people who have left home.)

The fact that the people desired him without envisioning anyone in particular only made him freer and more unlimited in his possibilities. But the mother's avowal, even if part of a deliberate deceit, had the effect of diminishing him; it took from him the wealth of his invention; it confined him to a will-less imitation; it reduced him to the individual he was not: it made him an impostor. And now, undermining him more subtly, came this Marina Mniszech, whose love was in itself a disavowal—since, as it later turned out, she believed not in him but in anyone. I cannot of course swear that all this was dealt with in the story. But it seems to me part and parcel of what was told.

But even setting that aside, this incident is far from dated. We can easily imagine modern writers who would revel in those last moments; and they would not be wrong in doing so. So much is going on there: from deepest sleep he leaps to the window and out of it into the courtyard among the sentinels. He can't get up by himself; they have to

---

* *Written in the margin of the manuscript.* [Rilke's note]

help him. His foot is probably broken. Leaning on two of the men, he can feel that they believe in him. He looks around: the others believe in him too. He almost pities them, these giant *streltsy*. Things have changed so drastically for them: they have known Ivan Grozny in all his reality, and still they believe in *him*. A part of him would like to disabuse them, but if he opened his mouth he'd only scream. The pain in his foot is agonizing, and he thinks so little of himself in this moment that all he registers is this pain. And then there is no time. They are crowding in, he sees Shuisky, and behind him all the others. Soon it will be over. But now his guards close ranks around him. They aren't giving him up. And a miracle occurs. The belief of these old men takes deeper root and spreads; suddenly not one of them is willing to press forward. Shuisky, facing him, calls in desperation to an upper window. The false czar does not look around. He knows who is standing up there; he realizes that a silence has fallen, fallen all at once. He waits now for that voice, that shrill, false, overstraining voice he knows of old. And then he hears the czarina mother disavowing him.

Up to this point the tale tells itself; but now, please, we need a storyteller, we need omniscience: because from the few lines that remain to be written there must emerge a force that will overcome all skepticism. Even if it is not overtly stated, you must find yourself willing to swear that in the interim (infinitely compressed) between shout and pistol shot, he was inhabited once more by the will and the power to be everything and everyone. Otherwise you won't grasp how instinctively right it is that they should bore through his nightshirt and stab his body in place after place, to see if they would strike the hard core of a personality. And that in death, for three whole days, he should still wear the mask that he had almost set aside.

~

When I think about it now, it seems curious to me that in this same book there was a story about the end of someone who remained his entire life a single person, the *same* person, hard and unchangeable as granite and weighing more and more heavily on those who supported him. There is a portrait of him in Dijon. But even without it, we know that he was brusque, headstrong, contentious, and despairing. Only the hands are perhaps not the way we would have pictured them. They are frightfully warm hands, continually seeking to cool themselves and instinctively resting on cold surfaces, outspread, with air between the fingers. Blood could surge into these hands the way it sometimes rushes to one's head, and when clenched they were truly like the heads of madmen, raging and brainsick.

To live with that blood required unbelievable caution. The duke was locked up inside himself with it, and at times, when it paced around in him, dark and aggrieved, he was afraid of it. Even to him it could seem fiendishly alien, this adroit, half-Portuguese blood he scarcely knew. Often he feared it would attack him in his sleep and tear him apart. He behaved as if he had it under his control, but in truth he always stood in terror of it. He never dared love a woman, for fear it would become jealous, and it was so wildly impulsive that he never let wine touch his lips; instead of drinking, he appeased it with rose jelly. One time, however, he did drink, in the camp at Lausanne, when Granson was lost; there he was sick, and all alone, and downed a great deal of undiluted wine. But then his blood was sleeping. During his last years, when he was out of his mind, that blood would some-times fall into a heavy, bestial sleep. Then it would be obvious how completely he was in its power; for when it slept, he was nothing.

At those times no one from his entourage was allowed to enter; he wouldn't understand what they were saying. Nor could he receive the foreign envoys, empty as he was. So he would sit and wait for it to waken. And usually when it did it would leap up and burst from his heart and howl.

In deference to this blood, he hauled around with him all sorts of things that he cared almost nothing about. The three great diamonds and all the precious stones; the Flemish laces and the Arras tapestries, stacked in heaps. His silk pavilion with its cords of braided gold and four hundred tents for his retinue. And pictures painted on wood, and the twelve apostles in pure silver. And the Prince of Taranto and the Duke of Clèves and Philip of Baden and the Lord of Château-Guyon. For he wanted to convince his blood that he was emperor and that nothing was above him: so that it would fear him. But his blood did not believe him, in spite of all such demonstrations; it was a distrustful blood. He may have managed to half-persuade it for a while. But the horns of Uri were his undoing. After that, his blood knew that it was in a lost soul: and it wanted out.

That's how I see it now; but back when I read it as a boy, what most compelled me was their search for him on the day of the Epiphany.

The young Duke of Lorraine, who the previous day had ridden into his poor city of Nancy after that strange battle that was over so quickly, roused his entourage very early in the morning and asked after the Duke of Burgundy. Messenger after messenger was dispatched, and from time to time the young prince himself appeared at the window, restless and concerned. He couldn't always make out who the men were that they were bringing in on their carts and litters; but he saw always that the duke was not among them. Nor was he among the wounded, and none of the stream of prisoners being brought in had seen him. But the fugitives brought with them rumors from everywhere, and were confused and frightened, as if they might encounter him. It was already growing dark, and still nothing had been heard of the duke. The news that he had vanished proliferated throughout the long winter evening. And wherever it spread, it birthed in everyone a sudden, exaggerated certainty that he was still alive. The duke had perhaps never been as real in everyone's imagination as he was on that night. There was no house in which they didn't stay awake and watch for him and anticipate his knock on their door. And if he didn't show up, it was because he had already passed by.

It froze that night, and the idea that he still existed seemed to freeze also; it became that unyielding. And years and years were to pass before it melted. All those people, without really knowing it, depended on his being alive. The fate to which he had consigned them was bearable only through the figure he had stamped upon them. The lesson that he *was* had been difficult to learn; but now that they knew it by heart, they found him easy to picture and impossible to forget.

But the next morning, the seventh of January, a Tuesday, the search began yet again. And this time they had a guide. He was one of the duke's pages, who from a distance apparently had seen his master fall; now he was going to show them the spot. He himself hadn't said a word; the Count of Campobasso had brought him and had spoken for him. Now he walked at their head, and the others followed close behind. Anyone who saw him this way, muffled and oddly unsure of himself, would have found it hard to believe that it really was Gian-Battista Colonna, who possessed the beauty and the slender wrists of a young girl. He shivered from the cold; the air was stiff with night frost, and the crunching of snow under their feet was like the grinding of teeth. They were all freezing, for that matter. Only the duke's fool, whom they had nicknamed Louis-Onze, seemed immune. He was in constant motion. He played at being a dog, ran ahead, came back, ambled for a while on all fours at the side of the boy; but whenever he saw a corpse in the distance, he bounded over to it, bent down, and urged it to pull itself together and be the man they were looking for. He gave it a little time for reflection, but then returned disgruntled to the others, complaining and cursing and fulminating about the obstinacy and indolence of the dead. And they walked on and on, and there seemed no end to it. The town was scarcely visible now, since in the meantime the air had thickened, despite the cold, and had become gray and impenetrable. The landscape lay there flat and indifferent, and the small, huddled group looked more and more lost the farther it traveled. No one spoke; only an old woman who had tagged along after them muttered something, shaking her head; perhaps she was praying.

Suddenly the boy leading them came to a halt and looked around. Then he turned abruptly toward Lupi, the duke's Portuguese physician, and pointed into the near distance. A few paces farther on there was an expanse of ice, a sort of depression or shallow pool, and in it lay ten or twelve corpses, half immersed in the ice. They were almost completely stripped and plundered. Lupi walked from one to the next, bent over and looking closely. And now you could see Olivier de la Marche and the chaplain as they walked separately among the corpses. But the old woman was already kneeling in the snow, whimpering, as she bent over a large hand whose outspread fingers pointed stiffly back at her. They all came running. With some of the servants Lupi tried to turn the corpse over, since it was lying facedown. But the face was frozen into the ice, and when they tried to pull it out one cheek ripped off, thin and brittle, and the other had apparently been gnawed by dogs or wolves; and the whole face had been split open by a great wound that began at the ear, so that you really couldn't speak of a face at all.

One after another they looked around; each thought he would find the Roman right behind him. But they saw only the fool running toward them, angry and bloodied. He was holding a cloak at arm's length and shaking it, as if to make something fall out; but the cloak was empty. So they set about looking for identifying marks, and found several. They had made a fire, and washed the body with warm water and wine. The scar on his neck became visible, as did the places where the two large abscesses had been removed. The doctor was no longer in doubt. But there was more evidence. A few paces farther on, Louis-Onze had found the carcass of Moreau, the large black horse the duke had ridden in the Battle of Nancy. Louis-Onze sat astride it, his short legs dangling. The blood was still running from his nose into his mouth, and you could see him tasting it. One of the servants recalled that the duke had an ingrown toenail on his left foot; so they all began to look for that nail. But the fool squirmed as if being tickled and called out, "Ah, monseigneur, forgive these dunces for exposing your gross defects, when they could have recognized you from my long face, in which all your virtues are written."

*(The duke's fool was also the first to enter when the corpse had been laid out. It was in the house of one Georges Marquis, though no one could say why. The pall had not yet been spread, so the fool could take it all in. The white of the shirt and the crimson of the cloak stood in sharp, standoffish contrast between the two blacks of bal-

---

* *Written in the margin of the manuscript.* [Rilke's note]

dachin and bier. In front, scarlet riding boots stood pointing toward him with their long gilded spurs. And there could be no disputing that the thing up there was a head, once he had seen the crown. It was a large ducal crown set with various precious stones. Louis-Onze walked around and examined everything carefully. He even felt the satin, although he knew little about the quality of fabrics. It was probably fairly good satin, perhaps a trifle cheap for the House of Burgundy. He stepped back once more to take it all in. The colors seemed to clash oddly in the light reflected off the snow. He impressed each one separately on his memory. "Well disposed," he said finally, "if a bit ostentatious." Death seemed to him like a puppet master who quickly needs a duke.)

At some point it's best to acknowledge that certain traits are not going to change and simply are as they are, and to no longer regret their presence or even judge yourself harshly. Hence, for instance, it has become clear to me that I was never at heart a reader. In childhood, reading seemed to me like an occupation you took up later in life, when all the professions came along, one by one, for your consideration. To be honest, I had no clear idea when that might be. I trusted that I would recognize that the moment had come when life turned around, as it were, and now came from the outside only, just as formerly it had emanated from within. I imagined that from then on it would be clear and unambiguous and not possible to misunderstand. Not at all simple, on the contrary very demanding, probably even complicated and difficult, but at any rate *visible*. The strange undefined quality of childhood, its disproportions and that sense of nothing ever being quite anticipated—all that would have been left behind. (Though admittedly I couldn't see how.) But meanwhile my inner life kept increasing and closing up all around, and the more intensely I looked outward, the more material I stirred up within: God knows where it all came from. But apparently when it reached its maximum capacity it would dissolve once and for all. For it was obvious that grown-ups were hardly bothered by any of it; they went about making judgments and taking action, and if they ever got into difficulties, external circumstances were to blame.

So I resolved to postpone reading until those other changes began. When that time came I would deal with books as I would with casual friends; there would be occasions for them, intervals that would pass smoothly and pleasantly, just as much as there was time for. Some, of course, would be closer to me than others, and inevitably I would occasionally overstay a half hour or so with them, and maybe miss a walk, an appointment, the beginning of a play, or a letter that needed writing. But that my hair would get twisted and tangled as if I had been lying on it, or that my ears would burn and my hands would grow as cold as metal, or that the tall candle at the table I was reading at would burn all the way down into its candlestick—all that, thank God, was out of the question.

I mention these symptoms because I myself experienced them vividly during those holidays at Ulsgaard when I suddenly discovered reading. It quickly became clear to me that I wasn't up to it. I had of course begun prematurely, well before that time in the future for which I'd planned it. But that year at Sorø, living among so many boys about the same age as me, had made me wary of such plans. There I was ambushed by swift, unanticipated experiences that were clearly treating me as an adult. And they were life-sized experiences that met me with all their grown-up weight. But even as I felt the impact of their strong actuality, my eyes were opened to the infinite reality of my childhood. I knew now that it would never end, any more than the other world was only just now beginning. I told myself that of course everyone was free to divide experience into halves, but that the dividing lines were pure invention. And I lacked the ingenuity to devise any for myself. Every time I tried, life made it clear to me that it knew nothing of them. And if I convinced myself that my childhood was past, then at that same moment the whole future would vanish also, and I would be left with only as much to stand on as a lead soldier has beneath his feet.

This discovery obviously isolated me even more. It preoccupied me with myself and filled me with a kind of radical freedom, which I mistook for worry, since that other way of experiencing it was far beyond my years. I was also disturbed, I remember, by the thought that now, since nothing was scheduled for any particular phase of my life, there were any number of things that I might miss altogether. And so when I returned to Ulsgaard in this frame of mind and saw all the books, I fell upon them: in a great hurry, almost with a bad conscience. Somehow I had a premonition of what I've so often felt in later life: that you didn't have the right to open one book if you weren't prepared to read them all. With every line you made a break in the world. Before books, it was whole, and perhaps after them it would be whole again. But how could I, who didn't know how to go about reading, take them all on? There they stood, even in this modest library, hopelessly outnumbering me, shoulder to shoulder in closed ranks. Defiant and desperate, I plunged from book to book and fought through the pages like someone who has to perform a task out of all proportion to his strength. At that time I read Schiller and Baggesen, Oehlenschläger

and Schack von Staffeldt, Calderón and whatever was there by Walter
Scott. Some things came into my hands that I ought to have read as
a child, while for others it was still much too early; almost nothing
seemed exactly right for my present needs. And nevertheless I read.

In later years I would sometimes wake up at night and the stars
would be standing there so real and advancing with such clarity of
purpose that I couldn't understand how people inured themselves
to so much world. I had a similar feeling, I think, when I'd glance
up from my books and look outside—where the summer was, where
Abelone was calling from. It was an unexpected turn for us that she
had to call and that I didn't answer. It was in the midst of our happiest time. But now that reading had set its hooks, I feverishly clung to
it and hid myself away, obstinate and self-important, from our daily
holidays. Awkward as I was at entering into those many (though often
unspoken) moments when the two of us enjoyed a natural happiness, I rationalized that our growing rifts would create the promise
of future reconciliations, and that they would be all the more moving
the longer they were deferred.

As it happened, I woke up from my reader's trance one day as
abruptly as I had entered it; and then we had a thorough falling-out.
Abelone had been reacting to whatever I would say with sarcasm or
condescension, and whenever I tried to join her in the arbor she would
declare that she was reading. On that particular Sunday morning a
book was indeed lying closed beside her, but she seemed almost overly
occupied with the red currants she was carefully separating from their
small clusters with the help of a fork.

It must have been one of those early mornings that sometimes appear
in July—fresh, rested hours when joyful and spontaneous events are
happening all around. From a million small irrepressible movements a

mosaic of life at its most persuasive is being composed; objects vibrate one into another and out into the air, and their cool freshness gives the shadows a clarity and lends brightness and spirit to the sun. In the garden there is no central focus; everything is everywhere, and to miss nothing you would have to be diffused in everything.

This whole epiphany was repeated in Abelone's small action. It was so perfect that she was doing exactly what she was doing, and in exactly the way she was doing it. Her hands, bright in the shade, worked together so lightly and dexterously, and the round berries leapt playfully from the fork into a bowl lined with dew-soaked vine leaves, where other berries were already heaped, red ones and blond ones, lustrous, with good seeds in their tart flesh. Standing where I was, I wanted only to go on watching; but since I would probably be called out if I did, and in order to appear at ease, I picked up her book, sat down on the other side of the table, and, after leafing through it briefly, began to read some random page.

"You could at least read out loud, bookworm," Abelone said after a while. That didn't sound nearly so quarrelsome as usual, and since I suddenly felt that it was high time we made up, I immediately started reading out loud, and continued all the way to the end of the section, and then on to the next heading: "To Bettina."

"No, not the replies," Abelone interrupted, and laid down the little fork as if exhausted. Then she laughed at the way I was looking at her.

"My God, how badly you read that, Malte."

I had to admit that I hadn't been paying the slightest attention to what the words said. "I was only reading so you would interrupt me," I confessed, and blushed and turned back to the title page of the book. Only then did I see what it was. "And why not the replies?" I asked, curious.

It was as if Abelone hadn't heard me. She sat there in her bright dress, as if everywhere inside her she was growing as dark as her eyes had become.

"Give it to me," she said suddenly, as if in anger, and took the book out of my hand and opened it right to the place she wanted. And then she read one of Bettina's letters.

I don't know how much of it I understood, but it was as if a solemn promise were being made to me that one day I would understand it all. And while her voice grew, until finally it was almost that same magical voice I listened to when she sang, I felt ashamed that I had entertained so petty an idea of our reconciliation. For I well understood that *this* was it. But now it was happening on a higher plane, far above me, in a place I couldn't reach.

The promise is still in force. At some time or other that same book got in among my own books, among the very few that I'm never without. Now it opens for me also at the passages I'm thinking of, and when I read them I can't be sure whether it's Bettina or Abelone who comes to mind. No, Bettina has become more real in me; Abelone, whom I knew in the flesh, was like a preparation for her, and now she has entered into Bettina as if into her own instinctive being. For this strange Bettina in all her letters created space, made room for the most essential forms. From the beginning she disseminated herself throughout the whole of things, as if she had her death behind her. Everywhere she was present in everything, became an essential part of it, and whatever she experienced was eternally part of Nature; there she knew herself, and it was almost painful when she had to reformulate herself as something separate from it, piecing herself together again, laboriously, guessing her way back as if from stories and old records that had survived—conjuring her separate self like a ghost and enduring it.

Such a short time ago you were *here*, Bettina. I recognize your traces. The earth is still warm from you, the birds still leave room for your voice. The dew is different, but the stars are still the stars of your nights. Or is the whole world not yours? For how often you set it afire with your love and watched it blaze and burn up and secretly replaced it with another world while we were all asleep. You felt in such complete harmony with God when each morning you demanded of him a new world, so that all the ones he had made could have their turn. You thought it would be beggarly to save them and mend them; you used them up and held out your hands for more and more world. For your love was equal to everything.

How is it possible that there aren't stories everywhere of your love? What has happened since that is more remarkable? With what, then, *are* people concerned? You, at least, knew the value of your love, and you spoke it aloud to your greatest poet, so that he would make it human; for in your telling, it still belonged to the elements. But in writing back to you, he persuaded people *not* to believe. Everyone reads those replies and gives them more credence, since to them the poet is easier to understand than Nature. But perhaps one day we'll see that these replies marked the *limit* of his greatness. This woman in love was placed before him as his task, and he was not equal to the challenge. What does it mean that he could not respond? Love such as this needs no response; it contains both call and reply in itself; it answers its own prayer. But he should have humbled himself before this love in all his magnificence and written what she dictated, with both hands, like John on Patmos, kneeling. There was no choice in the presence of this voice which "performed the office of the angels" and had come to enwrap him and carry him off into eternity. Here was the chariot for his fiery ascension. Here, prepared against his death, was the dark myth he left empty.

~

Fate thrives on figures and intricate designs. Its difficulty lies in its complexity. But life is difficult by reason of its simplicity. It has just a few elements whose magnitude is out of all proportion to our little existences. The saint, refusing fate, chooses life and comes face-to-face with God. But because woman, in accordance with her nature, must make the same choice relative to man, she calls forth the doomed nature of all love relationships: resolute and fateless, like an eternal being, she stands firm beside the one whose nature is to change. The woman who loves always surpasses the man who is loved, because life is greater than fate. Her self-abandon desires the infinite: that is her happiness. The nameless suffering of her love, however, has always been: that it is demanded of her to put limits on that abandon.

It's the only lament that has ever been lamented by women. The first two letters of Héloïse contain only this, and five hundred years later it rises from the letters of the Portuguese nun; one hears it like a familiar bird call. And suddenly present life lights up, as the far-off figure of Sappho streaks through it, she whom all the past eras failed to find, since they looked for her not in life but in fate.

~

I've never dared to buy a newspaper from him. I'm not always sure he even has copies with him, as he shuffles slowly back and forth outside the Jardin du Luxembourg, all evening long. He pushes his back against the railings and his hand rubs against the stone ledge from which the bars rise. He presses so flat against that barrier that many people pass by every day and never even see him. He still has the remnant of a voice in him, and it calls out the price; but to those who hearken it's like a noise in a lamp or a stove or the sound of water when it drips at odd intervals in a cave. And the world is such that there are people who all their lives pass by unsuspectingly during those intervals he makes when, more silently than any moving thing, he moves on—like the hand of a clock, like the shadow of that hand, like time itself.

How wrong I was to resist looking. I am ashamed to write that often when I found myself close to him I adopted the pace of the others, and walked by as if I didn't know he was there. Then I'd hear something inside him say "*La Presse*," and then say it again, and then a third time, with scarcely a pause in between. And the people next to me would turn and look everywhere for the source of that voice. But I had hurried on, faster, ahead of the rest, as if I'd noticed nothing, as if I were deeply preoccupied with thoughts of my own.

And in truth I was. I was preoccupied with picturing him to myself; I had undertaken the task of imagining him, and sweat had broken out on my brow from the effort. For I had to piece him together the way you would re-create a dead man for whom no evidence exists and no remains survive, whose every facet is to be achieved entirely within yourself. I realize now that it helped me a little to think of all those demounted Christs of striated ivory that you find in every antique shop. The memory of some Pietà came and went—: all this probably just to call up that certain angle at which he was holding his long face, and the hopeless stubble of beard in the hollows of his cheeks, and the final grievous blindness of his closed expression, turned obliquely upward. But there was so much more that was uniquely his; for even then I understood that nothing about him was incidental: not the way that his coat, slumping back from his shoulders, exposed the whole of his collar, that low collar which in a wide arc circled his pitted, elongated neck without ever touching it; not the greenish-black cravat fastened loosely around all this; and most especially not his hat, an old, stiff, high felt hat that he wore as all the blind wear their hats: without regard to the lines of their faces, with no intent to create a new external persona by adding this accoutrement; but merely putting it on as some agreed-on thing that people do. In my cowardly determination not to look, I went so far that finally the image of this man, often for no reason at all, intensely and painfully contracted inside me to create an aversion so extreme that eventually I was unable to bear it any longer; as a last resort I resolved to counteract this growing independence of my imagination by forcing it to confront the thing itself. It was toward evening. I ordered myself to walk slowly by and look at him closely.

It's important for you to know that spring was in the air. The wind had died down, the side streets were long and contented; where they met other streets, buildings gleamed as new as fresh cuts in some white metal. But it was a metal that surprised you by its lightness. In the broad thoroughfares many people were out walking, almost without thought of carriages, which seldom rolled past. It had to be a Sunday. The towers of Saint-Sulpice stood out bright and unexpectedly tall in the windless sky, and the narrow, almost Roman alleys yielded brief glimpses into the season. In the park and outside it so large a crowd was milling about that I didn't see him immediately. Or was it that I didn't recognize him at first amid all those people?

I knew at once that my image of him was worthless. The abject self-surrender in his wretchedness, unmitigated by any trace of caution or dissembling, was beyond my means. I had understood neither the angle of his posture nor the terror which the insides of his eyelids seemed to keep spilling into him. I had never even considered his mouth, which was shaped like the spout of a drain. It's possible that he had memories; but now nothing found its way into his soul except the inert feel of the stone ledge behind him, against which his hand was gradually rubbing itself out. I had come to a halt, and as I was registering all this almost in a single moment, I realized that he was wearing a different hat, and what was undoubtedly a Sunday cravat; it was patterned in diagonal squares of yellow and violet, and as for the hat, it was a cheap new straw one with a green band. The colors are of no importance, of course, and it is petty of me to have remembered them. I would only want to say that on him they were like the softest down on a bird's breast. He himself took no pleasure in them, and who among all these (I looked around me) could possibly think that this finery was meant for them?

Dear God, it struck me violently, so you really *do* exist. I know there are logical proofs of your existence, but I have forgotten them all and never demanded one, for what an immense obligation the certainty of you would confer. And yet that is what is now being shown to me. *This* is your liking, *this* is your pleasure. If only we could teach ourselves to bear, and not to judge. Which are the heavy things? Which are winged with grace? You alone know.

When winter comes again and I need a new coat—grant that I may wear it just like this, for as long as it is new.

It's not that I want to differentiate myself from them when I go about in better clothes that have always been mine, and make such a point of having a place to live. It's simply that I'm not as far along as they are. I don't have the courage yet for their life. If my arm were to wither, I know I would hide it. But *she* (I don't know anything about her), she appeared every day in front of the café terraces, and though it was very difficult for her to take off her coat and get herself out of her layers of ill-defined outer garments, she didn't shy away from the task and took so long removing them that with each piece you could hardly believe there could be another. But then finally she stood there before you, modestly, with her dry, withered stump, and you saw that it was special.

No, it's not that I want to distinguish myself from them; in fact I would be grossly overestimating myself if I claimed to be like them. I'm not. I have neither their strength nor their fortitude. I eat on schedule, and thus exist from meal to meal, completely without mystery; but they subsist within themselves, like eternal beings. They stand on their daily corners, even in November, and don't cry out during the coldest winters. The fog comes in and renders them indistinct and uncertain: but when it clears, there they still are. I left on a long journey, I fell ill, many things were lost to me: but they didn't perish.

*(I don't even know how it's possible for schoolchildren to get up in the morning in their bedrooms full of gray-smelling cold. Who gives them the strength, these pell-mell little skeletons, to dash out into the grown-up city, into the murky dregs of the night, into the

---

* *Written in the margin of the manuscript.* [Rilke's note]

never-ending school day, always so small, always full of presentiment, always getting there late? I have no idea what source of sustenance is constantly replenishing them.)

This city is full of people who are slowly sliding down to their level. Most of them put up a struggle at first; but then there are those faded, aging girls who constantly, for all their strength, are letting themselves slip over without resisting, their untapped souls still waiting, girls who have never been loved.

Perhaps you expect me, O Lord, to dispense with everything and love them. Why else do I find it so hard not to follow them when they walk past me? Why do I suddenly think up the sweetest, most evocative words of night, while my voice hesitates timidly between my heart and my throat? Why do I imagine holding them to my breath with indescribable tenderness, these dolls that Life has played with so roughly, flinging their arms open, spring after spring, for nothing and again for nothing, until they grow loose in the shoulders? They have never fallen from very high a hope, so they are not broken, but they are badly damaged and Life is bored with them. Only stray cats come to them in their rooms at night and secretly knead them and sleep on them. Sometimes I'll follow one of them for a couple of streets. She'll walk along past the houses, clumps of people will gradually form and make it hard to track her; farther on she'll vanish behind them as if she had never been there at all.

And yet I know that if someone tried to love them, they would lean on him with all their weight, like people who have been walking too long and can go no farther. I believe that only Jesus could bear that burden, because he still has resurrection in all his limbs; but he cares nothing for them. Only women in love attract him, not those who wait, with their small need to be loved, as with a lamp grown cold.

~

[On Charles VI of France] I know that if I am destined for the worst it won't help me to disguise myself in my better clothes. Didn't he, even though he was a king, descend among the lowest of the low? He who, instead of rising, sank to the very bottom? It's true, at times I have believed in the other kings, although their parks prove nothing. But it is night, it is winter, I am freezing, I believe in him. For glory is but one moment, and we have never seen anything longer-lasting than misery. But the king shall endure.

Isn't he the only one who bore up under his madness like wax flowers under a bell jar? People prayed in churches that the others might live long lives; but the chancellor Jean Charlier de Gerson wished for him life everlasting—and this was when he was already the most abject of them all, base and wretchedly poor despite his crown.

That was in the days when anonymous men with blackened faces would sometimes attack him in his bed to rip off the shirt which had rotted into his sores and which he had long since come to think of as part of his own body. It was dark in the room, and they tore away the foul rags from under his stiff arms whenever their hands found them. One of them fetched a light, and only then did they find the purulent sore on his chest where the iron amulet had sunk in, since each night he pressed it to him with all the strength of his faith; now it lay deep in his flesh, grotesquely precious, in a pearly bed of pus, like a miracle-working remnant in the hollow of a reliquary. Hardened thugs had been picked for the job, but even they weren't proof against nausea when the aroused worms stretched up and reached for them from the Flemish nightshirt and, falling from its folds, began climbing here and there up their own sleeves. Things had undoubtedly grown worse

with him since the days of the *parva regina*; for she had still been willing to lie with him, young and radiant as she was. Then she had died.
And now no one could imagine bedding another concubine next to
this carrion. She had not left behind the words and endearments with
which the king could be comforted. There was no one now who could
penetrate the wilderness of his mind, no one to help him out of the
ravines of his soul—and thus no one to understand when suddenly
one day he got up all on his own and stood there sanely with the
round-eyed gaze of an animal heading out to pasture. And when he
recognized the pensive face of Juvénal, he remembered the kingdom
and what it had been like the last time he was aware of it. And he
wanted to be filled in on all that he'd missed.

But it was in the nature of the events of these times that nothing
could be left out in the telling of them. When something happened,
it happened with its full weight, and everything seemed connected
when you tried to relate it. For how could you gloss over the fact that
his brother had been murdered, and that yesterday Valentia Visconti,
whom he had always called his dear sister, had knelt before him all
in black, lifting her widow's veil from a face contorted by lament and
accusation? And today an unbearably loquacious lawyer had stood
there for hours proving that the princely murderer was in the right,
until the crime grew transparent and the act seemed to rise brightly to
heaven. And justice meant saying that everyone was in the right, for
Valentina of Orléans died of grief even though vengeance had been
promised her. And what good did it do to pardon the Burgundian
duke, and pardon him yet again; the black rutting of despair now
possessed him; for weeks he had been living in a tent deep in the forest of Argilly, insisting that only the stags belling in the night gave
him solace.

As he thought all this through, over and over and from beginning to end (though the events themselves were brief), the people were
clamoring to see him, and see him they did: bewildered. But they
rejoiced nonetheless; they realized that this was the king: this silent,
patient human being, who was only there so that a dilatory God could
act above him with pure suddenness when the time arrived. In these
lucid moments on the balcony of his Hôtel de Saint-Pol, the king
perhaps had an intimation of his own secret progress; he recalled the
day of Roosebeke, when his uncle de Berry had taken him by the
hand and led him to the place of his first military triumph; there, in
that November day's light, which stretched eerily into dusk, he had
surveyed the mass of the Ghentians, who had strangled themselves
in their own tight formation when his cavalry had attacked from
all sides. Twisted into one another like a giant brain, they remained
there in the knots of those formations they created in order to stand
firm as a single mass. His breath failed him when everywhere he
looked he saw their smothered faces; he couldn't help imagining the
air being sucked straight up and far above these corpses (which were
still packed together, standing erect) by the sudden flight of so many
despairing souls.

They had impressed this scene upon him as marking the inception
of his glorious reign. And it had stayed with him. But if that had been
the triumph of death, then this—standing here with his knees trembling, alone and erect in all these eyes: this was the mystery of love.
He had seen through the eyes of those grown-ups that the battlefield
could be comprehended, monstrous as it was. But what was happening now resisted understanding; it was as much a miracle as that stag
with the golden collar he had seen with his own eyes, years ago in
the forest of Senlis. Only now he was the vision, and all those others

were lost in wonder. Nor did he doubt that they were holding their breath, filled with the same vast expectation that had overcome him on that boyhood day of hunting, when that quiet face, peering at him intently, had stepped out from the branches. The mystery of its visibility spread over all its gentle form; it held perfectly still, as if it would vanish if it moved; the thin smile on its broad, simple face projected a natural abidingness, like the smiles carved on stone saints; and there was no effort in maintaining it. That is how *he* offered himself up now to all these people, and it was one of those moments that are like eternity foreshortened. The crowd could scarcely bear it. Strengthened, fed with an inexhaustibly multiplied solace, it broke the silence with a cry of joy. But above, on the balcony, the single figure of Juvénal des Ursins remained, and he shouted into the next interval of quiet that the king would be coming to the Brotherhood of the Passion on the rue Saint-Denis, to see the Mysteries.

On such days the king was full of gentle consciousness. Had a painter of that time been searching for some analogue of life in paradise, he could have found no more perfect model than the king's quiet figure as it stood at one of the high windows of the Louvre under the downward arc of its shoulders. He was leafing through the pages of Christine de Pisan's little book *The Path of Long Study*, which was dedicated to him. He was not reading through the learned disputations of that allegorical parliament, which had set out to determine what sort of prince would be a worthy ruler of the world. The book always opened for him at the simplest passages, where it spoke of the heart that for thirteen years had stood like a flask over the fires of pain, its only purpose to distill the water of bitterness for the eyes; he grasped that true consolation began when happiness lay far in the past and was gone forever. Nothing was more precious to him than this solace. And while his gaze seemed drawn to the bridge beyond, he loved seeing the things of that long-ago world through Christine's heart, which had been taken in hand by the powerful Cumaean and schooled in the dimensions of greatness: the perilous seas, those cities with their strange towers held shut by the pressure of distances, the ecstatic solitude of the congregated mountains, and the endless heavens that were searched so anxiously and that only now were closing like an infant's skull.

But when someone entered he was jolted out of his reverie and his mind slowly clouded over. He allowed himself to be led away from the window and given something to keep him occupied. They had accustomed him to spending his hours leafing through illustrations, and he was happy doing so, although it frustrated him that you could only look at them one page at a time, and they were bound so tightly into the folios that you couldn't move them around. Noting his vexation, someone remembered a game of cards that had been completely forgotten, and the king lavished favor on the man who brought them in, since they were colorful and crowded with figures and could be moved at will and were thus very much to his liking. And while card playing became the fashion among his courtiers, the king sat in his library and played alone. Just as he now turned up two kings side by side, so too God had recently paired him with the Emperor Wenceslaus; sometimes a queen died, and then he laid an ace of hearts on her, like a gravestone. It didn't surprise him that in this game there was more than one pope; he put Rome over there at the far edge of the table, and here, under his right hand, was Avignon. Rome was of no interest to him; for some reason he imagined it as round, and left it at that. But Avignon he knew. And scarcely had he thought of it than his memory re-created the tall, hermetic palace and afterward experienced a deep weariness. He closed his eyes and had to take a breath. He was afraid he would have bad dreams that night.

On the whole, though, it really was a calming occupation, and they were right to return him to it again and again. Such hours strengthened in him the conviction that he was the king, King Charles VI. Not that he exaggerated his importance; in his own mind he was nothing more than a card like those laid out before him. But he felt increasingly that he was a *particular* card, perhaps a bad one, perhaps one that was played in anger, one that always lost: but always the same card, never any other. And yet, after a week of such repeated self-corroboration, he began to feel confined by what he was. His skin grew taut across his brow and at the nape of his neck, as if he were suddenly experiencing his own sharp outlines. No one knew what temptation he gave in to then, when he asked about the Mysteries and could scarcely wait for them to begin. And when the time came at last, he spent more time on the rue Saint-Denis than in his own palace at Saint-Pol.

The fateful thing about these acted-out poems was the way they kept increasing and adding to themselves until they grew to tens of thousands of verses, so that the time in them ultimately became real time, much as if someone were to make a globe whose dimensions duplicated those of the earth. The hollow platform—with hell beneath it, and above it, built onto a pillar, the open scaffolding of a balcony without a balustrade that stood for heaven—only demystified its illusions. And in truth this century *had* made heaven and hell mundane: it battened on the energies of both to feed its appetites.

These were the days of Avignon Christendom, which had drawn together around John XXII a generation earlier, when so many had instinctively sought refuge with him, that at the site of his pontificate, immediately after he settled there, the mass of that palace had arisen, closed and heavy, like an emergency body for the homeless soul of all. As for himself, this small, slight, spiritual old man still lived openly and unafraid. Yet when, scarcely having settled in, he began to institute reforms swiftly and without delay in every quarter, dishes spiced with poison were suddenly discovered on his table; the first cup always had to be poured away, since the piece of unicorn was discolored when his cupbearer drew it out. Perplexed, not knowing what to do with them, the seventy-year-old pope hid on his own person the wax effigies that had been fashioned to hasten his destruction; and he scratched himself on the long needles that impaled them. They could be melted down of course. But these secret simulacra had instilled such dread in him that, overriding his strong will, the thought persisted that doing so would bring about his own death, and he would vanish in the flames just like the wax. This fear made his shriveled body become even drier—and more enduring. And now the body of his empire was being threatened; from Granada the Jews had been incited to slaughter every Christian, and this time they had hired more fearsome executioners. No one, from the very first rumor, doubted that the lepers were conspiring; several citizens had already seen them throwing bundles of their horrible putrefaction into the wells. People accepted this as possible with a readiness that was more than light credulity; on the contrary, belief had grown so heavy that it had plunged from their trembling hands and dropped into the bottom of the wells. And once more the zealous old man had to protect his blood from poison. Back when his bouts of superstition first started, he had prescribed the Angelus for himself and those close to him, to fend off the demons of twilight; and now every evening this calming prayer rang throughout the whole agitated world. But otherwise all the bulls and letters he issued were more like spiced wine than medicinal tea. The empire had not put itself in his hands for treatment, but he never tired of diagnosing its illnesses; and already from the farthest East people were turning to this imperious physician.

But then something incredible happened. On All Saints' Day he had preached longer and more ardently than usual; possessed by a sudden need, as if to see it again for himself, he openly displayed his special belief; slowly, with all his strength, he lifted it from the eighty-five-year-old tabernacle and set it on the pulpit: and instantly they cried out against him. All Europe cried out: this was an evil belief.

With that, the pope disappeared. For days no decree went out from him; he remained on his knees in his oratory, searching the mystery of why it is that those who take action do damage to their souls. Finally he emerged, exhausted by his heavy meditations, and recanted. Over and over he recanted. Recanting became the senile passion of his soul. Sometimes he even had the cardinals wakened in the middle of the night so that he could speak with them of his remorse. And perhaps what ultimately prolonged his life so far beyond the normal span was no more than the hope of abasing himself before Napoleon Orsini, who despised him and refused to see him.

Jacques of Cahors had recanted. And one might think that God himself had wanted to underscore his error, since so soon afterward he summoned to himself the son of the Count of Ligny, who seemed to await his coming-of-age on earth only so that he could relish with the full virility of a mature soul heaven's sensual delights. Many were alive who remembered this radiant youth during his cardinalate, and how, on the threshold of adolescence, he had become a bishop and had died, scarcely eighteen, in an ecstasy of perfection. The dead walked: for life in its pure state now floated in the air around his tomb, and it had a long and vivifying effect on the corpses. But was there not a measure of injustice in that precocious sanctity? Was it not a wrong done to all, that the pure fabric of this soul had only briefly been dipped in life, just long enough to dye it in the rich scarlet vat of an age where radiance and blood were everything? Didn't people feel something like a recoil when this young prince leapt away from the earth to make his passionate ascension? And why did these radiant spirits not linger among the hardworking candlemakers? Was it not this inequity that had led John XXII to assert that there could be no beatific vision, not anywhere, not for anyone at all, even among the most radiant of the blessed, *before the Last Judgment had taken place?* And indeed, how much tenacious arrogance would it take to insist that while such dense confusion reigned on earth, in some other realm the faces of the destined few were basking in God's light, reclining on angels and already relishing their inexhaustible view of him.

~

I sit here in the cold night writing all this and somehow living it. Perhaps it feels alive to me because of that man I crashed into once when I was little. He was very tall; I think he must have turned heads on account of his height.

As unlikely as it may seem, I had somehow managed to get out of the house alone one evening. I was running, I turned a corner, and in the same moment I collided with him. What occurred next took only about five seconds to happen: I still don't understand how. I'll try to be brief, but the telling of it will take much longer. In running into him I had hurt myself; I was small, it seemed to me quite something that I didn't cry, and I was standing there waiting instinctively to be comforted. Since he did nothing of that sort, I assumed he was embarrassed; perhaps he couldn't think of some jesting remark that would make things right again. By then I was perfectly willing to help him out, but to do so I would have to look him in the face. I have said that he was tall. He had not, as would have been natural, bent down to me, and as a result he was standing at a height for which I was unprepared. In front of me there was still nothing but the smell and scratchy texture of the suit I had hit. Suddenly his face appeared. What was it like? I don't know, and I don't want to know. It was the face of an enemy. And beside that face, right up next to it, at the same height as his terrifying eyes, there loomed, like a second head, his fist. Before I had time to lower my own gaze I was already running; I dodged past him on the left and ran down an empty, fearful street, the street of an alien city, a city in which nothing is forgiven.

In those seconds I was experiencing something I now understand: the heavy, massive enmity of that long-ago era. That era in which the kiss that reconciled two men was the signal to the murderers lurking close by. The two drank from the same cup, they mounted the same horse before all eyes, and it was rumored that they slept in the same bed: and all this intimate contact made their repugnance for each other grow so desperate that whenever one saw the pulsing veins of the other, a nauseating disgust rose up in him, as at the sight of a toad. That era in which one brother attacked the other brother and kept him prisoner because he had inherited the larger share. True, the king did intercede on the ill-used brother's behalf, seeing to it that his freedom and property were restored to him; and the elder brother, caught up in fates that played out in other, faraway places, left him in peace and in letters regretted the wrong he had done. But for all that, the brother who was freed never regained his equanimity. The century shows him in pilgrim's habit, wandering from church to church, making pledges that seemed more and more insane. Hung about with amulets, he whispered his fears to the monks of Saint-Denis, and for a long time afterward their accounts recorded the hundred-pound wax candle he thought it would be good to dedicate to Saint Louis. He never recovered a life of his own; to the very end he felt his brother's wrath and envy revolving in a twisted constellation over his heart. And that Count de Foix, Gaston Phoebus, admired by all—had he not openly killed his cousin Ernault, the English king's captain, at Lourdes? And what was that obvious murder compared to the horrible "accident" that happened when, having forgotten to put down a razor-sharp penknife he held in his famously beautiful hand, he reached out in a spasm of reproach toward the naked throat of the son who lay before him? The room was dark; a light had to be brought to detect the blood that had come from so long a line and was now leaving a noble family forever, as it issued secretly from the tiny wound on that exhausted boy.

Who could be strong and not think of murder? Who in that era didn't fear that the worst was unavoidable? Here and there one whose glance had unwittingly met the lustful gaze of his assassin would later that day feel a strange foreboding. He would withdraw, lock the door behind him, write his will, and conclude by ordering the lit-ter of woven willow, the Celestine cowl, and the strewing of ashes. Strange minstrels appeared at his castle, and he gave them princely rewards for their song, which eerily spoke to his vague premonitions. When the dogs looked up at him there was doubt in their eyes, and they attended him with less confidence. From the motto that had served him all his life, a new, insidious meaning uncannily emerged. Many long-standing customs suddenly seemed obsolete, and it was as if no substitute would ever come to replace them. If projects arose, he threw himself into them without any real belief; certain memories, by contrast, took on an unexpected finality. In the evenings, by the fire, he felt he might give himself up to them. But the night outside, which was no longer familiar to him, suddenly became very loud as he listened. His ear, which had become finely tuned by nights both safe and treacherous, could sort out the separate elements of a silence. And yet this time it was different. Not the night between yesterday and tomorrow, but instead: a night. Night. Beau Sire Dieu, and then the Resurrection. Even a hymn in praise of a beloved could scarcely penetrate such hours: all his women were masked in albas and sirventes, unrecognizable under long, overwrought forms of address. At most, barely there in the gloom, like the full feminine upward glance of a bastard son.

And then, before a late supper, over the silver washbasin, those thoughts about hands. Your own hands. Was there any rationale for their actions? Any logic, any principle that governed their reaching and refraining? No. All men strove for both the thing and its opposite. All gestures canceled themselves out: there was no such thing as action.

There was no action except among the missionary brothers. The king, having seen how they comported themselves, drew up their charter himself. He addressed them as his dear brothers; no one had ever affected him so deeply. They were given express permission to mingle with the laity as the characters they played; for the king wished nothing more than that they might infect the many and draw them into this powerful and ordered action. As for himself, he longed to learn from them. Did he not wear, just as they did, the tokens and costume intended to convey a meaning? When he watched them, he believed it must be possible to learn these things: how to enter and how to leave, how to speak out and how to turn away in a manner that left no doubt. Enormous hopes flooded his heart. Every day he would go to that restlessly lighted, strangely nondescript hall of the Hospital of the Trinity and sit in the best seat and leap up excitedly and calm himself down again like a schoolboy. Others wept; but he was filled with shining inner tears and only pressed his cold hands together in order to endure it. Occasionally at key moments, when an actor who had finished speaking suddenly exited his wide gaze, the king looked up and was startled: how long had *he* been standing there: Monseigneur Saint Michael, advanced to the edge of the scaffolding, in his silver armor that gave back bright reflections . . .

At such moments he sat up straight. He looked around him as if on the verge of an understanding. He was so close to *seeing* it: that other action, the counterpart of this one onstage, that great, fearful, profane passion in which he himself played a part. But then it was gone. Everyone was moving pointlessly. Open torches were coming toward him, and formless shadows cast themselves into the vaultings above. People he did not know were pulling at him. He wanted to perform his role: but nothing came from his mouth, and his motions failed to create gestures. They crowded around him so strangely that he began to think he should be carrying the cross. And he wanted to wait for them to bring it. But they were stronger than he was, and slowly they herded him out.

Outwardly, much has changed. I do not know how. But within, and before you, Lord, within ourselves and before you who are our spectator: are we not without a plot? We discover quickly that we don't know our part; we look for a mirror; we would like to remove our makeup and all that is false and be real. But somewhere a piece of disguise we forgot about still sticks to us. Some trace of exaggeration remains in our eyebrows; we don't see that the corners of our mouths are twisted. And thus we go about, laughingstocks and shambling halves: with neither real existence nor a part to play.

~

It was in the amphitheater at Orange. Without really looking up, only vaguely conscious of those huge cracked stones of its façade, I entered by the attendant's small glass door. I found myself among prone columns and small mallow shrubs; but they only briefly hid from me the open shell of the tiered auditorium, which lay there, divided by the afternoon shadow, like an enormous concave sundial. I walked quickly toward it. As I climbed up among the rows of seats, I felt how small I was becoming in these surroundings. Above, somewhat higher, scattered tourists were gazing about in idle curiosity; their clothes stood out unpleasantly, but their presence was negligible amid these dimensions. For a while they stared at me, marveling at my smallness. That caused me to turn around.

Ah, I was completely unprepared. A play was taking place. An immense, indeed a more-than-human drama was in progress, the drama of that awesome backdrop, whose threefold vertical structure was now visible, a cliff of sheer magnitude, almost annihilating, and yet somehow measured in its immeasurability.

I sat down, overcome by a kind of joyful shock. What towered before me now, the shadows collecting at the center like its mouth, the cornice at the top like its curled locks—was the antique mask that covers everything, and behind which the scattered world coalesces into a face. Here, in this vast, inward-curving circle of seats, an existence reigned where all was expectancy, emptiness, absorption. The poles of action met there: the gods and fate. And when you looked up high, you saw, coming lightly over the wall's rim: the eternal entrance of the sky.

That hour, I realize now, shut me out of our theaters forever. Why should I frequent them? What should I do before a stage set where this wall (the icon screen of Russian churches) had been done away with, since we no longer have the strength to press the gas-like action through its hardness till it comes forth in full, heavy drops of oil? Now plays fall in pieces through the crude sieve of our stages and form little heaps and are swept away when we've had our fill. It's the same underdone reality that litters our streets and houses, except more accumulates there than can be crammed into a single evening.

*(Let's face it: we don't have a theater, any more than we have a God: for both require community. Instead we have our own singular brainstorms and apprehensions, and we let the others see only as much of them as suits our purposes. We continually dilute our understanding so there'll be enough to go around, instead of crying out for the wall of a mutual need, behind which the incomprehensible would have time to gather force and prepare for action.)

⌒

[On Eleonora Duse] If we did have a theater, would *you* define it, tragic woman, standing there time and again so slight, so exposed, so

---

* *Written in the margin of the manuscript.* [Rilke's note]

completely without the pretext of a role between you and those who sate their hasty curiosity with the spectacle of your grief? You who draw from us such inexpressible emotions: you created an emblem of your own contradiction when, that time in Verona, still almost a child playing at theater, you held a spray of roses up before you like a glorious full-face mask that only heightened your concealment.

It's true that your parents were actors, and when they performed they wanted to be seen; but you were of a different breed. This calling was to be for you what nunhood was for Mariana Alcoforado, even though she didn't know it: a disguise, tough and durable enough to let you be relentlessly despairing behind it, with the same unreserved passion with which the invisibly blessed ones are blessed. In all the cities you visited they would describe that gesture of yours; but they didn't understand how you, growing more reclusive every day, were holding up a work of poetry before you, constantly, to see if it offered you concealment. You held your hair, your hands, anything opaque, before the translucent places. You clouded over with your breath those that were transparent; you made yourself small; you hid, the way children hide, and then gave that brief, happy cry—and only an angel should have had leave to look for you. But when you glanced up warily you saw that they'd been watching you the whole time, all those beings in that ugly, hollow space that was filled with eyes: you, you, you, and nothing else but you.

And you wanted to crook your arm toward them and reach out with the sign on your fingertips that wards off the evil eye. You wanted to snatch back your face, which they were feeding on. You wanted to be yourself. Your fellow actors were afraid of you; they crept along the backdrops as if they'd been caged with a lioness, and tried to speak their lines without rousing you. But you dragged them forward and set them there and interacted with them as if they were real people. The flimsy doors, the false curtains, the props and settings that had no reverse side, all brought out in you a spirit of opposition. You felt how your heart rose ceaselessly toward an immense reality, and almost in panic you tried once again to pull their gazes off you, as if they were long strings of gossamer that were holding you back—. But already, in their fear of the very worst, they were breaking into applause: as if to avert, at the last moment, a silence that would force them to change their lives.

～

Women who are loved live poorly and in danger. Ah, if only they might transcend themselves and become women who love. Around women who love there is a force field of security. No one distrusts them any longer, and they cannot betray themselves. In them the mystery has grown inviolate: they cry it out like nightingales, and there is no division in it. Their lament is for one person; but all nature joins in: it becomes the lament for an eternal being. They hurl themselves after the lost loved one, but with their first steps they are racing past him, and only God is out ahead. Their legend is that of Byblis, who pursued Caunus as far as Lycia. Her heart spurred her on, following him through many lands, until at last she reached the end of her strength; but so powerful was the emotion at her core that, as she sank to earth, she reappeared beyond her death as a spring, quickening, as a swiftly quickening spring.

And didn't the Portuguese nun also deep within become a spring? And you too, Héloïse? And all you loving women whose laments have reached us: Gaspara Stampa, the Countess of Die, and Clara of Anduze; Louise Labé, Marceline Desbordes, Élisa Mercoeur? But you, poor fleeing Aïssé, you began to falter and at last gave in. Weary Julie de Lespinasse. Sad story of the happy park: Marie-Anne de Clermont.

I still remember vividly how one day long ago at home, I found a jewel casket; it was two hand's breadths wide, fan-shaped with a border of flowers impressed in the dark green morocco. I opened it: it was empty. I can put it this way now, after so long a time. But when I opened it back then, I saw only the substance of that emptiness: velvet, a little mound of light-colored velvet that was no longer fresh; and at its center that depression which, holding nothing anymore except a faint trace of melancholy, vanished into it. For that short moment it was bearable. But for those loved ones who are left behind, perhaps that is how it always is.

Women: Leaf back through your diaries. Wasn't there always a time in earliest spring when the year's flowering struck you like a reproach? You felt an urge to flower also, but when you walked out into the open there was a trembling in the air, and your steps became uncertain, as on a ship. The garden was beginning; but you (that was it, that was the problem) you brought winter with you, along with the previous year; for you it was at best a continuation. You waited for your soul to join in, but suddenly you felt the weight of your limbs, and a presentiment of becoming ill forced its way into your open anticipation. You blamed it on your thin dresses, you pulled your shawls more tightly around your shoulders, you ran all the way to the end of the avenue:

and then you stood, hearts pounding, in the wide turnaround, straining to be one with this new life. But a bird sang out, and it was alone,
and it excluded you. Ah, would you have had to have died?

Perhaps. Perhaps what is new is that we survive it: the year, and
love. Flowers and fruit are ripe when they fall; animals experience
themselves and find each other and are content with that. But we, we
who have brought God into the equation, we can never be done. We
postpone our nature's promptings, we need more time. What is a year
to us? What are all the years? Even before we have embarked upon
God, we are already praying to him: Let us survive this night. And
then the illnesses. And then love.

That Clémence de Bourges had to die in the dawn of her life. She
who was without equal; she who was herself more beautiful than the
sound of all those instruments she could play with an accord no one
else possessed, unforgettable even in the softest tone of her voice. Her
girlhood was a time of such great resolve that a woman in the full
flood of her love could dedicate to this rising heart a book of sonnets in which every line sang of unrequitedness. Louise Labé was
not afraid of frightening this child with the long agonies of love. She
revealed to her the nightly ascent of longing; she promised her pain
like a greater world; and she sensed obscurely that she herself, in spite
of all the griefs she'd experienced, was far short of what darkly awaited
this bright girl and made her beautiful.

Girls in my homeland: May the loveliest of you, on some summer
afternoon in the darkened library, find that little book that Jean de
Tournes printed in 1556. May she take that cool, lustrous volume out

with her into the buzzing orchard, or across to the field of phlox, in whose oversweet fragrance a distillation of pure sweetness waits. May she find it when she is young. In those days when her eyes are just beginning to reflect, while her mouth, still childish, can bite off pieces of apple that are much too big and be happy.

And then, girls, when the time of more passionate friendship arrives, may it be your secret to call one another Diké and Anakto-ria, Gyrinno and Atthis. May someone, a neighbor perhaps, an older man who traveled in his youth and has long been thought odd, con-fide these names to you. May he sometimes invite you into his home to taste his famous peaches, or to view, up in the white hallway, his equestrian prints by Ridinger—which are so widely talked about that you simply must see them.

Perhaps you'll persuade him to reminisce. Perhaps (who knows?) there will be one among you who can induce him to bring out his old travel journals. That same girl who one day will draw from him that certain fragments of Sappho have come down to us, and who won't rest till she's learned what is almost a secret: that this reclusive man loved once to spend many of his spare hours translating those fragments of verse. He must confess that he hasn't thought about his translations for a long time now, and that what he did achieve, he assures her, is not worth mentioning. Yet when they insist, he is happy to recite a stanza to these ingenuous friends. He even discovers the Greek original in his memory, and he recites that also, since in his opinion the translation captures nothing, and he wants these young people to hear an authentic fragment of that massive, jewelry-like lan-guage that was forged in such strong flames.

All of this warms him again to his work. He is granted evenings that are beautiful, almost youthful—autumn evenings, for instance, that augur long stretches of silent night. Then the lamp burns late in his study. He isn't always bent over his pages; often he leans back, closes his eyes over a line he has been rereading, and its meaning courses through his blood. Never has he been so confident of antiquity. He almost smiles at the generations that have mourned it like a lost play in which they wish they could have acted. Now in a flash he grasps the dynamic significance of that early unified world, which was something like a new, simultaneous infolding of all human inquiry and endeavor. It doesn't trouble him that their civilization, with its almost total commitment to what could be made manifest, appeared to many who looked back from later ages to form a perfect whole— and as such, to be wholly past. It is true that there the celestial half of life fitted perfectly on the semicircular bowl of earthly existence, the way two full hemispheres come together to form a golden ball. Yet scarcely had this been achieved when those spirits confined in it felt that such absolute realization was no more than a conceit; the massive star grew weightless and rose into space, and in its faraway golden curvature it reflected the melancholy of everything that still could not be *seen*.

As he thinks through these things, this man alone in his night, thinking and understanding, he notices a bowl of fruit on the window seat. He takes an apple from it, casually, and places it before him on the table. How my life centers on this fruit, he thinks. Around everything that is complete, the unachieved collects and spreads.

And then, out beyond the unachieved, there rises before him, almost too swiftly, that slight figure straining toward the infinite, the one everyone meant back then (according to Galen) when they spoke of "the poetess." For just as, after the labors of Hercules, the slow destruction and remaking of the world rose up, demanding its enactment: so too, from the stores of being, all the ecstasies and despairs that would play out through the ages thronged toward the deeds of her heart, so that they might be lived *now.*

Suddenly he understands that resolute heart, which was prepared to make good on the whole of love—to the very end. It doesn't surprise him that they had misconstrued it—that in this woman in love, who was so entirely of the future, they saw only excess, not the new measure for love and heart-grief. That they read her life's legend in the only way those times could make sense of it; that finally they blamed her for the death of those women whom the god incites, each alone, to pour themselves forth into a love that can never be requited. Perhaps even among the women whom she brought to love, there were some who failed to understand: that at the height of her action she lamented not a man who had left her embraces empty, but the one who was no longer possible, that *other* who was her love's *same.*

Here he stands up from his thoughts and walks to his window. Even the high ceiling of his room feels too close to him; he would like to look up and see stars. He does not deceive himself: he knows that this emotion fills him because among the young girls of the neighborhood there is one especially about whom he cares. He has wishes (not for himself, no, but for her); because of her he has understood, in a passing hour of the night, the demands of love. He promises himself to say nothing to her about it. It seems to him that the utmost he can do is to remain alone and wakeful and for her sake reflect how right the poetess was when she grasped that the pairing of two people can mean only an increase in solitude; when she lifted the temporal veil of sex and saw its infinite purpose; when in the darkness of embracing she delved not for satiety but for longing; when she abhorred the notion that of two people one must be the lover and the other a loved

one—taking frail beloved women to her bed and kindling them into
women in love, who then left her. Through such sublime farewells her
heart became Nature itself. Beyond fate, she sang the epithalamia of
each seasoned lover; praised marriage to them; magnified the coming
bridegroom, so that they might prepare themselves for him as they
would for a god, and perhaps even surpass him in glory.

~

Once, Abelone, during these last years, I felt your presence again and
saw into you—unexpectedly, after I had long stopped thinking of you.

It was in Venice, in autumn, at one of those salons where passing foreigners gather around the lady of the house, who is herself a
foreigner. These people stand with their cups of tea and are flattered
whenever some in-the-know neighbor points them discreetly toward
the door and whispers a Venetian-sounding name in their ear. They
expect the most stunning entrance; nothing can surprise them, for
as frugal as they may usually be with their experience, in this city
they eagerly await the most extravagant possibilities. In their normal
lives they constantly confuse the extraordinary with the forbidden,
so that the expectation of the marvelous that they now allow themselves shows on their faces as an avid licentiousness. The true emotion
that back home may sometimes secretly course through them—at
a concert perhaps, or alone with a novel—in these flattering realms
they counterfeit shamelessly for all to see, as if it were a fundamental
condition. Just as, totally incautious, ignorant of any danger, they let
themselves be carried away by the almost deadly confessions of music,
as if by physical indiscretions: so, without even beginning to sense
the deep truth of Venice, they give themselves up to the pleasurable

swoon of the gondolas. Couples no longer newly married, who during the whole trip had only snappish replies for each other, sink into a kind of heedless compatibility: the husband yields to the agreeable loosening of his morals, while she feels young and nods encouragingly to the indolent locals, smiling as if she had teeth of sugar that were always dissolving. And if you eavesdrop, it turns out that they are departing tomorrow or the day after tomorrow or at the end of the week.

So I stood there among them pleased not to be leaving. Soon it would be cold. The soft, opiate Venice of their preconceptions and demands would vanish with these somnolent foreigners, and one morning the other Venice would be there, the true one, awake, lucid, glassy almost to the point of shattering, above all not dreamlike: a Venice willed into being on sunken forests in the midst of nothingness, a testament to sheer force and in the end so incontrovertibly *there*. The hardened body, honed to its bare essentials, through which the sleepless Arsenal pumped the blood for its labor; and this body's spirit, penetrating and constantly expanding, so much stronger than the scent of aromatic lands. The resourceful state, bartering the salt and glass of its poverty for the treasures of nations. The world's exquisite counterweight, full of latent energies that spread into the tiniest, most intricate details of its ornamentation like a complex network of nerves—: *this* Venice.

The consciousness of knowing this city filled me, among all these self-deluding people, with such a spirit of opposition that I looked up, hoping somehow to share my thoughts. Was it possible that in these rooms there wasn't some one person who was unconsciously waiting to be enlightened about the nature of these surroundings? Some young person who would grasp immediately that what was being offered by this city was not a saccharine enjoyment but a display of sheer willpower, more strict and exacting than could be experienced anywhere else? I wandered about impatiently; this truth of mine had made me fractious. Having seized me here among so many people, it demanded to be spoken, defended, *proved*. The grotesque notion arose in me that in the very next moment I would start slapping my hands together out of hatred for all their chattered misunderstanding.

It was in this ridiculous mood that I saw her. She was standing alone before a window filled with light and was watching me—not exactly with her eyes, which were serious and pensive, but more pointedly with her mouth, which was ironically mimicking the obvious disapproval on my face. I felt at once the tense annoyance in my features and put on a calm face, in response to which her mouth resumed its natural haughtiness. After a moment of reflection, we smiled toward each other simultaneously.

She brought to mind, if you will, a certain portrait of the young Benedicte von Qualen who played a part in Baggesen's life. You couldn't look into the dark stillness of her eyes without intuiting the clear darkness of her voice. The braiding of her hair and the neckline of her bright dress were moreover so reminiscent of Copenhagen that I was prepared to speak to her in Danish.

But I was still too far away when a flood of people pressed toward her from the other side; our guest-happy countess herself, in her warm, effusive distractedness, rushed upon the young woman with a band of accomplices, resolved to carry her off on the spot to sing. I was sure she would make her apologies by saying that no one present could possibly be interested in hearing someone sing in Danish. And so she did, as soon as she was able to get a word in. The crush around this bright figure grew more insistent; someone knew that she also sang in German. "And Italian," a laughing voice added wickedly. I could think of no excuse to wish for her, but I was sure she would resist them. Already an expression of dry vexation was beginning to replace the prolonged smiling on the wearied faces of the persuaders, and already the good countess, in order not to lose face, was taking a step back with an air of pity and forced politeness—and then suddenly, just when it was clear that the girl had won the field, she yielded. I could feel myself growing pale with disappointment; my eyes filled with reproach, but I turned away; there was nothing to be gained by letting her see that. But she worked herself free of the others and was suddenly standing next to me. Her dress shone on me; the flowery scent of her warmth enveloped me.

"I really am going to sing," she said in Danish, close to my cheek. "Not because they want me to, not for appearance's sake: but because now I *must* sing."

In her words I heard the same bitter frustration from which she had just freed me.

Slowly I followed the group with whom she moved away. But at a tall door I hung back, allowing the rest to maneuver and settle into place. I leaned against the reflecting black of the inside of the door and waited. Someone asked me what was happening, whether there was going to be a recital. I pretended not to know. But before I had completed my lie, she had already begun to sing.

I couldn't see her. Space gradually widened around one of those Italian songs that foreigners hold to be so very authentic precisely because they are so patently conventional. She who was singing did not believe it. She lifted it like something of great weight, and labored to imbue it with seriousness. You could tell when it was over by the applause in front. I was sad and ashamed. There was random movement, and I resolved that as soon as someone left I would follow them out.

But suddenly everything grew still. It was a stillness that a moment earlier no one would have thought possible; it stretched on, it grew taut, and now, inside it, that voice arose. (Abelone, I thought. Abelone.) This time it was strong, full, and yet not heavy; of a piece, without a break, without a seam. It was an obscure German song. She sang it with remarkable simplicity, as if it was inevitable. She sang:

> *You whom I don't tell that at night*
> *I lie weeping,*
> *whose existence calms my thoughts*
> *like a cradle.*
> *You, who do not tell me when you lie awake*
> *because of me:*
> *what if we meshed these wakeful hours*
> *and together bore them*
> *unrequitedly?*

(a brief pause, then hesitantly:)

> *Look at the lovers:*
> *when they first begin to confess their feelings*
> *how soon they lie.*

Again the silence. God knows who made it. Then the people stirred, bumped into one another, apologized, coughed. They were on the verge of devolving into a kind of universal obliterating hubbub when suddenly the voice burst forth, resolute, broad, and urgent.

You make me alone. I transpose you endlessly.
For a while it is you, then it's the leaves rustling again,
or it's a scent without remainder.
Ah, in my embrace I lost them all,
you, you only, are born again and again:
because I never took you in my arms, I hold you fast.

No one had expected it. They all stood bowed, as it were, before that voice. And in the end there was so great an assurance in her that it was as if she had known for years that she would be called on at that precise moment.

~

Sometimes I used to ask myself why Abelone didn't direct the calories of her magnificent emotion toward God. I know that she longed to divest her love of everything transitive, but could her truthful heart deceive itself into regarding God as only a direction love takes, not as an object love seeks? Didn't she know that no reciprocating love from him need be feared? Didn't she understand the restraint of this superior loved one, who calmly puts off desire so that we, slow as we are, have time to achieve our whole heart? Or did she want to avoid Christ? Was she afraid that he would intercept her halfway, and make her a loved one? Was that why she didn't like to think of Julie Reventlow?

I almost think so, especially when I consider how women in love as forthright as Mechthild, as passionate as Teresa of Ávila, as self-excoriating as Blessed Rose of Lima, could sink back into this alleviation of God, compliant and beloved. Alas, the Christ who was a help to the weak does these strong ones an injustice; where they were anticipating nothing more than the endless road, once again a living form steps out to meet them in that tense forecourt of heaven, spoiling them with refuge and troubling them with manhood. His heart's powerful lens once more causes their already parallel heart-rays to converge at a point, and they, whom the angels had hoped to preserve for God, blaze up in the drought of their desire.

*(To be loved is to be consumed in flames. To love is to shine forth with inexhaustible oil. To be loved is to perish; to love is to endure.)

Even so, it is possible that in later years Abelone tried to think with her heart, so that she might enter inconspicuously into a direct relationship with God. I could imagine that there might be letters from her that recall the keen introspection of Princess Amalie Gallitzin; but if those letters were addressed to someone she had been close to for years, how he must have suffered from that change in her. And as for herself: I suspect what she feared most was that ghostly transformation that we never become aware of because all the evidence for it seems to have so little to do with us that we simply let it pass by.

It would be difficult to persuade me that the story of the Prodigal Son is not the legend of a man who didn't want to be loved. When he was a child, everyone in the house loved him. He grew up not knowing that it could be any other way, and became accustomed to their tenderness—when he was a child.

But as a boy he wanted to cast off his customary ways. He couldn't

---

* *Written in the margin of the manuscript.* [Rilke's note]

have put it into words, but when he spent the whole day roaming the countryside and didn't even want the dogs with him, it was because they too loved him; because in their eyes there was watchfulness and sympathy, expectation and concern; because in their presence also he couldn't do anything without making them happy or disappointing them. But he was impelled in those days by the passionate indifference of his heart, which from time to time, when he was out in the early morning fields, would seize him with such purity that he broke into a run, so that he might escape himself and be no more than a weightless moment in which the morning becomes conscious.

The secret of the life he had yet to live lay spread out before him. Spontaneously he left the trail and went running deeper into the fields, arms outstretched, as if in that wide reach he could take several routes at once. And then he lay himself down behind some hedge or thicket and no one cared how he felt or what he did. He stripped a willow branch and made himself a flute, he threw a rock at some small animal, he leaned down and caused a beetle to reverse its course: none of this had anything to do with fate, and the sky passed over him as over nature. Finally afternoon came with all its whims: you could be a pirate on the island of Tortuga, without being obliged to live that life; you could besiege Campeche, capture Veracruz; it was possible to be an entire army or a general on horseback or a ship at sea: whatever entered your head. If it occurred to you to kneel, then you quickly became Deodatus of Gozon and had slain the dragon and, still hot from battle, were being made to understand that without obedience such heroism was mere vanity. For you left out nothing that was part of the role you played. But no matter how many scenes arose, there were always intervals when you could simply be a bird—you didn't even have to know what kind. Eventually, though, it was time to go home.

My God, how much there was to cast off and forget; and you really did have to *forget*; otherwise you'd betray yourself when they persisted. No matter how long you lingered and nosed around, in the end the gable always rose on the near horizon. The topmost window fixed its eye on you; there was likely someone standing there. The dogs, in whom anticipation had been rising all day, tore through the hedges and herded you together into the person they recognized. And the house did the rest. You had only to walk into its full smell and almost everything was decided. Little details might still be altered, but on the whole you were already the person they took you for; the person for whom they had long since made up a life out of your small past and their own wishes; the creature whom they all owned in common, who stood day and night under the influence of their love, between their hope and their doubts, before their approval or their blame.

It does no good for such a person to climb the steps with utmost caution. They will all be in the living room, and the door only has to creak for them to look his way. He remains in the dark, he tries to wait for their questions. But then comes the worst. They take him by the hand, they pull him in and lead him over to the table, and all of them, however many there are, lean forward inquiringly toward the focus of the lamp. It's fine for them, they're still in the shadows, while on him alone falls, along with the light, all the infamy of having a face.

Will he stay and lie his way through this approximate life that they've prepared for him, and come to resemble them with the whole of his face? Will he divide himself between the delicate truthfulness of his will and the crude deceit that sickens him even as he grows adept at it? Will he give up becoming what will surely hurt those of his family whose weak heart is all they have left?

No, he will go away. For example, while they are busy arranging on his birthday table all those ill-chosen gifts that once again are supposed to make up for everything. Go away forever. Not until much later will he realize how fiercely determined he was back then never to love, that he might never put anyone in the terrible position of being loved. Years later he will think back and reflect that this resolution, like all his others, had proved impossible to keep. For in his loneliness he had loved again and again, each time lavishing his whole being while fearing unspeakably for the other's freedom. He had learned to let the rays of his emotion shine quietly through the beloved, rather than consume her all at once in them. And with what delight he'd watched, through her ever more transparent form, vast territories slowly open to his boundless will to possess.

How he could weep for whole nights, longing to be suffused by such rays himself. But a woman who yields is still far from a woman who loves. Oh those desolate nights, when the gifts that had flooded forth from him would be returned to him in discrete pieces heavy with transience. How often then he was reminded of the troubadours, who feared nothing more than being answered. All the money he had acquired and increased he gave away, so as not to experience that as well. He offended them with his gross offers of payment, more and more afraid that they might attempt to reciprocate his love. For he had lost all hope of experiencing the woman whose love would crash through to him.

Even at that time when poverty alarmed him daily with new hardships, when his head was misery's favorite plaything and quite worn out, when all over his body sores were opening like emergency eyes against the blackness of affliction, when he was revolted by the filth into which he had been thrown because that was where he belonged: even then, when he thought about it, his greatest terror was that someone would respond to him. What were all the darknesses he'd gone through, compared to the intense sadness of those embraces in which everything was lost? Didn't he wake up feeling that he had no future? Didn't he go about pointlessly, with no right even to the slightest of dangers? Didn't he have to promise a hundred times not to die? Perhaps it was the persistence of that one most painful memory—which wanted to make sure that each time it returned there would be a place reserved for it—that caused his life in the dunghills to go on. Finally, he found his way out. And it was not until then, not until his years as a shepherd, that his tumultuous past found peace.

Who can describe what happened to him then? What poet is skillful enough to reconcile the length of those days with the shortness of life? What art is broad enough to call forth both his slender, cloaked form and the vast space of those enveloping nights?

That was the period that began with him feeling nameless and generic, like a convalescent slowly recovering. He did not love, except insofar as he loved existing. He took for granted the humble attachment of his sheep; like light falling through clouds, it scattered all around him and shimmered softly over the meadows. Following the innocent trail of their hunger, he strode silently over the pastures of the world. Strangers saw him on the Acropolis; and perhaps he was for many years one of the shepherds at Les Baux, and saw petrified time outlast that noble family which, for all its luck with sevens and threes, was helpless against the sixteen rays of its own star. Or should I imagine him at Orange, leaning against the rustic triumphal arch? Or picture him in the soul-inhabited shade of Alyscamps, among those sarcophagi that lie open like the graves of the resurrected, his eyes following the path of a dragonfly?

No matter. I see more than him. I see the whole of his existence, which was then embarking on that long, silent, goalless labor of loving God. For he who had wished to hold himself back forever, was overcome once again by his heart's irrepressible need to call out. And this time he hoped to be heard. His deep being, which during his long solitude had grown composed and far-seeing, assured him that the One he was now turning to was indeed capable of loving, with a penetrating, radiant love. But while he longed to be loved at last with such mastery, his emotion, so conversant with distances, felt the extreme remoteness of God. There were nights when he imagined hurling himself into space toward God; hours filled with discovery, when he felt strong enough to dive for the earth and lift it up on the storm tide of his heart. He was like someone who hears a magnificent language and feverishly resolves to write in it. Still ahead was the dismay of learning how difficult this language was; at first he refused to believe that a long life could be spent constructing those first short practice-sentences that mean nothing at all. He threw himself into this schooling like a runner into a race; but the density of what had to be mastered slowed his pace. It was impossible to imagine anything more humbling than this apprenticeship. He had found the philosopher's stone, and now he was being compelled to transmute ceaselessly the quick gold of his inspiration into the dull lead of patience. He who had adapted himself to infinite space now burrowed like a worm through long winding passages without exit or direction. Now, as he learned to love so laboriously and with such pain, he was forced to understand how all the previous love he thought he had achieved was peremptory and trivial; how nothing could have come of it, since he had not begun to work upon it and translate it into something real.

During those years great changes took place in him. He almost forgot God in the hard work of approaching him, and all that he hoped in time perhaps to attain from him was "*sa patience de supporter une âme.*" The accidents of fate that human beings set such store by had long since fallen away from him, but now even the essentials of pleasure and pain lost their sharpness and became gentle and nourishing to him. The sturdy evergreen plant of a fertile joy sprang from his roots. He was wholly engrossed in mastering every aspect of his inner life; he wanted to leave nothing out, for he was certain that in all of it his love was still alive and thriving. Indeed, his inner composure was so great that he decided to take up again the most important of those things that earlier he'd been unable to achieve, the ones that he'd been forced to put on hold. He thought in particular of his childhood; the more calmly he reflected on it, the more unfinished it seemed to him. All its memories had the sense of vague presentiments, and the way they'd been relegated to the past almost pushed them into the future. To take all this upon himself once more, and to do so truly, was the reason this son who had become a stranger returned home. We don't know whether he stayed; we know only that he came back.

Those who have told the story try at this point to picture for us the house as it then was; for only a little time has passed there, a short run of countable time—everyone in the house can say exactly how much. The dogs have grown old, but they are still alive. Some say that one of them started barking joyously. All the work of the day comes to a halt. Faces appear at the windows, faces that have aged or matured and bear a touching resemblance to faces he remembers. And in one ancient face, suddenly pale, recognition breaks through. Recognition? Is it only recognition?—Forgiveness. Forgiveness for what?—Love. My God: love.

It had no longer occurred to him, preoccupied as he was, that it might still exist. It is understandable that from all that happened then, only this has been handed down: his gesture, the incredible gesture that no one had ever seen before, the gesture of entreaty with which he threw himself at their feet, imploring them not to love. Confused and shaken, they raised him up. They interpreted his vehemence in their own way, forgiving him. He must have felt an incredible relief when he saw that they all misunderstood him, in spite of the desperate clarity of his posture. Apparently he could stay. For each day he realized more clearly that the love of which they were so vain and to which they tacitly encouraged one another, had nothing to do with him. He almost had to smile at the efforts they made, and it became obvious how little access they had to his thoughts and feelings.

What could they know of him? He was fearfully difficult to love now, and he felt that only One was capable of it. But He was not yet willing.

End of the Notebooks

NOTES

page

1   **11th September, rue Toullier:** RMR's first address in Paris (1902–1903) was 11 rue Toullier. Note how the italics, with no more than a slight numeric shift (or a one-word insertion), cross from space into time, from the autobiographical past of RMR to the fictive present of MLB.

1   **Maison d'accouchement:** Maternity hospital.

1   **Asyle de nuit:** Night shelter.

2   ***Ah tais-toi, je ne veux plus:*** "Oh be quiet, I've had enough!" There is a parallel utterance (though the tone may be opposite) later in the narrative, when MLB's mother recalls the dying Ingeborg's long-ago words, "*Ich mag nicht mehr*," still trying to understand them. (She, like the reader, has no access to their interior dimension.)

4   **Faces are faces:** An intricate, surreal motif of faces and/as masks runs through the whole of *Malte*: cf., for instance, MLB's experience of the "inside" of the sitting woman's face; the face of the man MLB sits next to in the hospital waiting room; the mother's salvific visage in the child's dark room; the beautiful death mask of the drowned woman; MLB's experience with the mask and the mirror in the costume room at Ulsgaard; the mask that the false czar dies in; the masking gestures of Eleonora Duse; the antique mask that materializes for MLB at the amphitheater at Orange; and the face torn from the frozen body of Charles the Bold.

4   **Hôtel-Dieu:** Large hospital (the oldest in Paris) on the Île de la Cité near the cathedral of Notre-Dame.

5   ***brocanteuse:*** Junk dealer.

5   **the Cité:** One of two islands in the Seine near the center of Paris.

8   **Ulsgaard:** The family estate of the Brigges.

23 **"our little Anna Sophie":** Anna Sophie Reventlow (1693–1743) eloped bigamously with King Frederick IV (1671–1730) in 1712. They

remarried shortly after the king's legitimate wife died in 1721. Members of the Danish royal family were interred in the medieval cathedral of Roskilde.

34   *"Chou-fleur, Chou-fleur"*: Cauliflower.

36   **crémerie:** Small café, often a little stopover dairy café.

38   *têtes-de-moineau*: Small chunks of coal burned in stoves (literally, "sparrows' heads").

38   **Duval:** A famous chain of inexpensive restaurants slightly more upscale than the crémeries.

40   **not one word will be left upon another:** Mark 13:2 (Christ's prophecy of the sack of Jerusalem): "There shall not be left one stone upon another, that shall not be thrown down."

40   *Mécontent de tous . . . méprise*: From Baudelaire's prose poem "A une heure du matin": "Disgusted with everyone and disgusted with myself, I should like to redeem myself and take some pride in myself in the silence and solitude of the night. Souls of those I have loved, souls of those I have sung, strengthen me, sustain me, keep far from me the lies and the corrupting vapors of the world; and You, my dear God, grant me the grace to produce a few beautiful poems that will prove to me that I am not the lowest of men, that I am not worse than those I despise."

41   **"They were the children of fools":** Job 30:8–9, 12–13, 16–18, 27, 31.

41   **Salpêtrière:** The huge Hospice de la Salpêtrière, since 1656 a hospital complex in Paris (forty-five blocks of buildings) where beggars and prostitutes were cared for, and later also aged women and the insane. By the late nineteenth century it was especially known for its treatment of psychological disorders. Freud studied there with Charcot in the 1880s.

43   *chapeau à huit reflets*: A shiny, elegant top hat.

46   *"Riez! . . ."*: "Laugh! Go on, do it, laugh, laugh!"

46   *"Dites-nous le mot: avant . . ."*: "Say the word: before . . . Can't hear you. Once again . . ."

55   **the Panthéon:** A mausoleum, originally a church, where famous men from French history are buried. There is a mural there by Puvis de Chavanne depicting Saint Geneviève, the patron saint of Paris, watching over the sleeping city; there are also paintings by Chavanne near the crypt that RMR found especially beautiful.

55   **"Une Charogne":** "A Carcass." In Baudelaire's poem (from *Les Fleurs*

du mal) the male speaker recalls to his lover the time they encountered, while out on a romantic walk, a dead animal rotting on the path they had taken. The speaker describes to her the putrefaction they witnessed in unflinching, almost impudent detail, and then embraces that process in the final stanza as the permanence (however ironic) of his art. It may be this last gesture that MLB objects to as wrong or false.

56   **"Saint Julien l'Hospitalier"**: One of Flaubert's *Three Tales* from 1877. Julian, after many brilliant successes, in the last part of his life attempts a series of expiations (he had unwittingly killed his parents in his wife's bed) that commit him to extreme forms of poverty and servitude. They culminate in his warming a leper, skin to skin, in his own bed.

58   *mouleur*: Molder (in this case, a maker of plaster casts).

58   **the young drowned woman**: The reference is to the death mask of an unknown woman who in the 1880s drowned herself in the Seine. The mask achieved celebrity status (for its beauty and its haunting, elusive expression), and she became known as "l'Inconnue de la Seine."

59   **the seed of Onan**: See Genesis 38:9: "And Onan knew that the seed should not be his; and it came to pass when he went in unto his brother's wife, that he spilled it on the ground, lest that he should give seed to his brother."

61   **those ships' figureheads . . .**: Rilke explained to his Polish translator that he had seen painted figureheads from the prows of old ships set up like this in the gardens of Danish sea captains.

63   **What did it matter. . . . What did it matter**: Plot elements that figure in the surface conflicts of different plays by Ibsen.

64   **There was a rabbit . . .**: An escalation of realistic details from successive Ibsen plays.

73   **To undergo once more . . . hearing myself narrate it**: MLB, of course, as the adult narrator of the story we are reading, is doing exactly this.

99   **There are tapestries here**: The six famous sixteenth-century *Dame à la licorne* tapestries, which RMR would have seen at the Musée de Cluny in Paris.

101   ***"A mon seul désir"***: "To my sole desire."

102   **château Boussac**: Castle owned by Pierre d'Aubusson (1423–1503), Grand Master of the Order of St. John (i.e., the Knights of Malta). The tapestries bear the coat of arms of the Le Viste family, and may have been commissioned as an engagement gift.

104   **Gaspara Stampa**: An Italian noblewoman, Gaspara Stampa (1523–

1554) fell in love with Count Collatino di Collato at the age of twenty-six and was deserted by him three years later. She responded by recording the story of their love and her experience of solitude and loss in a series of some two hundred sonnets. RMR invokes her again in the first *Duino Elegy*.

104   **the Portuguese nun:** Mariana Alcoforado (1640–1723). At twelve she entered a nunnery, where at twenty-five she met Albert de Chamilly, who became her lover and then eventually left her. Her five passionate letters to him appeared anonymously in book form in 1669, and became a publishing sensation. The authenticity of the letters was challenged almost immediately, and both their truth and her authorship have been sources of controversy ever since. RMR wrote an article on them in 1908, and translated them in 1913.

106   **points d'Alençon . . . Valenciennes . . . Binche:** Types of French and Belgian needlepoint.

114   **Bredgade:** An upscale street in Copenhagen.

116   **Swedenborg:** Emanuel Swedenborg (1688–1772), a Swedish mystic and theosophist.

117   **"Saint-Germain":** The Comte de Saint-Germain (1710–1784), also known as the Marquis of Belmare (among several other variant titles). He was a famous adventurer, international diplomat, composer, and political intriguer of the eighteenth century. He was also "adept" in alchemy, and was said to be able to remove the flaws from diamonds, to transmute metals, and to have discovered an elixir of life—he himself claimed to be over a thousand years old. He died in the town of Eckernförde in Schleswig-Holstein.

118   *jardin d'acclimatation:* Parisian amusement park with zoo. The site of several of RMR's most famous *New Poems* (1907–1908), including "The Panther."

119   **the Bernstorff circle:** A group of political and intellectual figures close to the Danish crown and led by Count Johann Hartwig Ernst von Bernstorff (1712–1772) and his nephew Count Andreas Peter von Bernstorff (1735–1797).

120   **"Julie Reventlow":** Countess Frederike Juliane Reventlow (1763–1816) belonged to the Bernstorff circle and was the center of a large group of writers and intellectuals. She was intensely religious, but was only "poetically" a saint.

122   **"the perforation of the heart":** The practice of piercing the heart (at

the request of the deceased) just before interment, apparently to ensure against being buried alive. At the time, the procedure was not uncommon in much of Europe.

123 **the shattering of the helmet:** A custom performed at the burial of someone who was the last in the line of a noble family. MLB utters the words that conclude the ceremony, even though logically they would be uttered on the occasion of *his* death.

124 **Langelinie:** A promenade and pier in downtown Copenhagen ending in a small lighthouse.

126 **"*Døden . . . Døden*":** Death . . . Death.

129 **Félix Arvers:** 1806–1850; a French poet, the centenary of whose birth took place while Rilke was in Paris.

130 **Jean de Dieu:** Juan de Dios (1495–1550); a Portuguese saint who founded a hospital in Granada for the poor. In 1886 he was denominated patron saint of hospitals by Pope Leo XIII.

142 **those fantastic paintings:** The reference is to early Flemish paintings. *The Garden of Earthly Delights* by Hieronymus Bosch (c. 1450–1516) seems especially relevant.

145 **"Grisha Otrepyev":** Grigory Bogdanovich Otrepyev (c. 1582–1606); a fugitive monk who passed himself off as Dmitri Ivanovich, the youngest son of Ivan the Terrible. Dmitri had died in 1591 at the age of nine under suspicious circumstances. Otrepyev appeared in Poland in 1603, claiming that he was Dmitri and had survived not an illness but an attempted assassination. When Boris Godunov died in 1605, Otrepyev's claims were accepted, and he reigned as czar until he was exposed in an uprising in 1606. History refers to him now as "the False Dmitri," or "the Pseudo-Dmitri." Shortly after his death a second "False Dmitri" appeared, and after that a third, and after that a fourth.

146 **Maria Nagoi:** Seventh wife of Ivan the Terrible, and mother of Dmitri. After his death she became a nun. Her public pronouncements of Otrepyev first as "true" and later as "false" are cruxes of the story.

146 **Marina Mniszech:** A Polish noblewoman (1588–1614) who was married by proxy to the False Dmitri in November 1605. She was crowned on May 8, 1606, nine days before the uprising. She also married the second False Dmitri.

147 *streltsy:* Bodyguards of the czar.

147 **Ivan Grozny:** Ivan the Terrible (1530–1584).

147 **Shuisky:** Prince Vasily Ivanovich Shuisky (1552–1612). A former gen-

eral under Godunov, he had been sent by the latter to investigate Dmitri's death in 1591, and had reported it a suicide. He seemed initially to
have courted Otrepyev's favor, but ultimately conspired against him,
incited an uprising, and succeeded him as czar.

148   **the end of someone:** Charles the Bold (1433–1477); Duke of Burgundy from 1466. He had ambitions to turn Burgundy into a kingdom
that would rival France, and after a series of bloody, merciless conquests
seemed poised to do so. He conquered Lorraine in 1475, but the next
year suffered defeats at Granson and Morat and then, on October 6,
at Nancy, the capital of Lorraine. He responded to this last defeat by
besieging the city with a hastily reconstituted army; in a one-sided battle against the combined forces of Switzerland and Lorraine that took
place there deep in winter, he perished along with most of his soldiers.

149   **Uri:** A Swiss canton. During the Battle of Morat, in which the forces
of Charles were routed by the Swiss, he would have heard blasts from
the famed and dreaded battle horns of Uri sealing his defeat.

151   **Louis-Onze:** "Louis the Eleventh." The name is meant to mock
Charles's great enemy, the French king Louis XI. It may be RMR's
fictive invention.

151   **Olivier de la Marche:** Charles's secretary and, later, his chronicler.

152   **the Roman:** Gian-Battista Colonna, one of Charles's pages; he came
from Rome.

157   **"Bettina":** Bettina von Arnim, née Brentano (1785–1859), sister of
Clemens Brentano and wife (after 1811) of Ludwig Achim von Arnim,
both well-known German Romantic poets. She was a talented writer
and composer, as well as a close friend of Beethoven and an admired
acquaintance of some of the leading musicians of the time. When she
met Goethe in 1807 (she was twenty-two; he was in his late fifties),
she already adored him from his work and responded to him passionately. Goethe did not reciprocate her love, but he did enter into a correspondence with her, in which he tactfully attempted to counteract
her unbridled passion with something like "reality." In 1811 he broke
off all contact with Bettina, partly at the urging of his wife, whom he
had married earlier that same year. In 1835, three years after Goethe's
death, Bettina published their correspondence as *Goethe's Correspondence with a Child.*

160   **with both hands:** cf. RMR's uncollected poem "The Words of the
Lord to John on Patmos" (1915): "And you shall write without looking

down: / for that too is why you're here: for writing. / Place your left hand on the stone's left / and your right one on its right: so I can use them both."

160   **the chariot for his fiery ascension:** Cf. 2 Kings 2:11, which describes Elijah's ascent into heaven in a whirlwind, borne by a chariot of fire.

160   **Héloïse:** Héloïse d'Argenteuil (1101–1164), student and lover of the famous scholastic philosopher Peter Abelard. When she became pregnant they secretly married, but her uncle exposed the affair and had Abelard castrated. Héloïse withdrew to a convent, and Abelard to a monastery, where he wrote *Historia Calamitatum* (The Story of My Misfortunes) in the form of a letter. After reading the book, Héloïse wrote to him, and there ensued an exchange of passionate love letters (seven survive: three by Héloïse and four by Abelard).

160   **the Portuguese nun:** See note to page 104.

162   **Saint-Sulpice:** Church in Paris near the Luxembourg Gardens.

166   **he, even though he was a king:** Charles VI of France (1368–1422). He inherited the throne at age eleven, and reigned from 1380. In 1393 he suffered the first of many violent attacks of insanity.

166   **Jean Charlier de Gerson:** 1363–1429; theologian and chancellor of the University of Paris.

167   *parva regina:* "little queen"; Odette de Champdivers, for a time the king's concubine, who while they were intimate (according to reports) was able to calm his madness through the sheer force of her goodness. She bore him two daughters during their brief time together.

167   **Juvénal:** Jean Juvénal des Ursins (1369–1431), one of Charles's most loyal counselors; his son wrote *The History of Charles VI and of the Memorable Events During the Forty-Two Years of His Reign* (1430).

167   **his brother:** The king's brother, Louis, Duke of Orléans (1372–1407), whose murder by hirelings of his cousin John the Fearless, Duke of Burgundy (1371–1419), precipitated a civil war.

167   **Valentina of Orléans:** Valentina Visconti (1371–1408), Louis's widow, and the daughter of the Duke of Milan and Princess Isabelle of France.

168   **Hôtel de Saint-Pol:** A royal residence built in 1361 by Charles V southwest of the immediate environs of Paris.

168   **Roosebeke:** In this battle (1382), the forces of Charles VI (who was only eleven) crushed a revolt by an alliance of several Flemish cities.

169   **the Brotherhood of the Passion:** A guild of lay actors founded in Paris in 1402 for the performance of the mystery plays.

169   **Christine de Pisan's:** c.1364–1430; a prolific, protofeminist woman
        writer of the early Renaissance. Her *Path of Long Study* is an allegorical
        dream-narrative in which the Cumaean Sybil (guard of the shrine of
        Apollo, who had previously guided Aeneas into the underworld) leads
        the author on a journey across Europe and Asia and into heaven.

170   **the Emperor Wenceslaus:** Wenceslaus (1361–1419); Holy Roman
        Emperor and King of Bohemia. He and Charles had met in 1397 to
        discuss the schism in the papacy.

171   **Avignon Christendom:** In 1309 the French pope Clement V had
        moved the papal residence from Rome to the Provençal town of Avi-
        gnon, where subsequent popes continued to reside until 1377. In 1378
        the College of Cardinals, under pressure to return the seat of power
        to Rome, elected as pope Urban VI, who promptly set up residence in
        Rome; but then, four months later, the cardinals declared their deci-
        sion invalid and elected Clement VII instead. For the next forty years
        (the Western Schism) there were two popes, one ruling from Rome and
        the other (the "antipope") from Avignon.

171   **John XXII:** Jacques Duèze of Cahors, the second pope to reside at
        Avignon. The "belief" he preached on All Saints' Day 1331 was that it
        would not be until the Resurrection and the Last Judgment that the
        virtuous dead, no matter how impeccable their lives on earth, would
        experience salvation and enter into heaven and behold the face of God.
        Those who died before then would be taken into "Abraham's bosom,"
        where they would obliviously sleep out the interim.

173   **Napoleon Orsini:** Cardinal Orsini (1263–1342), one of John's bitter-
        est political and doctrinal foes.

177   **albas and sirventes:** Popular genres of love poems in the early Renais-
        sance. In an alba (aubade), the poet is parting from his beloved at
        dawn, after a night of lovemaking. In a sirvente, the poet pledges his
        service in extravagant terms to a woman he worships.

179   **the amphitheater at Orange:** Second-century Roman amphitheater
        built against a hill in the Provençal town of Orange.

180   **icon screen:** The iconostasis (an altar screen) that separates the nave
        from the sanctuary in Russian Orthodox churches.

180   **tragic woman:** Eleonora Duse (1859–1924) was celebrated through-
        out Europe as one of the greatest actresses of her time. RMR saw her
        perform, would eventually meet her in 1912, wrote at least one poem
        about her ("Portrait," in *New Poems: The Other Part* [1908]), and ded-

icated to her the revised version of his symbolist tragedy, *The White Princess* (1904).

181   **Verona:** In a legendary performance in Verona in 1873 of *Romeo and Juliet*, Duse (she was only fourteen) made stunning use of a bunch of pink roses to heighten her performance.

182   **Byblis:** Her story is told in Ovid's *Metamorphoses*, where Caunus is her twin brother.

183   **Louise Labé:** 1526–1566; a French poet of the Renaissance, well known and admired by her contemporaries. RMR translated some of her sonnets.

183   **Sad story of the happy park:** Marie-Anne de Bourbon-Condé, Princesse de Clermont (1697–1741), met and fell in love with Louis de Melun, Duc de Joyeuse, in the forest of Chantilly; not long after their secret marriage in 1719, he was killed there mysteriously in a hunting accident (his body was never found). Marie-Anne never remarried.

184   **Clémence de Bourges:** 1535–1561; a talented French poet of the Renaissance (her work has not survived), and a younger friend and correspondent of Louise Labé. Labé dedicated her complete works to her in 1556. De Bourges supposedly died of grief following the death of her fiancé during the siege of Beaurepaire (1561).

185   **Diké and Anaktoria, Gyrinno and Atthis:** Companions of Sappho named in her poems.

186   **that slight figure:** Sappho.

189   **the sleepless Arsenal:** The Arsenal was Venice's shipyard and armory, founded in the early 1100s. Cf. RMR's poem "Late Autumn in Venice," in *New Poems: The Other Part*.

190   **Benedicte von Qualen:** 1774–1813. Jens Baggesen (1764–1826) was a highly regarded Danish satirical poet. He met von Qualen in 1795 while his wife was dying of a long illness, and fell in love with her— while she, in turn, became a close friend of his wife Sophie. Two years later, shortly after his wife's death, he proposed to von Qualen. She turned him down.

194   **Princess Amalie Gallitzin:** 1748–1806; daughter of a Prussian general, wife of the Russian ambassador to Paris and The Hague. Early on she was an enthusiast of the Enlightenment, and was friends with Voltaire, Diderot, and Goethe. In her later years she returned to the Roman Catholic Church.

198   **Les Baux:** A small village with an imposing castle, built in the Middle Ages out of an especially rocky part of Provence. It thrived in the Middle Ages, but by the time RMR saw it in 1909, there was little of it left but stone ruins and rubble. He saw it as a powerful image of time as both force and object of pure erosion.

198   **that noble family:** The wealthy dynasty that ruled at Les Baux traced their lineage to King Balthazar, one of the three wise men (their motto was "*Au hazard, Balthazar*"), and took as their emblem the sixteen-rayed star of Bethlehem. The princes, unfortunately, regarded sixteen as an extremely unlucky counter-number, and attempted to offset its influence by embracing the holy number seven and acquiring their riches in lots of four and three.

198   **Alyscamps:** An ancient cemetery near Arles. Its uncovered sarcophagi reappear movingly in Part 1, sonnet 10, of RMR's *Sonnets to Orpheus* (1923), along with a note linking them to *Malte Laurids Brigge*.

199   **the philosopher's stone:** For the medieval alchemists, the philosopher's stone transformed lead into gold.

200   **"*sa patience de supporter une âme*":** "his patience in enduring a soul." RMR told his Polish translator that he thought the quotation was from Saint Teresa of Ávila.

201   **But He was not yet willing:** The German reads, "*Der aber wollte noch nicht*," and thus allows the novel to end literally with "not yet"—a crucial gesture impossible to replicate in an English translation.